A Londoner by birth, Colette . ⁣ ⁣ ⁣ ⁣ ⁣ ⁣ ⁣ ⁣ university in Bath and made it her home. Her academic career consisted of a First-Class Honours Degree, a Master's Degree awarded with Distinction, and a scholarship to undertake a Doctorate in Political Science. Her thesis, New Labour, New Language; Ideas, Discourse and Policy, was published in 2001.

Writing is a second career for Colette. In addition to her novels, she has had award winning Flash fiction, short stories and poetry, published in popular magazines and anthologies.

ALSO BY COLETTE DARTFORD

Learning To Speak American

An Unsuitable Marriage

The Mortification of Grace Wheeler

Colette Dartford

First published in 2022 by whitefox

Copyright © Colette Dartford, 2022

www.wearewhitefox.com

ISBN 978-1-915036-57-5
Also available as an ebook
ISBN 978-1-915036-58-2

The moral right of Colette Dartford to be identified
as the author of this work has been asserted in accordance
with the Copyright, Designs and Patents Act 1988.

All rights reserved. No part of this publication may be
reproduced, stored in a retrieval system or
transmitted in any form or by any means, electronic,
mechanical, photocopying, recording or otherwise,
without prior written permission of the author.

Designed and typeset by Typo·glyphix
Project management by whitefox

Mortification *(noun)*

1. great embarrassment and shame
2. the action of subduing one's bodily desires

ONE

In many ways it was a perfect day. Late summer sun, buttery and low, showered gold dust on the river as it rippled over shallow rocks. A riot of insects flitted over the deeper water, tempting unsuspecting fish to the surface. Josh stood knee-deep in his waders and cast out with a long swish of his rod.

Grace sat on the riverbank, a tartan blanket spread out beneath her. The book her mother, Ruth, had given her lay face down on the picnic hamper – *The Empty Nest: A Survival Guide*. Ruth meant well, but even the title troubled Grace. It foreshadowed the vacuum Josh's absence would create, and the spotlight it would shine on her marriage. From tomorrow, Grace's own nest would be empty, and reading about it wasn't how she wanted to spend this last day with her son.

Her husband, Cal, couldn't understand why she had given up her entire Saturday, when she could have just dropped Josh at the river and gone shopping, or 'whatever it is you girls do'. His faux ignorance implied women were a strange and mysterious species, unknowable except to each other. In his sixty-eight years, Cal had chalked up two wives and three daughters, so he knew perfectly well what girls did. Grace shoved the book in her bag, determined not to let negative thoughts intrude. This place was beautiful and so was her boy. Nothing would spoil that for her. As if he had read her mind, Josh turned his head and smiled. God, she would miss him. How did Cal not get that? Whenever she confided her apprehension about their only child leaving home, he told her not to be silly. He didn't mean to be dismissive, and yet she felt dismissed. What she needed was a reassuring hug, not the foreboding sense that she was in this alone. Yesterday's quip said it all: 'Come on, Gracie, he's going to Exeter, not joining the Foreign Legion.' So much for empathy.

Only last week, Cal had made it seem as if she was the reason Josh had decided against a gap year. Christina had dropped by for coffee, Cal hovering as always, clearly impressed that her own son, Adam, was off to do charity work in Uganda. *Grace would be a basket case if Josh did anything like that*, Cal had said, rolling his eyes for effect. Poking fun at Grace was something of a pastime for him – harmless in his estimation, irritating in hers. Usually she ignored such comments, but being disparaged in front of her closest friend incited a rare stab of resentment. She wanted to say that Josh had never expressed any interest in a gap year, that his medical degree meant a long slog at university, and he was eager to get started. She wanted to defend her innate maternal instinct to protect her child, while making it clear that she would never allow it to stop him following his dreams. She wanted to say how boys his age believed they were immortal, making them vulnerable to their own poor judgement. Not a criticism, she would have stressed to Christina, simply a function of youth. She wanted to confess the fears she harboured about what might lie in wait for a boy like Josh – an innocent, trusting boy. She wanted to say so many unsayable things, but the words just boiled inside her.

The only person she had admitted this to was Ruth, whose advice was not to dwell. But it was in Grace's nature to dwell and each time she felt aggrieved at Cal, she remembered all the people who had warned her against marrying him in the first place. Her family, several of her friends, those of her co-workers who were brave enough to offer an opinion, since he was their boss, and Grace's too. It was a long list. Even his ex-wife, Marilyn, had dripped poison in her ear. *He's literally old enough to be your father. You're the same age as Beth, for God's sake. Have you no decency?* Apparently she didn't, because Grace had ignored them all, certain she knew what she was doing. The folly of youth had a lot to answer for.

She didn't want to think about that – not this afternoon. If she hadn't married Cal, she wouldn't have Josh, and he was everything to her. She watched him now, casting out further, to where the river was dark and flat. The feathery fly landed on the water before disappearing beneath the surface. A sudden tautness on the line preceded the twisting and thrashing of a fish, desperate to get free. Josh pulled the rod up towards his chest, and let the fish wear itself out before he reeled it in. Grace sprang up and hurried along the bank, wanting to share her son's moment of triumph – his only catch of the day.

'Can I see?' she called.

Josh scooped the fish into his net and waded over to the bank.

'What is it?' she asked, pushing her sunglasses onto her head to get a better look.

'Brown trout,' he said, carefully removing the hook from its mouth. 'Three or four pounds, I'd say.'

He held it up with both hands, as though presenting her with a gift. Its belly's silvery scales glinted in the fading sunlight. It had given up trying to wriggle free but its mouth still gulped helplessly.

'Are you going to put it back?' said Grace, hoping he didn't intend to bring it home for supper.

She hated to see him dispatch the poor creatures (via a sharp blow to the head with a truncheon-like object, bizarrely called a 'priest'), and then attend to the messy business of gutting it.

'Yep,' said Josh, lowering the fish back into the water. 'It's catch and release here, not catch and kill.'

They watched it dart swiftly between the rocks, before disappearing from sight. The sun had dipped behind a far row of trees, and the air had a creeping chill to it. Grace inhaled the rushing sound of the river and felt a rushing of her own – a sadness so quick and sharp it tightened the flesh on her bones.

'We should probably call it a day,' said Josh, scrambling onto the riverbank.

Grace watched intently, hoping to seal the image in her brain. Tomorrow he would leave, and never need her in quite the same way again. Perhaps it was unreasonable to expect Cal to understand. How could he? For him it was a case of 'job done', but for her it was an ending. She swallowed hard and forced a smile.

'Yes,' she said. 'We probably should.'

TWO

Leaving Josh at Exeter was even harder than Grace had imagined. The air hummed with excitement and the promise of new challenges. On the open day last year, the three of them had walked around St Luke's Campus, admiring its bold mix of modern and traditional buildings. Arched cloisters nestled proudly alongside their glass-fronted neighbours. The idea of Josh actually living there had been distant and theoretical, yet here she was, saying goodbye. Grace forced a smile as she hugged him, but he pulled away before she was ready, sensing perhaps that she never would be. Cal ushered her into the car, saying something about traffic on the M5. She watched Josh get smaller and smaller in the rear-view mirror, until all of a sudden he was gone.

Cal patted her leg as if to say, *Well done*, and chatted happily about Josh's room being a good size, and how he hoped he would pace himself, not go crazy in freshers' week like he had. The idea of Cal as a student, or going in any way crazy, was difficult for Grace to envisage. He was already in his late forties when they met, handsome in a daytime-TV sort of way, with mid-brown hair, greying at the temples. His physique was muscular and solid – a legacy from his rugby-playing days. To her, he seemed like a proper grown-up – confident, sensible, reliable (although his ex-wife and daughters might beg to differ on that score). Grace had never known him as a young man, and however much she pored over old photographs, all she gleaned was how he looked, not who he was. The young Cal was as unknowable to her as the pop stars whose posters adorned her teenage bedroom wall.

Their car trundled down the motorway in the middle lane, taking Grace away from her only child. Cal finally abandoned any attempt to engage her in conversation and turned on the radio. It was tuned to one of those tedious talk-sport programmes, with listeners phoning in to air their opinions. Under normal circumstances she would have suggested music instead, but she couldn't summon the will to object. Putting on a brave face all day had drained her.

It was after six when they finally got back to Bath. She had dreaded returning to an empty house – being enveloped by the silence, the unnatural stillness that lay in wait. It had always seemed too small for them (Marilyn got the four-bed detached in the divorce, and it was as much as Grace and Cal could do to scrape together a deposit for their narrow end-of-terrace), but now it felt too big. Cal walked past her into the kitchen and took a bottle of wine from the fridge. He had stopped drinking after his heart scare, but that was over a year ago and the habit had crept back in. He rationed himself to a couple of glasses of wine, two or three times a week, but no beer and no binges.

'Here you go,' he said, handing her a glass of white and chinking his own against it. 'Cheers.'

Nothing about this moment seemed remotely celebratory to Grace. She took a long, deep drink, barely tasting the wine but longing for the loose lightness it would induce. She knew Cal was looking at her but didn't meet his gaze.

'We've done a good job, Gracie,' he said tenderly. 'Josh is a credit to us both, you especially. He's a fine lad and he'll make a fine doctor. I'm proud of him.' He raised his glass. 'To Josh.'

Coming from a man quietly disdainful of *all that touchy-feely stuff*, this caught her unawares. He wasn't given to heartfelt expressions of emotion, something she tried not to take personally. It was a generational thing, her mother had explained, often understanding him better than Grace did. Cal and Ruth were the same age, both baby boomers raised in post-war austerity. *We were taught to be grateful for what we had*, she cautioned Grace, *not examine it too closely*. Perhaps that was why Cal's brief but unexpected soliloquy was so touching. She wondered if he was bereft too, and trying to be strong for her. Josh was his only son, after all, but at least he had the girls nearby. Josh was a hundred miles away.

The sorrow she had been bottling up brought a sluice of hot tears spilling down her cheeks. She wiped them away with the heel of her hand, knowing how Cal hated it when she cried. He had seen too much crying when he left Marilyn and the girls. If Grace felt weepy, she retreated to the bedroom or bathroom so as to spare his feelings. Her own too, since unravelling in front of him made her feel silly and self-conscious. Rather than seeing a good cry as a natural emotional outlet, she had somehow imbibed Cal's aversion, and felt ashamed at not being able to control herself. Yet here she was, blubbing right in front of him. When he patted her upper arm in a 'there, there' gesture, she asked if he could fetch a box of tissues from the bedroom, giving him an excuse to leave.

She tore off a piece of kitchen roll and blew her nose. The wall clock seemed to tick louder than before – an ominous countdown to something, although she didn't know what. For eighteen years her life had revolved around Josh, and without him she was adrift. Dread stirred in the pit of her stomach, even as she poured another drink to try to dampen it down. She wanted to feel anything other than this emptiness. Don't overthink it, she told herself, taking the wine glasses upstairs to the bedroom.

Cal was in his boxer shorts, his clothes in a pile at the foot of the bed. His torso was broad and barrel-shaped, his chest covered with wiry grey hair. His legs were hairy too, and thick with muscle. Grace handed him a glass.

'It was nice, what you said about Josh.'

'I meant it,' he said. 'Feeling better?'

She nodded.

'It's just hard.'

'I know it is.'

She felt close to him in that moment, as if maybe he did understand a little of what she was going through. When she put down her glass and kissed him, it was slow and deep, like a couple in love. They hadn't kissed like that in a long time. Cal pulled away, his surprised expression confirming that such advances were totally out of character for Grace.

'What was that for?' he said, as if every intimacy needed to be accounted for.

'Can't I be spontaneous?' she said, rapidly going off the idea.

'Of course, it's just, you were so upset a minute ago and now –'

'And now what?'

'And now this.'

'Well, if you don't want to,' she said, turning away from him.

'Hey,' he said, pulling her back. 'I want to very much, as long as you're sure.'

Was she? That he even posed the question underscored her lack of interest in the physical side of their marriage. She didn't know if sex would make her feel better or worse, but when she glimpsed the long evening ahead, it seemed like a wasteland.

It was night-time when she woke. Her head felt fuzzy and her mouth sour and dry. She squinted into the semi-darkness and spotted two wine glasses on the dressing table below the window. The blinds were down and Cal's side of the bed was empty. An unwelcome image of him on top of her, sweaty and out of breath, popped into her head.

'Thought you might be hungry,' he said.

He was standing in the doorway with a tray, like a waiter bringing room service. When he placed it down next to Grace, she saw two thick slabs of low-fat Cheddar, a jar of

Branston pickle, a packet of Sainsbury's crackers, and a green apple cut into quarters.

'Sit up then,' he said brightly. 'Don't know about you, but I've worked up quite an appetite.'

Grace found these post-coital references crass and cringey. And did he have to look so grateful? She half expected a thank-you card. Arranging the pillows behind her head, she made sure the duvet covered her breasts. They didn't sleep naked as a rule, or have supper in bed, or sex for that matter. She felt vaguely self-conscious at having initiated it.

Cal plonked himself down, turned on the TV and flicked through until he found a channel showing golf. Grace picked up a dry cracker and asked if there was any more wine. He didn't complain about going back downstairs to bring up the bottle from earlier. There was only one glass left, which he gave to her – he'd already had his quota. She wanted to rekindle the closeness she had felt earlier, when he spoke so tenderly about being proud of their son.

'Do you think I should text Josh?' she said. 'Make sure he's settled in OK?'

'It's only been a few hours,' said Cal, not taking his eyes off the golf. 'Give the poor lad a break.'

And there he was – the Cal she knew and loved. Or not. Grace could feel a headache tightening across her temples but took a long hit of wine anyway. She watched Cal stack cheese on a cracker and spoon a generous dollop of pickle on top.

'Anyway, we should make the most of it,' he said.

'What do you mean?'

'Well, this for a start.'

He patted her thigh under the duvet and gave it a suggestive squeeze. 'Couldn't do this with Josh around.'

He turned his attention back to the golf and munched his cheese and cracker.

'It's just the two of us now,' he said, eyes glued to the screen.

Indeed it is, thought Grace, draining her glass. She looked around the bedroom, with its plain walls and plain carpet, Cal's clothes in an untidy heap, a faint hint of aftershave in the air. He still wore the same brand as when they married, twenty years before. Her husband was nothing if not a creature of habit. She realised she had been dreading today, not only because of Josh, but also because of Cal. Josh was the glue that held them together, and already she sensed herself peeling away.

When the little white ball disappeared into the hole, Cal applauded rapturously. She envied him his happiness. With Josh they had been a family, but now they were a couple again and she wasn't sure how that would work. There was no real intimacy between them anymore. Even lying naked in bed, with Cal bringing her food and wine, didn't feel romantic. If anything, she was struck by the wrongness of it. Their sex life had dwindled to the occasional shag (she hated that word, the crudeness it implied, but sadly it was apt). They had no shared interests beyond the well-being of their son, and she couldn't remember the last time they had really laughed together. And perhaps she could have lived with those things if she hadn't started to see Cal as old. Not that she would ever say so out loud – even thinking it made her feel callous – but there it was. He was a good man, a loyal husband, a devoted father, and that had always seemed enough. Now she wasn't so sure. There were so many different types of love and if she did love Cal, it wasn't the romantic kind. That had faded long ago, replaced by a more pedestrian version usually afforded to old friends or second-tier relatives. She certainly wasn't *in* love with him. It was shocking to acknowledge that, even to herself. She glanced at his profile and thought how content he seemed. Everything would be so much simpler if she felt the same. Maybe it was the dull headache or the disappointing sex, and she would feel differently tomorrow. She certainly hoped so. But what if she didn't? What then?

THREE

'And you don't think you're overreacting just a tad?' said Christina, somewhat astonished.

They had met after work in All Bar One, which was busy for a Thursday. Grace and her friends only went there on weekdays, when it wasn't overrun with screeching hen parties. Being early autumn, the worst of the tourist invasion was over, or at least in a bit of a lull until the Christmas markets sprung up around the abbey, and Bath would be inundated again.

Grace sipped her Chardonnay.

'Maybe, probably,' she said. 'Oh, I don't know.'

Christina checked her watch.

'Do you have to be somewhere?' asked Grace.

'Not yet,' said Christina. 'I'm picking up Ellie from swimming club, but I've got forty minutes or so.'

'You see, this is the problem,' said Grace, already on her second drink. She had skipped lunch, so the alcohol was buzzing in her brain. 'Adam's gone, but you've still got three children at home. All I've got is Cal.'

'Yes, but you're not seriously thinking of leaving him?'

Grace drank more of her wine and shrugged.

'No, not really, but the idea of him sitting at home, waiting for me ...'

She didn't bother to finish that sentence. Her meaning was clear enough.

'Have you heard from Adam?' she said, tired of sharing her marriage woes.

'A two-word text,' said Christina. '*I'm fine*. Not even a kiss for his old mum. What about Josh?'

'We've spoken a few times. He's fine too.'

'You seem disappointed.'

Grace looked at her, eyebrows knitted together.

'Of course not. Why would you say that?'

Christina's phone pinged. She glanced at it before turning her attention back to Grace.

'It's been, what, ten days since he left?'

'Eleven,' said Grace.

'Not that you're counting.'

Grace sighed, which wasn't exactly a denial.

'Look,' said Christina. 'I know how close you two are, only child and all that. You were obviously going to feel a bit down and dejected when he left.'

'Go on.'

'And I wonder if maybe you're muddling that with your feelings for Cal, you know, thinking it's all about him when really it's more about having an empty nest.'

'My mum gave me a book about it,' said Grace. 'You can borrow it if you like.'

'A bit premature,' said Christina, 'as Ellie's only eleven.'

'I wish I'd had more children, but Cal flatly refused.'

'And you know my thoughts on the subject,' said Christina.

'That I should have just done it anyway,' said Grace. 'Well, it's too late now.'

'Is it?' said Christina, fiddling with the chunky diamond stud in her earlobe. 'Women have babies in their mid-forties, and I know Cal's a lot older –'

'Twenty-three years older.'

'But you still have sex. I mean, thank God for Viagra, right?'

'Wrong,' said Grace. 'Firstly, he's on beta blockers so he's not supposed to take it, and secondly ...' She screwed up her face. 'Thank goodness. A rampant Cal is the last thing I need. I don't even find him attractive anymore.'

'I imagine most people in long-term relationships don't find their partners particularly attractive. Harry's hardly an Adonis, but it's habit, isn't it, and comfort and intimacy, all that stuff.'

'I suppose,' said Grace, finding it easier to agree than to debate the subject.

'And Cal's pretty good for his age,' said Christina. 'Reminds me a bit of that *Great British Bake Off* rogue, Paul Hollywood. I'd shag him in a heartbeat.'

'No you wouldn't,' said Grace, amused. 'You and Harry are the perfect couple.'

'No such thing,' said Christina, checking her watch again. 'Look, Josh leaving home was bound to be unsettling. I wouldn't read too much into it. Yes, Cal's older, and his jokey put-downs must get tiresome, but he adores you.'

'Does he?' said Grace, genuinely surprised.

She didn't feel adored.

'My advice,' said Christina, 'is find something you enjoy, something just for you. And don't overanalyse things. It's not healthy.'

She gathered up her jacket and slipped her phone into her bag.

'I'm sorry to drink and dash, but Ellie panics if I'm late.'

She pecked Grace on the cheek and glided towards the door, turning admiring heads as she went. It was twenty-five years since Christina had graced a catwalk, but her posture and deportment were still faultless. Grace realised she should get home too, but she thought of Cal plonked in front of the television and ordered another drink instead – a small one this time. She envied Christina her big, noisy family. How wonderful to be the epicentre of all that unconditional love. It had been difficult enough persuading Cal to have one child, let alone a brood. He argued that he had three kids already, but as Grace pointed out, the girls were Marilyn's children, not hers. What sort of man would deny a woman's natural desire to be a mother, simply because he was already a father? She gave him an ultimatum – no children, no wedding. He relented, the compromise being one child only, and stupidly, Grace had agreed. That was before she understood the intensity of maternal love. It had washed over her like a tsunami the very first moment she held Josh in her arms, and never lessened. Maybe if she'd had other children, it would have diluted a little, been less heart-achingly intense, but Cal had remained adamant. *I don't want to be like those ageing rock stars having kids in their dotage.*

There was a time, when Josh was a toddler, that Grace considered 'forgetting' to take her pill and letting nature take its course. When she flicked those little white tablets from their blister pack, she would stare at them with loathing. She hated that they denied her the baby she longed for, although really it was Cal doing the denying, so she hated him a little bit too.

Those early years with Josh were the happiest of her life. He was such an easy child – smiley, undemanding, affectionate. Then one day Grace found herself buying a school uniform, and all that happiness became something else entirely. When she dropped him off for his first day at St Julian's, she wasn't the only mother wiping away a few tears, but for Grace it heralded a descending darkness. She would drag herself home from the school run and curl up on Josh's bed, as if weighed down by an invisible force. It sapped her strength, made her limbs too heavy to move. When it was time to go back and fetch him, she mingled with the other mothers at the school gates, playing the role of a normal, sane person, which she feared she absolutely was not. On a rational level she knew she cherished her family as much as she always had, but that knowledge didn't translate into a feeling. There *was* no feeling – she was numb. Cal seemed not to notice at first, or if he did, he said nothing. It was sex, or the lack of it, that finally pushed him to ask what was wrong. When she said she didn't know, he accused her of punishing him for not wanting another baby. She responded by going to bed and staying there for three days. Cal enlisted Ruth's help – *listen to your mother if you won't listen to me* – and between them they persuaded Grace to see her GP. Cal took the morning off work to make sure she went, but when her name was called, she insisted on going in alone.

The doctor – a serious young Asian man with sad eyes behind heavy-framed glasses – asked what seemed to be the problem. It was a simple enough question, but not one she could answer. She mumbled something about this being a mistake, but he looked so concerned that she felt she ought to at least try to explain. If she didn't, he might feel he had failed in some way. 'My family made me come,' she said. 'They're worried about me.' He nodded sagely and asked why. Grace swallowed hard and shrugged, tears brimming in her eyes. The doctor pushed a box of tissues towards her and waited. She said her husband didn't like it when she cried, an admission that made her cry harder. The diagnosis of depression was almost a relief – there were pills she could take, people she could talk to. Cal led her to the car as if she was breakable, a firm arm around her waist. He clicked her seat belt into place, just like he did with Josh.

Grace swallowed the last mouthful of Chardonnay, feeling guilty that she had moaned about him to Christina. Yes, Cal had his shortcomings, but who didn't? Reflecting on those dark days reminded her of so many small acts of kindness. He started bringing her tea in bed every morning, made sure she took her pills, kept Josh entertained so she could rest. Once she was 'on the mend', as he put it, he had a word with his old friend Marty Devlin, a property developer on the lookout for an admin person. Cal believed it unhealthy for Grace to have so much time on her hands. It would do her good to get out of the house, he said – meet new people, have new challenges. She resisted at first, but Ruth weighed in on Cal's side, so it was two against one.

The morning she walked into Marty's office in smart black trousers and an ivory silk blouse, she was so nervous she almost walked straight out again. He had spotted her, though, so it was too late. Once her nerves had settled, the interview didn't feel like an interview at all – more like an interesting conversation with an acquaintance. Marty often discussed his business with Cal, who had briefed Grace the previous evening. When Marty said she was perfect for the role and could work school hours, four days a week, she surprised herself by accepting. Afterwards, she wondered if she had got the job on her own merits, or because Marty and Cal were friends, but decided it didn't matter. They agreed a three-month trial period, and thirteen years later she was still there.

A text from Cal arrived as she was waiting for her Uber.

When will you be home?

Leaving now x

The acrid smell of burnt toast greeted her at the front door. Cal was in his recliner chair, television blaring, the remote control in his hand.

'Hi, love,' he said, glancing up from the screen. 'You're late.'

'I told you I was meeting Christina for a drink. Have you eaten?'

'Just some toast to keep me going. What's for dinner?'

Grace sighed, thinking how nice it would be to come home to a cooked meal. She blamed herself for Cal's lack of culinary skills. The kitchen was small and he was big, so it was easier just to shoo him out rather than have him under her feet, trying to help.

'Pasta,' she said, because it was quick and required minimal effort.

Grace's mother had taught her to cook when she was a child. A simple pasta dish took no thought at all, allowing her to reflect on Christina's advice to find something she enjoyed, something just for herself. On the short taxi ride home, she had begun a process of elimination: yoga (not flexible enough), swimming (chlorine dried out her skin and hair), art classes (no talent), volunteering (possibly). The one thing she always enjoyed was fly fishing with Josh. Watching him from the riverbank induced a rare sense of serenity. Her heart tugged when she set two places for supper instead of three. She poured a couple of glasses of wine and called Cal.

'This looks nice,' he said, poking the sauce with his fork.

'It's vegetarian bolognese,' she said, in case he was hunting for mince.

Red meat was bad for his heart, a treat confined to their Sunday roast. He had left the television on in the sitting room, the sound turned up so loud she could follow the news report he had been watching.

'You should probably have another hearing test,' she said.

'Pardon?' he said, with a jokey smile. 'I was thinking, you don't work on Fridays so why don't you come to the golf club tomorrow, get signed up for lessons.'

It wasn't the first time he had suggested it, despite knowing she had zero interest in playing golf, watching golf, going on golfing holidays, or any other golf-related activity. A lack of time was her go-to excuse, but she had three days off and no plans. That was when it came to her.

'Actually, I'm going fishing.'

'Fishing?'

'Yes. I've decided to take lessons.'

He turned his head and stared at her.

'I always enjoy watching Josh, and I thought if I learn too, then it's something we can do together when he's home.'

'You never said anything.'

'It was Christina's idea. She said I should try something new.'

'I've been trying to get you to take up golf for ages.'

'Something I enjoy.'

'How do you know you won't enjoy golf if you don't give it a chance?'

'I'm sorry, but that's your thing, not mine. There's something beautiful and peaceful about being by the water.'

Cal huffed as he dumped two large helpings of Parmesan onto his spaghetti. Grace resisted mentioning his cholesterol in case it seemed like she was nagging. And anyway, he was well aware that cheese was on the 'unhealthy' side of his list of heart-healthy foods.

'Right,' he said testily. 'Well, it's up to you, of course. I just thought it would be nice for us to have a hobby we could do together. I mean, Josh isn't even here.'

As if she needed reminding. She had cooked enough food for three.

'Lots of men at the club play with their wives,' said Cal, unwilling to let it go.

He took a slug of wine and said golf courses can be beautiful and peaceful too, sounding more petulant than he probably intended.

They ate in silence for a while, before Cal started complaining for the hundredth time about how long it was taking to get Brexit done. Grace had voted Remain. Officially they agreed to disagree, but that didn't stop him lecturing her on the tyranny of the EU. She didn't know if it was the wine or listening to Cal drone on, but she felt weary to her bones. He offered to load the dishwasher but always made a hash of it, cramming pans together so the water couldn't circulate, or angling wine glasses too low to drain. She sent him back to the sitting room and did a quick Google search on her phone, finding three local fly-fishing instructors. Now she had told Cal about it, she felt obliged to follow through. The first one was a discontinued number, the second wasn't taking new clients, but the third – David Gill – could fit her in tomorrow morning.

'That soon?' she said.

It had seemed like a good idea in theory, if only as an excuse not to play golf, but she didn't have any of the gear – rods, reels, waders, flies. Josh had taken all his stuff with him (there was great fishing around Exeter, apparently). She explained this to David Gill, who assured her he had everything she needed, and that her son was right, he'd be spoilt for rivers around Exeter: the Teign, the Dart, the Yealm, the Avon.

'Uh-huh,' said Grace, not expecting him to actually list them. This was happening too fast. Now that it came to it, she wasn't sure she did want fishing lessons after all. Josh made it look so easy, but what if it wasn't? Don't commit, she told herself.

'Let's call this a trial session,' she said. 'In case I'm

absolutely useless and can't face humiliating myself on a regular basis.'

She giggled nervously and winced, wondering what this David Gill person must make of her. Oh well, she would find out soon enough. When she set up an alert in her iPhone, she scrolled idly through her calendar, and realised the date of her period had come and gone. She was never late. She checked again, but there was no mistake. It puzzled her that she hadn't noticed, but her emotions had been so volatile that she had even initiated sex that first evening without Josh. The memory was unwelcome, but prompted a thought that quickened her heart. It was crazy – of course it was crazy. She told herself this very sternly, even as a tiny kernel of hope grew inside her. Was a baby growing inside her too? She hadn't bothered with her diaphragm, and miracles did happen.

Cal came into the kitchen to ask if she'd seen his phone. She barely registered the question.

'You all right?' he said. 'You look a bit flushed.'

'I think I might be pregnant.'

He pulled his chin into his neck, clearly confused.

'You can't be.'

'Well, I'm late,' she said. 'And we didn't use anything, you know, the last time.'

She knew having this conversation with her husband shouldn't make her squirm, but it did.

'Surely you're too old,' he said.

She breathed deeply, letting her chest take the full force of the insult. Seeing a splodge of pasta sauce on his shirt was gratifying for some reason. Grace gathered her thoughts and pride, and quoted Christina.

'Lots of women have babies in their forties.'

'More likely you're starting the menopause,' he said, doubling down on the insult.

Did he have any idea how insensitive he was being, condemning her to a slow, sweaty decline? She was only forty-five. The desire to tell him to sod off was immediate and intense, but they weren't that kind of couple. They never argued in front of Josh, so had lost the knack of arguing. Perhaps that was why their marriage felt so flat and lifeless. Her innate aversion to conflict aside, she wondered if the occasional row might be good for a relationship. Surely it was better to clear the air rather than allow grievances to fester.

She swallowed her indignation and said she would buy a test tomorrow. He rolled his eyes, which struck her as an odd reaction. Why was he unwilling to entertain even the slim possibility that she was pregnant, if only to humour her?

'Do you think I'm trying to trick you into having another child?' she said. 'Is that it?'

'You do your test,' was his glib response. 'Oh, and give me a shout if you find my phone.'

Grace stood with her palms open, as if to say, *What the hell is wrong with you?* Something weird was going on, but she didn't have the first clue what. Fired up by Cal's casual condescension, she marched into the sitting room to demand answers. Josh wasn't around to overhear. They could argue to their heart's content – make up for lost time.

Cal was in his recliner chair, eyes glued to the television. Grace grabbed the remote and switched it off. He looked more surprised by that than when she'd told him she might be pregnant.

'What are you doing?' he said.

'I could ask you the same thing?'

He looked both astonished and confused.

'Why are you so calm about this?' she said, her head a swarm of questions.

She furrowed her brow, trying to figure it out as she went along.

'I mean, you always made it crystal clear you wouldn't even entertain the idea of more children. God knows I begged you enough times. Yet I've just told you I might be pregnant and you seem, I don't know – indifferent. It doesn't make sense.'

She was standing between him and the TV, holding the remote control hostage in her clenched fist. Her face was hot, her heart galloping. Cal shifted in his seat and sighed loudly, as if this whole scene was an unwelcome intrusion into his evening's viewing.

'I had a vasectomy,' he said.

Grace leaned forward a little, certain she had misheard.

'You what?'

'I had the snip.'

He made it sound as routine as his annual flu jab. She reeled back, barely able to comprehend the magnitude of what he was telling her.

'When?'

'Just after Josh started school – you remember how moody you got?'

'Moody? I was clinically depressed.'

She could feel blood gushing through her veins – hear it in her head.

'Yes, and I thought you might use it as an excuse to fall pregnant again.'

'So you went behind my back and made sure I would never have another child?'

'We agreed,' he said, as if he held the moral high ground.

Part of her couldn't quite believe he would do something so heinous.

'I would have noticed,' she said, desperate for it not to be true.

If it was true, the betrayal was beyond forgiveness.

'I told you I was going to a conference,' he said, 'and went to a private clinic.'

'Oh my God,' she said. 'You really did this.'

He didn't even have the decency to look sorry. She had endured the pill for years – blinding headaches, sore breasts, bloating that made her clothes too tight – and for what? Disbelief turned to righteous anger, and it was as much as she could do to breathe.

'Come on, Grace,' he said, trying to placate her. 'It was a long time ago.'

Was that his defence – the statute of limitations? Grace had never felt rage like it. She hurled the remote at the television, hoping it would smash Cal's precious screen to pieces.

FOUR

Grace lay on Josh's bed in a state of shock. Never in her entire life had she lost her temper like that. It was frightening to find she was capable of it, but also a tiny bit exhilarating – an exquisite moment of release. If she had tried to swallow Cal's act of treachery – be *civilised* about it – it would have burned a hole inside her. No, it was better to let it out, she knew that, but hated the way it had made her feel. Her heart kicked hard against her chest, and she couldn't stop trembling. She sat up and forced herself to take some slow, deep breaths, hoping she would calm down. It seemed to be working, too, until Cal opened the door, wearing an aggrieved expression.

'What are you doing in here?' he said.

Her heart started kicking again, forcing heat from her chest to her face.

'Well, there's not much space in the box room,' she said crisply, alluding to the fact that it was crammed with his stuff: golf clubs, old box files, rugby memorabilia and other assorted junk.

She had asked him to clear it out dozens of times, but he only ever seemed to add to it.

'There's plenty of space in our room,' he said.

Really? Did he honestly think they would curl up in bed together after what he had done? She wanted to tell him to fuck off, but Grace didn't swear. Cal found bad language offensive, especially in women. She remembered his youngest daughter, Lydia, describing an ex-boyfriend as a 'tosser', and Cal reprimanding her, even though she must have been twenty at the time. Christina often extolled the efficacy of a well-deployed expletive, but Grace could never bring herself to do it, at least not out loud.

'You broke the remote, by the way,' he said, loitering in the doorway as if unsure whether to venture further.

'Good.'

He shook his head.

'What's got into you, Grace, apart from too much Chardonnay?'

'What?'

'How much did you and Christina drink? And you had a few more glasses when you got home.'

She got to her feet.

'You think *that's* what this is about? That I had too much to drink?'

She could hear the incredulity in her voice, but Cal carried on regardless.

'If it's going to cause you to lose your rag like that, then maybe you should knock it on the head.'

She took a long breath to steady herself, and spoke as calmly as she could.

'I lost my rag, as you put it, because you had a vasectomy without telling me. Quite a big deal, I'd say.'

'It was a long time ago.'

'Not for me it wasn't. I've known for about half an hour, so forgive me if I'm struggling to get used to the idea.'

He sighed loudly, as though the whole tedious incident was trying his patience. She was trembling again, struggling to contain her rising anger.

'You watched for years as I took the pill, knowing all the health risks and side effects. And when I couldn't stand it anymore and we discussed birth control, you could have told me we didn't need to worry. But no, you were too much of a coward – a liar.'

She had had a coil fitted (agony) and removed (more agony) after three months of cramps and bleeding. The memory hit her like a punch. She clenched her fists so hard her fingernails pressed into the soft flesh of her palms.

'Look,' he said. 'I don't know if it's the wine, your hormones, a bad day at the office, whatever, but you can't behave like that, Grace, throwing things, breaking things. What's done is done. Now for all our sakes, pull yourself together.'

She glared at him, almost speechless with loathing. Almost.

'Oh, just fuck off, Cal,' she said, shutting the door in his face.

And it turned out Christina was right. That actually felt pretty good.

Grace had a horrible night, mostly spent staring at the ceiling. Josh's bed was a small double, pushed up against the wall. The room was too stuffy, but when she opened the window she could hear traffic and sirens from the nearby hospital, so had to shut it again. She threw off the duvet, but was still sticky and hot. The bedroom she shared with Cal was at the back of the house, away from any road noise. At around three-thirty she was so exhausted she considered sneaking back there to at least try to get a few hours' sleep. Cal slept like the dead so might not even notice. But then she thought about what he had done, the way he had spoken to her, and couldn't bear to be near him.

Just as Grace feared, Josh's absence had thrown their marriage into sharp relief, exposing its cracks and crevices. Their tacit agreement not to upset their son meant she had tolerated things she should have spoken up about: the fact that Cal was retired, yet she did most of the housework; the way he chastised her for drinking, like she was some sort of lush; his insensitive references to the menopause, even though it could still be years away. And did he honestly expect her not to be upset about the vasectomy? Perhaps this is how it would be from now on. No matter what he said or did, her reaction, however proportionate, could be dismissed as irrational or unhinged, simply because she was a woman. A middle-aged woman with hormones.

Marilyn was forty-six when Cal left her, a year older than Grace was now. He rarely talked about it, but she remembered him complaining that, at times, it had been like living with a madwoman. After tonight's debacle, he would probably say the same about her. She could imagine him comparing notes with his golf club cronies, each trying to outdo the other with tales of their wives' unreasonable behaviour. *Mine smashed the remote to smithereens and told me to F-off – top that!*

At six forty-five, Grace gave up on sleep altogether and got on with her day. She padded downstairs to make coffee and toast, feeling Josh's absence keenly. They would never have had that ugly fight if he had been at home. She sipped her coffee, aware of the weight of her heart. Cal was so vigilant about his, but Grace only noticed hers when it ached. Thinking about Josh made her feel ashamed of the way she had behaved last night, despite considering herself the injured party. Her calm, affable son wouldn't have recognised that woman. He would have been horrified by her outburst, and however hard she tried to justify it, Grace couldn't expunge the idea that she had let herself down. She considered Michelle Obama to be the epitome of poise and dignity, often pondering what Michelle would do in any given situation. *When they go low, you go high.* She thought about that for a moment. It seemed unlikely that Michelle would have destroyed the TV remote and told Barack to fuck off.

Grace took her tea and toast back upstairs to Josh's room, careful not to make any noise and wake Cal. The thought of coming face to face with him made her stomach churn. They never fought – this was uncharted territory. Hostile territory, and she didn't know the rules of engagement. Did he expect her to apologise, even though his transgression was far greater than hers? What Grace had broken could be fixed. She picked over the details as she sipped her coffee, still unable to believe Cal had done something so monstrous. Her earlier anger had flattened. It was heavier now and more dense, sapping her spirit in increments. She put down her cup and curled into the foetal position, aware of a creeping sense of déjà vu. Would Josh starting university beckon the same darkness that had consumed her when he started school? Cal would have her think so. Any unwelcome displays of emotion he framed as 'losing it', and laid the blame fairly on the female disposition.

The sound of the front door shutting startled her. She had only meant to close her eyes for a few minutes, but must have dozed off. Peering out of the window, she saw Cal loading golf clubs into his car. If he'd looked up he would have seen her, but he drove off without a backwards glance. Her relief was palpable. She didn't have to face him, for now at least. As she thought about trying to get some sleep, her phone pinged, reminding her that she had a fly-fishing lesson at ten. It had completely slipped her mind. Her first instinct was to cancel, but the thought of waiting around for Cal to come home filled her with a sick sort of dread. She told herself she would feel better after a shower, but didn't. If anything, the combination of steaming hot water and another comforting cup of decaf made her want to crawl back into bed. She was too tired to get dressed and drive all the way to Chew Valley Lake. It would probably be a waste of time anyway, since she wasn't in a fit state to concentrate. She found the instructor's number – David something? – and was about to call and cancel when the phone in her hand rang, startling her. Josh's name popped up on the screen.

'This is a nice surprise,' she said, her mood instantly lighter. 'You're OK, aren't you? I mean, there's nothing wrong?'

'Chill, Mum, I'm fine. Just calling to ask if you can look in my room for a box of PlayStation games. I thought I'd packed them, but they must still be at home.'

'Oh, right, hang on a minute –'

'Actually, I'm just heading into an anatomy class. You can text me later.'

'Or I'll give you a call and we can chat properly.'

She heard a girl's voice, high and excited, and then Josh laughed.

'Sorry, Mum, got to go,' he said.

Grace was about to sign off with 'love you', but he had already hung up. She stared at the blank screen, tears pricking her eyes. He sounded so happy, which of course was what she wanted, but missing him felt physical, like a weight she carried inside. She was about to look for the PlayStation games but remembered that before Josh rang, she was going to cancel her fishing lesson. Now she wasn't sure whether that was a good idea or not. Maybe the fresh air would help clear her head, although it did seem a lot of effort. She couldn't decide, which got her wondering if indecision was a symptom of the menopause – the old-hag version of baby brain? She buried her face in her hands. Cal had done this to her – made her question if what she felt was real, or a figment of her unruly hormones. Sod it, she thought, and got herself dressed.

The early-morning mist had cleared, revealing watery sunshine and a colourless sky. Grace presented herself at the office – a glorified shed with a wooden desk, a rack of leaflets and a refreshments area. A pinboard on the wall caught her eye. On it was a home-made poster advertising a charity pub quiz. It looked like a child's handiwork, with lots of stickers, glitter and smiley faces.

'Can I help you, miss?'

An elderly man (eighty, she would have guessed, with an abundance of facial hair and a completely bald head) stood next to her.

'Deserted my post to make a cuppa,' he said, raising his mug as evidence.

Grace explained that she was here for a lesson with David, apologising that his surname had escaped her.

'Gill. You want David Gill. Good timing – here he is.'

Grace turned to see a dark-haired young man dressed in the uniform of the country set: a hunter-green jumper with brown suede epaulettes, mud-coloured wellington boots with buckles on the side, and a tweed cap with a fishing fly pinned to it. It struck Grace that while his clothes were designed to blend into the scenery, the garish colours and loud patterns Cal wore for golf were designed to do the opposite. David Gill took a few steps towards her, his hand outstretched.

'Grace Wheeler?'

'Yes, hi.'

Their handshake was brief but cordial.

'OK, Reggie here will sort out the paperwork and then we can get started,' he said, leaving her with the octogenarian at the desk.

Reggie's grin exposed a lot of gum and very few teeth. By paperwork, David Gill meant payment. A one-hour lesson was forty pounds, which if memory served her correctly was a lot more than when she used to bring Josh here. Still, that was a while ago and they probably charged less for children. Reggie handed her the card machine and she keyed in her pin.

'Right,' said David. 'Let's get started.'

Grace followed him outside, but rather than heading towards the lake, he took her to a section of short, flat grass and handed her a rod.

'Did you bring sunglasses?' he said. 'To protect your eyes. And a hat, so the fly doesn't get caught in your hair.'

She remembered him telling her that on the phone, but with all the drama it had completely slipped her mind.

'I've got a pair of sunglasses,' she said, rummaging through her bag to find them. 'But I'm afraid I forgot to bring a hat. Sorry.'

'That's OK,' he said. 'You can borrow mine.'

He took off his flat cap and looked suddenly younger. It had hidden a thatch of boisterous waves, which he pushed back off his face with a quick sweep of his hand. Grace felt a little self-conscious putting on the cap, still warm from David Gill's head. She put on the sunglasses too, and thought how silly she must look, standing on grass with a fishing rod, shades and a flat cap at least one size too big.

'Right,' he said. 'We're going to practise casting here, and when you've got the hang of it, we'll head over to the lake.'

He explained about the reel, the line that ran along the length of the rod through a series of small metal loops, and the fly tied to the end. Grace tried hard to concentrate, but her head was fuzzy from a lack of sleep. The movement to execute a perfect overhead cast, he explained, was peel, pluck, pause and tap. Peel the line off the grass, pluck the rod back so it's pointing straight up, pause for a second before tapping the line forward. Grace doubted she would be capable of anything approaching a perfect cast, but gave it her best shot, which was abysmal. She started to apologise but David cut her off.

'It's just practice,' he said, reeling in the line, which had spewed out to her left, narrowly missing a nearby tree. 'Try to relax.'

'Right,' she said, taking a deep breath.

If she had been aiming for the tree then yes, her second attempt was a terrific cast, successfully hooking a tangle of leaves. She felt her face colour – a girlish blush, she told herself, definitely not the menopause. Bloody Cal. The M-word would never have occurred to her if he hadn't put the idea in her head.

Once David had retrieved the fly, taken the rod from Grace and reeled in the line, he showed her the sequence of movements again, this time in slow motion. When he handed the rod back, he positioned himself behind her, extending his arms so that his hands rested on hers. It felt strange to Grace, being enveloped by this virtual stranger. He smelled of damp wool and coffee, and despite the morning chill, his hands were surprisingly warm. Out of nowhere came the feeling she might cry, and she had to swallow hard to staunch it. Was she on the verge of another breakdown? The first one had been about feeling empty and numb, but this – whatever *this* was – felt the opposite. Even the slightest thing caused an upsurge of emotion that threatened to overwhelm her. Who was this weepy woman, quick to anger?

'Ready?' asked David.

Grace cleared her throat.

'Yep,' she said.

He demonstrated how to cast, exerting just enough pressure on her hands so she could feel the movement and rhythm he wanted her to copy. Her own effort was slightly improved – she managed to miss the tree – prompting an encouraging 'well done'. They went through the same things several more times – David behind her, guiding her cast with his hands, and then Grace attempting it on her own – before he was satisfied with her progress and suggested they head to the lake. The banks were dotted with fishermen – not a woman in sight.

'So, Grace, what made you want to take up fishing?' he asked as they walked.

To avoid spending time with my husband.

'My son's a keen fisherman. He's just gone off to university – I think I mentioned that on the phone – and I wanted to surprise him when he came home.'

They had reached a spot (no trees nearby, thankfully) that David assured her had plenty of fish.

'Why isn't everyone here?' she asked.

Her question prompted a knowing smile.

'Too easy,' he said. 'The thrill is in the chase.'

Was he being flirtatious? Before she had time to ponder that unlikely notion, he told her to hold still and retrieved the fly pinned to his flat cap. He handed it to her, pointing out the feathery autumn colours and the small metal hook sticking out from its underside. His fingers were surprisingly deft as he demonstrated how to tie it to the fishing line.

'You're not going to ask me to do that, are you?' she said.

He treated her to another smile.

'I think I've given you enough to remember this morning,' he said, handing her the rod.

His expression was half curious, half amused.

'People go fishing to relax,' he said. 'You seem tense.'

She took a quick breath and shook her shoulders, wriggled her arms, opened and closed her fists.

'There,' she said. 'All better.'

This time his smile was broader, making his face look boyish and kind.

'Right,' he said. 'You ready?'

'Hope so,' said Grace.

She let out enough line for the fly to sit on the water, about twelve feet from the bank. In her eagerness she peeled back too far, forgot to pause, and cast with too much force.

'Sorry,' she said, cross at her own ineptitude.

It was only a half-formed thought, but she found herself wanting to impress David Gill.

'Here, let me help,' he said, taking up his position behind her again.

A sliver of sunlight pushed through the cloud, anointing them with brightness. Grace tilted her chin towards the sky, allowing another half-formed thought to take shape. She liked the sensation of this man's body against hers, the way they fitted together so effortlessly.

FIVE

'I come bearing gifts,' said Grace, handing Christina a plastic carrier bag.

Grace had called before she left the lake, asking if it was OK to stop by. Christina ushered her into the kitchen and peered inside the bag.

'It's a fish,' she said, bemused.

'Rainbow trout. I caught it this morning.'

'You caught it? Where?'

'Chew. I had a fishing lesson.'

'Really? And some beginner's luck, it would seem.'

'That, and a very helpful instructor.'

Christina laid the trout on the worktop and admired it for a moment, before swathing it in cling film.

'I wasn't even going to go,' said Grace. 'Cal and I had a horrible fight and I didn't sleep a wink, but then I thought –'

'Wait. You and Cal had a fight? You two never fight.'

'I think we made up for that last night,' said Grace, filling Christina in on the order of events.

She listened in stunned silence as Grace told her about the vasectomy, and how furious she had been.

'I'm not surprised,' said Christina.

'Cal was,' said Grace. 'Surprised and condescending. He put my outburst down to Chardonnay – namechecked you, in fact – and my age. Can you believe it? Said I was probably starting the menopause.'

Christina actually gasped.

'The nerve,' she said.

'He thinks women are irrational creatures governed by their hormones, unlike men.'

Grace made speech marks with her fingers when she said 'hormones'.

'Bollocks they're not,' said Christina. 'All that fighting and fucking – sheer testosterone. Who does he think starts all the wars? And have you never seen *Love Island*? It's a cross between the last days of Caligula and Sodom and Gomorrah.'

'You watch *Love Island*?'

'In a supervisory capacity. Lucy's addicted, also to *TOWIE* and *Made in Chelsea*. Not that dreadful new one the good folk of Ascot are up in arms about. I had to draw the line somewhere.'

Despite herself, Grace laughed. Christina's humour never failed to hit the spot – one of the reasons Grace was so fond of her. Some of the other mothers were intimidated by her looks and affluence, but it was this down-to-earth quality Grace admired. The rest was just window dressing.

'Slight change of subject,' she said. 'But do you have plans tonight?'

'Um, don't think so. Harry should be home around six. Why, what did you have in mind?'

'Pub quiz, no husbands.'

'Oh?' said Christina, surprised. 'Didn't know that was your thing.'

'It's not, but the guy I was fishing with this morning mentioned that they needed a few women on their team – you know, for the subjects men are clueless about.'

'Bit sexist, but I'll let that slide for the moment. So, he asked you to go with him?'

'Not *with* him. It's just to make up the numbers.'

'Oh my God, you're blushing.'

Grace touched her cheek.

'It's hot in here,' she said defensively.

Christina gestured for her to sit.

'Tell me everything,' she said.

'There's nothing to tell,' said Grace. 'I was upset after last night, but dragged myself to Chew, even though it was the last thing I felt like, and David was so nice.'

'David?'

'David Gill – the instructor.'

'How old?'

'Oh, I don't know. Mid-thirties, maybe.'

'Younger man. I like it. Carry on.'

'Well, he sort of – and please don't read anything into this – he sort of put his arms around me, and –'

'Wait. He put his arms around you?'

'No, not like that. He was demonstrating how to cast.'

'Of course he was.'

'Seriously. I just couldn't get the hang of it and ...'

'What?'

Grace turned her head towards the autumn light, diffusing through the French doors that opened onto the garden. She sighed, remembering the faint smell of coffee and damp wool.

'It felt good to do something different, with someone different. Everything with Cal is so stale.'

'I can imagine. And when this David asked you out –'

'He didn't ask me out. There was a notice advertising a pub quiz, and this sweet old guy asked if I was going.'

'So the old guy asked you out?'

'No one asked anyone out.'

'But?'

'But David did say it might be nice if I could go along – all very casual.'

'Mm,' said Christina. 'Well, I think I should chaperone and give this David chap the once-over.'

Cal's car was in the driveway. He prided himself on his excellent parking, so the narrow slot he'd left for Grace felt petty and deliberate. Now that they were about to come face to face, her insides spasmed with dread. She didn't know what to say to him. Ideally, she would avoid him altogether, but their house was too small for a dignified silence. She steeled herself to go inside but was met not by Cal, but by his middle daughter, Julia. She was in the hallway, putting on her coat.

'Hello,' she said, barely glancing at Grace. 'I was just dropping off Dad's birthday present.'

It must have been obvious from Grace's expression that his birthday had slipped her mind.

'It's tomorrow,' said Julia.

'Yes,' said Grace, with her well-practised stepmother smile.

When Julia asked what she had planned, Grace told her it was a surprise. The toilet flushed and Cal came downstairs, looking as uncomfortable to see Grace as she was him. Julia glanced from one to the other, but if she picked up on the icy atmosphere – and how could she not? – she didn't comment.

'Thanks for stopping by, love,' he said, pecking Julia on the cheek. 'And for the card and pressie.'

Grace waited for her to go before hanging up her Barbour and taking off her boots, determined not to be the one to speak first.

'So, what's my surprise?' he asked finally.

A new TV remote.

'It won't be a surprise if I tell you,' she said lightly, and trotted upstairs to get changed.

She was in her bra and knickers when he came into the bedroom. It felt awkward and intrusive, implying an intimacy she didn't feel. She wrapped herself in her dressing gown and tied it tight.

'I thought we could go out tonight,' he said. 'Save you cooking.'

'I'm going out with Christina,' she said.

'Since when?'

'Since I popped round there for coffee and she asked me.'

Grace never lied, but Cal had been lying to her for thirteen years so she had a lot of catching up to do.

'Look,' he said. 'Can't we just kiss and make up?'

She most certainly didn't want to kiss him, but making

up, or at least the appearance of it, might render the situation more bearable.

'Fine,' she said.

He exhaled – a short, sharp breath of relief.

'Good,' he said. 'So you'll cancel Christina and we'll go to that new place over by the abbey.'

'No,' said Grace firmly. 'I've already made plans for tonight. We can go tomorrow – celebrate your birthday.'

He looked like he was about to say something, but changed his mind. The set of his mouth suggested that this wasn't a compromise he was happy with, but one he was reluctantly prepared to accept.

'I'll book us a table then,' he said, with little enthusiasm.

She wondered what on earth they would talk about. Tomorrow's problem, she told herself, making a mental note to pop into Waterstones and buy him a book about sport.

Grace searched everywhere for her keys – handbags, coat pockets, drawers where they had no reason to be. Cal was the one always losing things, not her. They were communicating on a 'needs must' basis, but she should have already left for Christina's so asked if he could help her look. He found them in among the bags of recycling he had put by the front door. Grace said 'thanks' and threw him a grateful smile as she dashed out of the house.

'Glad to be of service,' he said, looking chuffed.

Despite being fifteen minutes late, when Grace arrived Christina wasn't ready. She followed Harry into the kitchen, where he offered her some wine. He topped up his glass from an open bottle of red.

'I'd love to but I'm driving,' she said.

Christina and Harry looked an unlikely couple, but then Grace and Cal probably did too. There wasn't an age gap, like in her own marriage – Christina and Harry had met at Oxford – but while she was beautiful and willowy with a glossy curtain of Titian hair, everything about Harry's appearance was average: his height, his build, his nondescript colouring. Christina was scouted by a modelling agency in her mid-teens and though she refused to take it too seriously, strutting along catwalks provided a decent income until she graduated and got what she considered a proper job. She joined the editorial team at *Vogue* before becoming fashion editor at *Tatler*. Grace had never understood what Harry did for a living, other than it involved investing other people's money. People with the Pearces' income and background usually educated their children privately, but Harry and Christina were ardent supporters of the local state schools. Christina once told Grace that Marx had really been on to something, but his theories were never properly applied. Cal said they were champagne socialists, by which he meant hypocrites. Grace couldn't see anything wrong with being wealthy and left-leaning, as long as you practised what you preached.

Christina breezed into the kitchen with Ellie in tow. Maybe it was because she was the youngest and the others tended to baby her, but Ellie seemed to crave her mother's constant attention. She was the one with Christina's colouring and, though only eleven, she was already lanky and arrestingly pretty. Christina had once told Grace that being beautiful was as much a curse as a blessing, and she worried for her flawless, needy daughter. Lucy and her twin, Rupert, favoured their father's looks. Lucy had taken to tinting her hair with henna, giving it a brassy reddish sheen that was the closest she could get to her mother's lustrous auburn. Adam, Christina's eldest, was often mistaken for Josh's brother. They were both a smidge under six feet tall, with dark blond hair that tended to curl. In height, build and jawline, Josh resembled Cal, but he had Grace's fair complexion and mild temperament.

'Right, we're off,' said Christina, submitting to a fierce hug from her daughter.

Grace noticed in passing that Christina didn't say goodbye to Harry, or even glance in his direction. Once they were on the road, she asked if everything was OK. Christina shrugged with her usual insouciance, and lobbed the question back to Grace.

'And you?' she said. 'What news from the home front?'

Grace braked to avoid a squirrel that darted in front of the headlights.

'We've agreed a truce. It's his birthday tomorrow. We're going out to dinner.'

'Good. You don't want him to suspect anything.'

Grace took her eyes off the road for a second and turned to her friend.

'There's nothing to suspect. Seriously, it's all perfectly innocent. I think it's for charity, actually.'

'You said that earlier – good to keep your story straight. Now step on it, would you? I'm gasping for a glass of mediocre wine.'

By the time they walked into the Lamb and Lion, Christina's teasing, however good-natured, had rendered Grace shy and self-conscious. The pub was an old-fashioned spit-and-sawdust place. A blackboard boasted sandwiches at lunchtime, but that seemed to be the only food offering, apart from crisps, nuts and pork scratchings. People were arranged in groups around wooden tables, but she couldn't see anyone she recognised. Christina was already on her way to the bar when Grace felt a tap on her shoulder. She spun around and came face to face with David Gill, wearing blue jeans and a crisp white T-shirt. He looked younger than he had in his flat cap and woolly jumper.

'You made it,' he said.

Grace realised how pale his eyes were, and how dark his lashes. The contrast was disarming.

'Yes,' she said, stating the obvious. 'I'm here with a friend. She's gone to get us a drink.'

'We're over there when you're ready,' he said, pointing to a table in the corner.

Grace found Christina paying for a bottle of Pinot Grigio, while flirting with the barman – a short, ruddy-faced guy with a prominent belly. She flirted as a public service – a selfless act of kindness to raise the spirits of those less fortunate in the looks department. There was nothing overtly sexual about it – more a case of teasing, flattering, buoying the spirits of the lucky recipient. She did it with Cal all the time, much to Grace's amusement. Once, when the four of them were out to dinner, he had looked so flustered that Harry told her to leave the poor man alone. His tone was playfully indulgent, as though watching his wife trifle with another man amused him. When they got home that evening, Cal made a point of telling Grace he wouldn't let *his* wife behave like that. As if.

The admiring customers at the bar parted for Christina, who rewarded them with a dazzling smile.

'Are you sure you want a bottle?' said Grace. 'I can only have one small glass.'

'All the more for me, then,' said Christina. 'Now, where's this gorgeous fisherman?'

'Please don't say things like that. I'm begging you,' said Grace, leading her over to David's table.

She introduced her to Reggie, the old man with the whiskery beard. He gave them a gummy smile and shifted along to make room. When Grace introduced her to David, he offered Christina his hand, just as he had that morning with Grace. It seemed oddly formal under the circumstances, but respectful too. They sat down and helped themselves to paper and pencils from a stash in the middle of the table. Grace took a sip from her small glass of wine. The team was eight strong, with David nominated to write down the answers. Each time the quizmaster asked a question, they fell into a huddle to confer. A faint odour of beer and leather hung in the air.

Sport was the first category – a topic that posed no problem for the Chew Fishermen. Grace didn't know any of the answers, despite the TV at home being perpetually tuned to either news or sport. It was just irritating background noise to which she paid no attention. Next was politics. The team didn't argue when Christina named Karl Marx's resting place as Highgate Cemetery, and 1975 as the year of the first EU referendum. Grace hadn't made a single contribution. Cal loved watching quiz shows and calling out the answers. Grace found them as dull as she did sport. Apart from Josh, she wondered what on earth they had in common.

'You OK?' asked David.

She took another sip of wine and nodded.

'Sorry I'm so useless,' she said.

'You apologise too much.'

'Do I?'

'You spent most of your lesson doing it.'

'Yes, I suppose I did. Sorry.'

His smile made her feel she'd got something right at last. Christina was in her element when it came to popular culture, naming cast members from *TOWIE* and which *Made in Chelsea* celebs had gone into the jungle. David put his mouth so close to Grace's ear, she could feel his warm breath on her skin.

'Your friend doesn't seem to be the type to watch trash TV,' he said.

'Teenage daughter,' said Grace.

History was Christina's forte. She rattled off the answers, leaning over to check that David had written them down correctly. Her flirting was shameless, tossing her hair over her shoulder, taking the pencil from his hand to correct a spelling mistake, even though her own pencil was right there in front of her. Grace pretended not to notice, and focused on trying to get at least one answer right. She guessed Sydney was the capital of Australia and felt irredeemably stupid when the rest of the team knew it was Canberra.

'Trick question,' David told her, as he wrote it down.

When the bell sounded, the teams swapped answers, confirming the Chew Fishermen as the winners. Their prize was a hundred-pound donation to the charity of their choice, and free drinks all round. They made a beeline for the bar but David – also a designated driver – stayed behind with Grace.

'Thanks for not giving up on me this morning,' she said, 'when all I could hook were leaves.'

'Everyone starts out like that,' he said. 'What did you do with your catch? You didn't seem too keen to take it home.'

'Gave it to Christina,' she said. 'I actually don't like fish that much, unless it's battered with fat chips and mushy peas.'

'Does that mean you're not coming back?' he said.

'Not at all,' she said. 'I enjoyed it, and I'm sure Christina will be grateful for anything I might catch. She has three growing children to feed.'

'What about you?'

'Just the one.'

'Your son at uni.'

She was touched that he remembered.

'That's right,' she said. 'And I don't have to feed him anymore.'

'Sounds like you miss him.'

'I do,' she said. 'My husband thinks we should be celebrating – you know, job done – but Josh has left a huge hole in my life.'

She gave her head a little shake.

'Sorry, I have no idea why I told you that. And there I go apologising again.'

'Some habits are hard to break,' said David.

She wondered if that was what her marriage had become. When she admitted to herself that she wasn't in love with Cal, it had felt significant, as if from that moment everything would change. But nothing had. She didn't share his interests or particularly enjoy his company, yet she went home to him every day, cooked his meals, washed his clothes, slept in his bed, listened to his opinions, his lame jokes, his not-so-harmless jibes. She judged herself for it, actually.

David was looking at her with those indecently blue eyes.

'Shall I put you down for the same time next Friday?' he said.

'Fishing or pub?' she said, trying to emulate Christina's flirty voice.

'Either,' said David casually. 'Or both. Your call.'

SIX

Cal was already in bed when Grace got home. The thought of getting in next to him made her feel queasy, like she had eaten something that didn't agree with her. But if another stuffy, anxious night in Josh's room was the only option, she had little choice. Not yet, though – she would have some wine first. A little quiet solitude was welcome after the raucous energy of the pub. It was embarrassing not to have answered a single question, and if not for David, it wouldn't have been worth the effort. *Weren't you just a teeny bit jealous when I fluttered my eyelashes at him?* This was what Christina had asked on the drive home, as if her flirting had been some kind of test. Grace laughed it off, but in truth she had felt a twinge of envy. Christina was gorgeous, clever, self-assured. She could have any man she set her sights on. Grace felt mousy in comparison, and Cal didn't exactly bolster her self-esteem. She couldn't remember the last time he complimented her appearance, and their love life (a blatant misnomer) was about him wanting sex, not wanting her.

'I thought we were being burgled.'

She hadn't heard him come downstairs. He stared pointedly at the wine glass but didn't comment. His silence implied restraint on his part. Her drinking implied the opposite. She felt the urge to justify herself, tell him she'd had only one small glass all evening, but why should she? It reminded her of being a teenager, when her mother would say, *I'm not cross, Gracie, I'm disappointed.* A million times worse. Nobody wants to be a disappointment.

'Are you coming up?' said Cal, heading back upstairs.

'In a while,' said Grace, hoping that if she left it long enough, he would be asleep. She was wide awake anyway, and it was another half-hour before she felt drowsy enough to slip into bed next to him. He turned on his side, passing wind as he did so. Grace pinched her nose and grimaced. She knew it was involuntary, a natural bodily function, but it still disgusted her. When she tried to visualise her life without him in it, she couldn't. It would be easier if he was a terrible husband – at least she would have a reason to leave. The truth was, she had simply grown tired of him. She felt trapped in some sort of marital limbo – not unhappy enough to go, not happy enough to stay.

Tired though she was, she couldn't slow her pattering heart, or the whirlwind of thoughts in her head. She forced herself to breathe slowly and deeply, and recalled what her mother used to tell her when she had bad dreams. *Just close your eyes, Gracie, and think of something nice.* She pulled the duvet up to her chin and thought of David Gill.

The sound of a phone ringing dragged her from a dream she didn't want to leave.

'Do you want to speak to Josh?'

Cal was calling from downstairs. Grace pushed off the covers and sat up, vaguely aware of having lost something beautiful.

'Yes,' she called back.

She grabbed her dressing gown and followed the smell of coffee to the kitchen. Cal handed her his mobile.

'This is a nice surprise,' she said, popping a pod into the Nespresso machine and reaching for a mug. 'I assumed students slept in late at the weekend.'

'I wanted to wish Dad a happy birthday.'

Grace glanced at him, loitering nearby. The volume was always on the highest setting, so presumably he could hear every word.

'That's so thoughtful of you,' she said, grateful for the prompt.

Josh asked about his PlayStation games, and she promised she would look for them today. When he mentioned he was going fishing, she thought of David Gill and remembered her dream. A plume of heat reddened her face and neck. She told Josh to have fun and handed the phone back to Cal.

'Why didn't you tell him you were learning to fish?' he said.

'I want to surprise him when he comes home,' she said. 'Oh, and happy birthday. I'll go get your present.'

As she brushed past, she realised he probably expected a kiss, but couldn't bring herself to do it. A smile was the best she could manage, and even that felt insincere. He had a vasectomy without consulting her. She was still staggered that he would do that and expect her to be OK with it, but his other two daughters were coming for lunch and she didn't want an atmosphere. Beth, the oldest, had never made any secret of her disdain for Grace. It embarrassed her to have a stepmother her own age. Truthfully, it embarrassed Grace a little too.

After she and Cal married, Beth refused to come to their house, or even see her father if his 'little wifey' was going to be there. Grace could have made a fuss and demanded her husband's loyalty, but she put his interests first and encouraged his relationship with the girls. Beth had a good deal of influence over her younger sisters and tried to impose her stance on them too. Cal finally put his foot down when Beth got married. She expected him to walk her down the aisle, but didn't want Grace at the wedding. 'You can't have it both ways,' he told her. 'We come as a couple, or not at all.' She relented at the eleventh hour, but made a point of ignoring Grace the entire day.

Beth's wedding was the first time Grace had seen Cal interact with Marilyn, who, physically at least, was her exact opposite. Where Grace was petite and fair, Marilyn was tall with thick ebony hair, inherited from her Spanish grandmother. The girls were tall and dark too, and it was only in Lydia, the youngest, that Grace could see a little of Cal. They both had a slight cleft in their chin, and wide fingernails with prominent half-moons.

Cal didn't like to talk about his first marriage. They had been together a year before he confided that Marilyn had once had a 'fling'. When he found out, he couldn't bear to be around her and moved in with Marty Devlin and his wife. Beth and Julia were in their early teens and intent on punishing their mother. They knew nothing of her affair, but were daddy's girls and blamed her anyway. Beth acted out by drinking, smoking and staying out half the night, driving Marilyn crazy with worry. Julia tortured her mother in a more creative way by refusing to eat. Mealtimes became a battleground, with fierce rows, tears and recriminations. Marilyn begged Cal to come home. She told him she couldn't cope on her own, and it was only a matter of time before something terrible happened to one of the girls. As emotional blackmail went, it wasn't exactly subtle, but he felt he had no choice. He told Grace that Julia's clothes hung off her like those emaciated girls in magazines, and Beth looked like jailbait in her miniskirts and make-up. Order was restored when he moved into the spare room, although when he described the atmosphere – the bristling tension between him and Marilyn, the girls' mood swings and marathon sulks – Grace's heart went out to him.

Matters came to a head at Christmas, with the arrival of Marilyn's sister. Cal had to vacate the spare room and either camp out on the sofa or swallow his pride and share a bed with his unfaithful wife. Either way, the parlous state of their marriage was a much-discussed topic between the two women. The girls gleaned enough from their eavesdropping to form their own opinions on the matter. *Not much fun being the only bloke in a houseful of women*, he had told Grace miserably.

He didn't mention relations between him and Marilyn, but she was pregnant by January, so they must have begun having sex again straight away. She feigned shock when two blue lines appeared on the pee-stick, but Cal wasn't fooled. He told Grace she had got pregnant deliberately in case he was thinking of leaving again. Marilyn knew he had always wanted a son, and told him it felt different this time – she was sure it was a boy. Eight months later Lydia arrived, purple-faced and screaming, as if furious to have been brought into the world to fix something already beyond repair.

Cal told Grace he didn't care about not having a son but cared very much that Marilyn had deceived him again, and in such a calculated way. She claimed scans weren't one hundred per cent accurate in predicting the baby's sex, but what did it matter as long as they had a healthy child? It mattered because of her lies. They had been childhood sweethearts, lovers, best friends. Now he didn't even like her. For him the marriage was over, but how could he leave her to cope with two stroppy teenagers and a colicky baby? To his credit he stuck it out until Lydia started school, by which time Beth was living in Bristol and Julia was at university. It came as no surprise to anyone when he finally moved out of the house. Like putting a dog out of its misery, was how he described it to Grace.

It must have galled Marilyn that Grace had given him a son, and for all his faults, he was a devoted father. Why else would he have stayed in a loveless marriage for five long years? It made her wonder if the vasectomy was his way of ensuring he never had to go through anything like that again. She was still a long way from forgiving him, but would make an effort to be pleasant, at least for today.

He seemed genuinely pleased with his birthday present – an illustrated hardback, recounting the best sporting moments of the decade. When he put his face close to hers, their lips touched in what could plausibly pass for a kiss. He leaned in for more, but she turned away. The ice might be melting, but the water was still chilly.

Breakfast was a rare feast of processed meat and cholesterol – bacon, sausage, black pudding, fried eggs. When he started talking about what he would do for his big birthday next year (seventy seemed so much older than sixty-nine – almost elderly), she told him not to wish his life away.

'One year at a time,' she said, determined not to think about the future stretching before her.

It was when she was leaving for Sainsbury's that she realised she had mislaid her purse. There wasn't much money in it – twenty pounds and change – but it did have her debit and credit cards inside. Her first reaction was panic – she emptied her bag on the kitchen table and rushed from place to place, searching – before forcing herself to calm down and think logically. She had taken it with her to the pub quiz, but Christina bought the wine, meaning Grace hadn't spent any money. Could someone have stolen it from her bag? David had sat on one side of her, Christina on the other, and her bag was on the floor by her feet. It seemed unlikely that there was a thief among the Chew Fishermen, but if the bag had been open it was possible her purse had fallen out. She called David, her heart thrumming as she waited for him to answer.

'Hi, sorry to bother you – it's Grace Wheeler.'

'Hi, Grace Wheeler. You got home OK then.'

His voice induced a warm sensation from chest to groin.

'I did, and poured myself a large glass of wine to make up for my abstemiousness.'

'Glad to hear it.'

'Listen, I seem to have mislaid my purse. I'm sure it was in my bag last night, but I can't find it. I don't suppose you remember seeing it at all?'

'Um, no, sorry. I could give the pub a quick ring if you like, ask if anyone has handed it in.'

'Would you? That's so kind. I'd really appreciate it.'

'I'll do it now and call you back.'

He rang off, leaving Grace to hunt through her coat pockets for the second time. She found a used tissue, a long receipt from Sainsbury's, a twenty-pence piece and a Costa loyalty card.

'What are you doing?' said Cal.

'Looking for my purse,' said Grace.

'You've lost it?'

'Mislaid.'

'First your keys, now your purse. What's going on?'

'Nothing,' she said defensively. 'These things happen.'

'To me, yes. Not to you.'

He was right. Grace never lost anything, let alone important stuff like car keys and bank cards. She didn't know what was wrong with her. There was a family history of dementia, but she was far too young for that – at least, she hoped she was. When her phone rang, David's name popped onto the screen. With Cal six feet away, she hesitated before answering, but thought it would look odd if she didn't.

'Hi,' she said casually. 'Any luck?'

'Sorry, no. It hasn't been handed in.'

Her heart sank.

'Right. Well, thanks for letting me know.'

She slipped the phone into her jeans pocket, determined not to lose that too.

'Who was that?' asked Cal.

'Guy from the pub. I called earlier on the off chance someone might have found it.'

She massaged her temples, where a headache threatened.

'I'm going to have to cancel my bank cards,' she said.

'But they might turn up.'

'I doubt it. Somebody could be out there now, having a shopping spree at my expense.'

'Not likely, unless they have your PIN,' he said. 'It wasn't written down, was it?'

'Of course not,' she said. 'I'm not stupid.'

'Sorry,' he said, raising his hands in mock surrender. 'Just trying to help.'

She took a breath and reminded herself to be nice.

'No, I'm sorry. I was about to go and buy food for lunch.'

'Here,' he said, handing her his own bank card. 'Use mine for now. You know the PIN. We'll call the bank on Monday if yours haven't turned up.'

'The car,' she said suddenly.

'What?'

'It could have fallen out of my bag in the car.'

She put on her jacket and went outside to do another thorough but fruitless search. Begrudgingly admitting defeat, she took Cal's debit card and set off for Sainsbury's, half an hour later than planned. Being Saturday, the traffic was terrible, the car park full and queues snaked back from every till. When she arrived home, laden with four bags of shopping, Beth was in the kitchen drinking coffee with Cal. She greeted Grace with a tight smile.

'Lydia not here?' said Grace.

'Not yet,' said Beth. 'But you know Lyd.'

Yes, she did. Unlike her older sisters, little Lydia had loved visiting her daddy and his pretty new wife. Grace crimped her hair, painted her toenails with sparkly polish, cooked her favourite macaroni cheese with bacon bits and toasted breadcrumbs. They watched Disney films in their pyjamas, went shopping together, sang pop songs at the top of their voices. Lydia was the daughter Grace never had. As she got older, she confided the agonies of adolescence – falling out with her best friend, the boy she liked who didn't like her back, wishing she was small like Grace, not the tallest girl in her class. And when Marilyn got sick, Lydia moved in with Grace and Cal for weeks on end while her mother was in hospital or enduring the horrors of chemotherapy.

'What's for lunch?' asked Cal, peeking into the carrier bags.

'Smoked salmon, roast chicken, salad, that sort of thing. Oh, and I got that crusty bread you like.'

'With Flora, I hope,' said Beth.

The years had taken a heavy toll on her, and it showed in the worry lines etched across her forehead. Her dark hair was dull, with a thick streak of gunmetal grey. Grace wondered why she didn't dye it, but wouldn't dream of asking. It was Beth who had borne the brunt of caring for Marilyn. She had moved back home each time the cancer returned to steal a little more of her mother. Beth's career and marriage had suffered from her long absences, and after Marilyn had died and Beth was grieving, her husband had told her he had been having an affair with the mum of one of their son's school friends. It had been going on for over a year, and not only was he moving in with her, their only son, Zac, had elected to go too. She told Cal that it didn't really hit her until she went to Zac's parents' evening, and her ex was there with his new partner and the two boys. They looked like a family, she said. A happy family. When Cal shared this with Grace, her heart broke for Beth. She couldn't imagine the pain of Josh choosing not to live with her. It reminded her to make allowances for her stepdaughter's hard edges and brusque manner. The sacrifices she had made had cost her dearly.

'Why don't you two go into the sitting room,' said Grace, shooing them away for some father-daughter time.

All the years Beth had shunned Cal were forgotten after Marilyn died. She needed her dad and he was there. It was the quality Grace most admired about him.

Lydia arrived with a small bunch of yellow roses for Grace and a bottle of Cal's favourite wine.

'They're lovely,' said Grace, finding a vase for the flowers. 'You're such a thoughtful girl.'

'Where's Dad?' said Lydia.

'In the sitting room with Beth.'

'Who else is coming?'

'No one,' said Grace, realising this was the first time Josh would miss a family birthday. 'Julia stopped by yesterday with his card and present.'

'What about your mum?'

'She volunteers at a charity shop on Saturdays.'

'Just us Wheelers, then,' said Lydia. 'Anything I can do?'

'Yes, you can go talk to your dad and sister.'

'Any wine on the go?'

'Why don't you open that?' said Grace, handing Lydia a corkscrew.

Lydia took the bottle and four glasses into the sitting room, Grace following with the food. She laid it out buffet style on the coffee table and had forgotten all about losing her purse until Cal asked for his bank card back, just in case she lost that too. His tone was light and jokey, but she wished he hadn't brought it up. He made her sound ditsy and scatterbrained, when he knew perfectly well she was the opposite. Grace was the organiser in the household. She had a spreadsheet with important dates and reminded Cal when their cars were due a service, or a family event was coming up. It was Grace who managed the household bills and shopped around on comparison sites to make sure they were getting the best deal. She hated being demeaned in front of the girls (something he would strenuously deny), but it might have seemed churlish to take offence, so she offered a meek smile and poured herself some wine.

When lunch was over and the girls had left, Cal thanked Grace for all the trouble she had gone to.

'I know things have been a bit off,' he said, resting his hands on her shoulders. 'But we're OK, aren't we?'

It was more of a plea than a question. The deceit of his vasectomy was still raw, but holding on to the anger wouldn't change anything. What was done was done. She remembered Christina saying she might be projecting her negative feelings about Josh leaving onto Cal. Maybe she had a point. The morning after their terrible row, Grace had admitted to herself that she would never have behaved that way if Josh had been home. Cal was watching her earnestly, waiting for a response. She nodded. When she told him to go watch some TV, he positively beamed with relief.

Thinking about Josh reminded her that she still hadn't looked for his PlayStation games. She went upstairs to his bedroom and had to stop herself ruminating on the sleepless night she had spent there, and the anger that had made her shake and swear. Cal was right about moving past it. Neither of them was cut out for that sort of drama. Missing Josh was as much as Grace could cope with right now. The sight of his empty wardrobe prodded the gnawing ache of his absence. Her boy's room, but without her boy. It didn't even smell like him anymore. Keep busy, she told herself, determined not to mope. Her search yielded nothing except a stray sock under the bed. The only other place to look was the small third bedroom, although she couldn't imagine why his games would be in there. Apart from a single divan against one wall, it was home to Cal's clutter. When Grace came across their wedding album, she perched on the bed and studied the photographs, hardly recognising the fresh-faced bride and grinning groom. Cal was broad and handsome, with a good head of hair. Grace looked gleeful and impossibly young. Far too young to get married.

She found Josh's games in a Sports Direct bag, not a box like he had said. When she pulled her phone from her jeans pocket to text him, something caught her eye. Poking out from under the divan, she spotted her missing purse.

SEVEN

Grace was going to let David's call go to voicemail but changed her mind at the last minute.

'Hi, Grace Wheeler,' he said breezily, like someone without a care in the world. 'Just checking to see if you found your purse. Only I could phone round the other guys and ask if any of them saw it.'

She cleared her throat.

'That's kind of you,' she said. 'But it turned up yesterday afternoon.'

Cal admitted he had hidden it, but insisted he intended to 'find' it later. When Grace looked at him askance, demanding to know why he would do such a thing, he said that when he found her keys before she dashed off on Friday night, she had actually seemed pleased with him for a change. Such was the state of their marriage. David's voice cut through that depressing thought.

'You don't sound too relieved,' he said.

She ran her fingers through her hair and sighed.

'Sorry. I'm just having a bad day.'

'I know a cure for that.'

'Pardon?'

'In my official capacity as your fishing instructor, I can confirm that nothing clears your head or improves your mood like a few hours by the water.'

An unexpectedly tempting offer. At least she would escape the turgid atmosphere at home. She and Cal were supposed to have eaten out last night, but after the purse incident, she told him to cancel the table. She knew he was looking forward to it and almost relented when she saw his wounded expression. But then she remembered him regaling the girls with tales of her forgetfulness and cancelled the table herself. She accused him of belittling her. He accused her of making him feel like an inconvenience in his own home. Their argument was ugly and loud and she hated every second. *I was going to give it back to you*, Cal had called after her as she retreated to Josh's room.

'You live in Bath, right?' said David. 'There's a beautiful spot near Midford where you can fish on Sundays.'

Even more tempting. She thought he had meant her to drive to the lake. And if it was a choice between David's company and Cal's, David's was infinitely preferable.

'Go on, say yes,' he said, and when she didn't say no, he told her he'd text the postcode and see her around twelve.

She quickly showered and dressed, before she could change her mind. Skulking out of the house like a criminal felt absurd, but she didn't want to be confronted by Cal. He would have heard her reversing out of the driveway, and she half expected him to phone and ask where she was going. Just as well he didn't. She could hardly tell him she was on her way to meet David Gill.

She recognised the place he had chosen. Josh sometimes fished there – a beautiful, secluded spot with meadow grass and gin-clear water. A muddy Land Rover was parked on the verge – David's, Grace assumed. She tucked her car right behind and tried not to question why she had agreed to meet a man she barely knew, instead of sorting things out with her husband. His explanation for hiding the purse had incensed her, but troubled her too. Was she so withholding that he would go to those lengths for a scrap of appreciation? And truthfully, it was the sort of thing he might do. Cal considered himself a bit of a prankster – all good clean harmless fun. He once hid her Christmas present in plain sight, knowing she couldn't resist taking a peek. The box was loosely wrapped and empty, except for a note saying 'Gotcha!'

A text from David arrived.

The fish are biting 🎣 🐟

Grace stepped onto the spongy verge, climbed over a stile that straddled the drystone wall, and followed a footpath down to the brook. Rain threatened, and a biting breeze stirred the trees. David saw her and raised his hand.

'You came,' he said, smiling. 'I wasn't sure you would.'

'Me neither,' she said, smiling back.

He waited while she slipped on her sunglasses and then handed her a rod.

'I can't remember how to do this,' she said. 'Peel, pause, something?'

'Peel, pluck, pause, tap. Here,' he said, moving behind her and extending his arms to take hold of the handle. 'Peel the line off the water, pluck it upwards, pause for a second, and then tap to cast.'

He matched each instruction with a corresponding movement and the fly plopped onto the water, about twelve feet out from the riverbank. She noticed he was wearing aftershave – a subtle scent of musk and leather.

'You got it?' he said, and she nodded.

He picked up his own rod and cast with a soft swish.

'I was right, wasn't I?' he said, grinning. 'I bet you feel better already.'

She replied with a coy smile, glad she was here with David and not at home with Cal. Half a dozen casts later, when she was really getting the hang of it, spits of rain started to pockmark the river, and the breeze became gusty and strong. David reeled in his line.

'We can't fish in this,' he said. 'It's too windy and rain muddies the water so the trout can't see the fly.'

Her heart hardened at the thought of going home. As if he had read her mind, David asked if she was hungry. She hadn't eaten since Cal's birthday lunch – a few slices of smoked salmon and some salad. She had been saving her appetite for the dinner that never happened.

'Starving,' she said.

David was already packing away his rod.

'There's a pub about a mile down the road that does a respectable Sunday roast. Why don't we grab a bite and pick this up afterwards, weather permitting?'

He made it sound very casual. Just two people having lunch while they waited for the rain to stop.

'OK,' she said, going along with the fiction that it wasn't a big deal.

She chose to ignore the censorious voice in her head telling her that fishing was one thing, even a pub quiz, especially as Christina was there, but this was different.

'Great,' he said, sounding pleasantly surprised for the second time that day.

The Goose and Gander sat proudly among a scatter of stone houses either side of a narrow lane. The bar was busy – mostly men dressed in varying shades of brown or green, as if they were in uniform. David led her up a few steps to a larger, brighter room, dominated by an inglenook fireplace and laid out with tables and chairs. On each table was a laminated menu, and a caddy with cutlery and paper serviettes. A chalkboard had the specials – leek and potato soup, roast rib of beef for two, raspberry crème brûlée.

'What can I get you to drink?' asked David, putting his wax jacket over the back of the chair.

'Sauv blanc,' she said, glancing around to see if there was anyone she knew.

In the far corner, snuggled on a cosy window seat, was a gay couple – the young Asian woman strikingly pretty, her raven-haired girlfriend with her back to Grace. She didn't recognise any of the older couples, and the people with children were too busy getting them to eat and behave to pay any attention to the blonde with a slightly furtive countenance.

'Here you go,' said David, putting down a carafe of iced water and two glasses of wine – a large red and a small white.

'Have you had a look at the menu?' he said. 'I'm happy to share the beef, if you're up for that.'

Grace would have preferred chicken but wanted to be amenable, so she said yes, the beef sounded good. She watched David go back to the bar to order, struck by how at ease he seemed. Grace wasn't. Now that she was here, it felt borderline illicit. Why else would she have scoured the restaurant to make sure there was no one she knew? When he sat down again, she asked what they were doing here.

He looked vaguely confused by the question.

'Having lunch.'

'But why? We hardly know each other.'

'I know you have a son at university, that he loves fishing, that your general knowledge leaves a lot to be desired, that you apologise too much, oh, and that you were having a bad day.'

He drank from his wine glass, studying her from under the dark sweep of his lashes. Blood rushed to her cheeks. She wasn't used to such scrutiny. It was a relief when their food arrived on a large wooden platter, something Cal would have complained was gimmicky.

'Looks good,' said David. 'Tuck in.'

He was right – it looked delicious. Thick slices of rare beef luxuriated in the centre, with a generous dollop of horseradish on one side. Nestled between two giant Yorkshire puddings was a mound of roast potatoes. Carrots and broccoli added a hit of colour, and steam rose off the gravy, served in an old-fashioned jug. Grace's argument with Cal had twisted her stomach into knots, but now she was ravenous. She impaled a roast potato with her fork, duck fat oozing sinfully as she chewed. Cal's strict diet dictated their meals at home. Grace did her best but low-fat, low-salt food wasn't the most appealing. It was a pleasure to see David eat with gusto. He had gone straight for the beef, smothered in horseradish.

'That packs a punch,' he said, his eyes watering.

Grace sipped her wine, glad she had agreed to this, despite her reservations. The convivial atmosphere, the hearty food and the company didn't disappoint either. David took a drink of water and wiped his mouth.

'You look deep in thought,' he said.

'I was wondering if you made a habit of spending time with middle-aged women in bad marriages.'

He had just taken another mouthful of beef – less horseradish this time – and made a point of chewing thoroughly before he answered.

'I try to,' he said, with mock seriousness. 'Angling is a great career choice if you want to meet unhappy middle-aged women.'

Grace giggled, relieved he had made a joke of it. 'Bad marriage' had slipped out unintentionally.

'That's better,' he said.

'Seriously, though,' she said. 'This does seem a rather unlikely friendship.'

She stumbled a little over 'friendship'. Was she being presumptuous?

'I like you,' he said, using the same tone he had used about the beef. 'You're learning to fly-fish so you have something to share with your son, and you're persevering, even though there's not much reward in the beginning.'

'I caught a trout,' she said indignantly.

'The lake had just been stocked. I would have been amazed if you hadn't. And while we're on the subject, this is where I confess that I used to go fishing with my mum too.'

'Really?'

'It was just the two of us but she didn't want me to miss out, you know, not having a dad around, so she took me to cricket matches, football practice, even mountain biking. Fishing was what I enjoyed most, so that was what we did.'

'Wait. Are you saying I remind you of your mother?'

'In terms of maternal devotion, yes, I suppose I am. It's a compliment, by the way.'

'Um, thank you, I think.'

She tucked into a puffed-up Yorkshire pudding, still crisp under a serving of thick gravy.

'It was just me and my mum too,' she said. 'So we have that in common.'

Grace rarely thought about her father, and mentioned him even less. Like her earlier reference to her marriage, she found herself unguarded around David Gill. He raised his glass.

'To mothers,' he said, and drained the last of his wine. 'And not wishing to pry, but you mentioned an unhappy marriage.'

She wished she hadn't. He must have read that in her expression because he apologised, said it was none of his business. Christina was the only person she had confided in about Cal. There was certainly no good reason to discuss it with David, and yet she felt she could.

'My husband and I had an argument yesterday. It was his birthday – he's a lot older than me.'

'How much older?'

'Twenty-three years.'

David didn't hide his surprise. She regretted telling him, as if it in some way reflected badly on her and now he would see her differently.

'He's very fit and young for his age,' she said, in case he imagined her with someone old and doddery.

It had been true until last year. Ageing, she realised, wasn't an even-handed process. It happened in fits and starts. Things like weight gain or hair loss accelerated it on the outside. With Cal, it was on the inside – a blocked artery requiring surgery to fit a stent. There were no complications and his recovery was textbook, but the whole episode had changed him. He wouldn't admit it, but Grace could tell he saw himself differently after that. The physical strength he had taken for granted was noticeably diminished. He was more cautious, less likely to run full pelt into the sea or smash his way to victory on the squash court. Now it was golf and television, and a slow but inevitable decline.

'Grace?'

A woman's voice behind her. She turned and saw Lydia, hand in hand with the pretty Asian woman.

'Lydia,' she said. 'What are you doing here?'

'Same as you, by the look of it.'

She studied David intently, as if trying to pick him out of a police line-up.

A burst of heat exploded in Grace's chest, turning her face scarlet. She couldn't have looked more guilty. And surprised. She and Lydia had always been close. How did she not know she was gay? A conversation for another time.

'David is teaching me to fly-fish,' said Grace brightly. 'So I can surprise Josh when he comes home.'

A pause followed, as if this unlikely explanation needed time to sink in. For David's benefit she said, 'Lydia's my stepdaughter.'

'Nice to meet you,' he said amiably.

Lydia didn't introduce her girlfriend.

'Is Dad here?' she said.

'Um, no,' said Grace.

'Why not?' said Lydia.

The answer wasn't one she would want to hear. She believed Cal and Grace to be rock solid – the two people who had been steadfast in her life. Through no fault of her own, Marilyn often couldn't take care of her, and Beth was too busy looking after her mother to cope with her little sister as well. Grace worried she might feel rejected, but Lydia always said she preferred it at her dad's house anyway.

'Can I get you girls a drink?' said David, with a charm-offensive smile.

'Women,' said Lydia tersely. 'We stopped being girls some years ago.'

She stared at him with haughty defiance. Grace hadn't seen that look since Lydia was a teenager, when she would lock horns with Cal over curfews and short skirts. What Grace wouldn't give to magically disappear. Nothing in her ordinary, conventional life had prepared her for this scenario.

'Noted,' said David. 'But the offer still stands.'

Grace looked imploringly at Lydia.

'Can we talk later?' she said.

Lydia's girlfriend spoke quietly.

'Come on, Lyd. Let's leave them to it.'

Lydia allowed herself to be steered towards the door, but not before Grace had registered her hurt and confusion. It pained her immensely that she was the cause.

EIGHT

'That was awkward,' said David, which was something of an understatement.

Grace poured herself some water.

'You must think I'm very hard work,' she said, because she was thinking it herself. First she had whined on about her husband, and then her stepdaughter had loomed over them, ruining a perfectly pleasant lunch.

'It's not your fault she got the wrong idea,' he said, carrying on with his food.

Grace couldn't eat another thing. She checked her phone – nothing from Lydia or Cal. She half expected Lydia to call her dad the first chance she got. What a mess. Grace felt as if she had been caught red-handed committing some heinous crime, when really it was all quite innocent. She excused herself and went to the Ladies. The harsh, unflattering light made her look pasty and tired. She found a cherry-red lipstick at the bottom of her bag, but it only emphasised how washed out she was. A mother blustered in with twin girls of about eight or nine. Grace remembered Lydia at that age – obsessed with ponies and all things pink. They had never fallen out – not once in all these years. She hadn't been a rebellious teenager, certainly not compared to Beth and Julia, but whenever she got into trouble for flouting Cal's rules, it was Grace she came to – her ally, a go-between to smooth things over. She hoped this misunderstanding about David could be smoothed over.

He had finished his lunch when she got back to the table, and was checking the bill.

'Allow me,' she said, delving into her bag for her purse. 'It's the least I can do.'

'We'll split it,' he said, putting his credit card on the table.

Grace did the same.

'I'm so sorry,' she said.

'What did we say about apologising all the time?'

'Don't.'

The waiter ran their cards through the machine and they left. Outside, rain was falling in stiff rods. Violent bursts of wind stripped branches of their remaining leaves.

'Autumn's here with a vengeance,' he said, pushing his hands into his pockets.

God, they were reduced to talking about the weather. And vengeance wasn't something Grace wanted to think about right now. A sudden gust sent her hair flying in all directions. She tried in vain to smooth it down, wretchedly aware of how dishevelled she must look. He jogged over to the Land Rover and waved half-heartedly as he drove away. She sat in her car for a while, wondering what she was heading home to. A prolonged and resentful silence?

Another hideous row? She checked her phone again. No missed calls, no messages.

Cal's car wasn't there. Thank goodness, thought Grace, grateful for the reprieve. She parked neatly and let herself in, heading straight to the kitchen for a large glass of wine. It tasted sharp and fruity, like liquid redemption. She nursed her glass, agonising over whether or not to phone Lydia. Better to take the initiative, surely, but supposing she wasn't ready to talk? And even if she was, what would Grace say? She decided to text, which seemed a reasonable compromise between speaking and silence.

Can we talk?

She sipped her wine nervously, waiting for a reply:

No

Short, but not sweet. Grace was pondering her next move when she heard the front door open. Her heart felt as if it had doubled in size. Cal walked into the kitchen holding a bunch of limp service station flowers. He put them on the table, as if handing them to her was a gesture too far.

'I'm sorry about your purse,' he said.

Compared to her run-in with Lydia, the whole purse thing seemed relatively minor now. She obviously hadn't spoken to Cal. He poured himself a glass of wine and sat down opposite her. In the spirit of domestic harmony, she said she was sorry about cancelling the restaurant. She knew couples who carried on an argument for days, weeks even. Not the Wheelers. Grace didn't know how long their detente would last – in many ways that was up to Lydia – but she was grateful for it. Cal looked relieved too. She was about to ask him where he had been, but stopped herself in case he asked her the same thing.

'I hate arguing,' he said. 'You know that.'

She drained her glass and nodded.

'Me too.'

'I thought Josh going to university would be a fresh start for us,' he said. 'But you seem to find reasons to spend less time together than we did before.'

He wasn't wrong. Perhaps she should make more of an effort. If not a game of golf, then at least a meal at the club house. That would cheer him up. His phone rang – Lydia's name on the screen. Grace felt sick.

'Hi, love,' he said.

She sat still, waiting.

'Yeah, she's here. I'll pass you over.'

Cal handed Grace his phone.

'Hi,' she said, turning down the volume.

'You're home then,' said Lydia, coldly matter-of-fact.

'Yes.'

'We need to talk about earlier,' said Lydia.

That being the case, she wondered why Lydia had called Cal and not her. To worry her, perhaps. Give her a fright.

'Good idea,' said Grace, forcing a pleasant tone for Cal's benefit.

'I'll meet you tomorrow after work. Caffè Nero.'

Grace always went to her mother's on Monday, but this was more important.

'Lovely,' she said, sounding even more false and bright.

She gave the phone back to Cal and worked her way through a second glass of wine.

When Marty called her into his office, Grace assumed it was to discuss a brownfield site that had been idling in the company's portfolio for almost a year. Getting permission to build was proving tricky, and it was Grace's job to solicit regular updates from the planning committee. She took her laptop and notebook in with her and sat down opposite her boss. He offered her a cup of coffee, but he always made it too strong, so she told him she'd just had one.

'Everything OK, Grace?' he said.

'Yes, fine. I chased up the chief planning officer's PA and am waiting to hear back.'

'Good,' he said, nodding. 'But I meant, with you. Is everything OK with you?'

Grace stared at him, confused.

'Um, yes. Why do you ask?'

'It's just I saw Cal at the golf club yesterday, having lunch on his own. And I know it's none of my business, but he didn't look so good.'

'In what way?'

'Oh, a bit washed out. Rather like you do, in fact.'

Grace shifted in her seat. She supposed Marty was entitled to express concern in his capacity as Cal's friend, but he was also Grace's employer and this was their workplace. Being here allowed some respite from her personal problems, but Marty had waved them in front of her.

'I think I might be coming down with something,' she said, hoping he would take the hint and leave it at that.

'Please don't think I'm prying,' he said when Grace clammed up.

She shook her head.

'No, of course not. Anyway, I'll let you know when that PA gets back to me.'

She stood to leave, but Marty hadn't finished.

'June reminded me it was Cal's birthday this weekend. She has all these things written down.'

'That's right,' said Grace, prickling at the mention of his offish wife.

June and Marilyn had been close friends. The four of them – Marty and June, Cal and Marilyn – used to go on holiday together when the children were young. Cal was so humiliated by Marilyn's infidelity, he didn't even tell Marty the whole story, which was why, when Cal finally left her, everyone assumed he was the guilty party. A mid-life crisis seemed the obvious explanation, only instead of buying a sports car, he married a girl in her twenties. June and her crowd regarded Grace with suspicion, as if she had lured Cal away from his wife and children. This fictional version suited Marilyn, who cast herself in the role of wronged wife and, by implication, branded Grace a homewrecker. It was all nonsense, but when did the truth ever get in the way of a nice juicy piece of gossip?

'Do anything special?' asked Marty.

'Sorry?'

'For Cal's birthday.'

'Oh, the girls came over for lunch on Saturday. We were going to go out for dinner but I was a bit off colour.'

'Well, look after yourself, Grace. And that husband of yours.'

She promised that she would and went back to her desk, peeved at Marty's interference. Her mobile showed a missed call from David. She cringed, thinking about what had happened at the pub. Despite his good manners, it was obvious he couldn't wait to get away. He hadn't left a voicemail and since she was curious to hear what he wanted, she called him back.

'Hi,' he said. 'Just sorting my lessons for this week and wanted to check you were OK for Friday?'

Friday seemed a long way off. A lot could happen between now and then. Might be best to see how coffee with Lydia went before committing to anything.

'Um, I'm not sure.'

'Well, I'm getting pretty booked up, so why don't I put you in for twelve and if you can't make it, let me know.'

The afternoon dragged, even though Grace was busy. The planners had at last got back to her, not with a decision, but with a list of supplementary queries that she was still working her way through as five-thirty approached. Under normal circumstances she would have stayed until she had finished, but she didn't want to be late for Lydia. Rushing along Broad Street, her short, spiky heels kept catching between the cobbles and threatened to pitch her face-first onto the ground. She spotted Lydia through the café's misty windows, hunched in a corner, chewing her nails. Grace hadn't seen her do that since she was a little girl. She had persuaded her to stop by painting the tiny bitten stumps with glittery pink polish. Grace hoped the habit hadn't returned after all these years.

The café was warm and humid, the air laced with aromas of ground coffee, cinnamon and vanilla. She smiled at Lydia, who didn't smile back.

'Can I get you anything?' said Grace, taking off her coat and dropping it on the chair.

Lydia pointed to her cup.

'Already got one.'

Grace got a decaf latte that she didn't really want and when she sat down, Lydia got straight to the point.

'Are you having an affair?'

Grace was taken aback.

'No, of course not.'

Lydia fixed her with a hard stare – a human lie detector.

'So what were you doing with that guy?'

Grace took a sip of her latte.

'I told you, he's teaching me to fly-fish.'

'And cosy lunches are part of the deal?'

Grace started to explain how the weather had turned, but Lydia interrupted her.

'Where was Dad?'

Lydia was picking the cuticle on her thumbnail and winced as a speck of blood appeared.

'There was an argument,' said Grace. 'We needed a bit of space, so he went to the golf club and I –'

Lydia interrupted again.

'Met a good-looking guy half his age.'

'We didn't plan to have lunch –'

'Why did you and Dad argue? You seemed fine when I saw you on Saturday.'

Grace wished they were in a wine bar, not a steamy coffee shop. A nice crisp Chardonnay would have slipped down a treat.

'I'd rather not get into that,' she said. 'It's private.'

Lydia scrutinised her, as if deciding whether or not to dig deeper.

'And speaking of private,' said Grace, seizing on a chance to shift the focus onto Lydia, 'you didn't introduce me to your girlfriend.'

Lydia hesitated, but only for a moment.

'Kiara,' she said.

Grace offered an encouraging smile.

'She's very pretty. How long have you been seeing each other?'

'A few months.'

'Why didn't you tell me you were gay?'

It was the nearest Lydia had come to a smile, albeit a sardonic one.

'Does it help you to put a label on it?'

Grace wasn't sure what she meant.

'You've seen me with guys so assumed I was straight, but now you've seen me with a woman, so I must be gay, right?'

Grace sensed it was a trick question and kept quiet.

'It doesn't have to be a binary thing,' said Lydia. 'An either/or. Why can't it be both?'

'Well, it can,' said Grace. 'Be whatever you want to be. You should have brought her on Saturday.'

Another sardonic smile.

'Mm, not sure Dad would approve.'

A distinct possibility. Cal was certainly old-fashioned

– conservative with both a small and capital C – but he loved his children unconditionally.

'You never know, he might surprise you,' said Grace. 'And anyway, you're a grown woman. You don't need your father's approval.'

'Don't we always need our parents' approval – fear disappointing them?'

'I suppose, but it works both ways, you know. Parents fear disappointing their children too.'

They let that linger for a while. By the time Grace took another sip of her latte, it was tepid and slightly sickly.

'Look, I don't know about you,' she said, 'but I could do with a glass of wine. Why don't we pop along the road to the Ivy?'

'I'm meeting Kiara.'

'OK. Well, I hope you introduce me next time.'

'And I hope you and Dad sort out whatever it is that's going on between you.'

As they stood to leave, Lydia gripped Grace's arm.

'Look, if you and Dad are going through some stuff, is it a good idea to be hanging round with someone like David?'

'What do you mean?'

'Someone young and hot?'

Ludicrously, Grace felt flattered, as though the compliment was hers as well. She may have even blushed a little.

'It's putting temptation right there in front of you,' said Lydia. 'A broad shoulder to cry on when things are bad at home.'

'Please don't say anything to your dad,' said Grace. 'There's no point upsetting him over nothing.'

Lydia buttoned up her coat. In her chunky-heeled boots, she was head and shoulders above Grace.

'As long as it *is* nothing,' said Lydia earnestly.

'It is,' said Grace. 'I promise.'

It was heartening to see Lydia's face soften. Grace just hoped she hadn't made a promise she wouldn't keep.

NINE

Grace's Monday-night supper with her mother was a long-established tradition. Cal and Josh would have a takeaway – a tradition of their own. Now Cal spent his Monday evenings with a microwave meal and Sky Sports, reminding Grace she wasn't the only one who missed their son.

The 1960s development on Bath's unfashionable fringes was a sprawl of small, boxy houses and a few low-rise blocks of flats. Compared to the city's grand Georgian architecture it was unimaginative and plain, but to Grace it had been home for more than half her life. The taxi passed the cul-de-sac where she had learned to ride her bike, the playground where she used to meet friends, the bus stop where she had her first kiss. Bobby Roberts was his name, which fourteen-year-old Grace didn't realise was funny. Some of the other kids weren't allowed to mix with him because his dad was in prison, but Ruth said it wasn't the boy's fault, just try to be careful. Grace had been careful her whole life. A good girl – rarely any trouble. The most outrageous thing she'd ever done was marry an older, divorced man with three children of his own. Her mum hadn't been quite so relaxed about that.

'Why didn't you use your key?' said Ruth, opening the front door and planting a kiss on Grace's cheek.

'Sorry. Easier to ring the bell.'

The house smelled of her childhood: baking, fresh laundry, lemon Flash.

'You look tired,' said Ruth.

'So I'm told,' said Grace.

'Everything all right?'

'Do you have any wine?'

'I always buy wine when you're coming round. Make of that what you will.'

Dinner was ready to dish up – lamb chops, new potatoes, carrots and peas. Ruth wasn't an adventurous cook, but her meals were tasty and wholesome and Grace looked forward to them. There was a jar of mint sauce on the table and a small vase of pink carnations. She thought of the flowers Cal had brought home yesterday – his peace offering. She was glad they were speaking again.

Ruth poured them both a small glass of wine – something on special from Aldi – and they chatted as they ate. When Grace admitted she had found these past weeks difficult, Ruth agreed that an empty nest took a lot of getting used to. The voice of experience. Grace had lived at home until she married, just her and her mum in their clean, cosy house. She had only vague memories of her dad – her little girl feet in his giant shoes, the silly voices he did when he read her stories, the stubbly roughness of his chin. He vanished from her life when she was six, and she didn't understand why. She had been sure he would come back as suddenly as he had left, and when he didn't, she allowed him to fade from her memory. A matter of self-preservation, perhaps. It had been easier to let him go than to live with the ache of wanting and waiting. Always one to grasp the silver lining, Grace had revelled in having her mum to herself. Her friends had to share theirs with dads and siblings, but she and Ruth coexisted in a bubble of love and contentment. A shadow of sadness would darken her mother's face whenever Grace asked about her dad, so she'd stopped asking. The last thing she wanted was to make her mum sad. Ruth was her world, and vice versa. They didn't have a fancy car or shop at John Lewis like lots of her school friends, but that had never bothered Grace. It had bothered her that some of her clothes came from charity shops, but she had kept that to herself. Instead of jetting off to the Med, they had spent summer holidays in Anglesey with her grandparents. She had loved playing on the fine-sand beaches, buying ice cream from a van, sleeping in an old feather bed with her mum. The rest of the year Ruth had worked from home, doing telephone surveys for a marketing company. The money wasn't good, but it meant Grace didn't come back to an empty house after school each day.

She had buried thoughts of her absent father until her engagement to Cal, when they floated to the surface again. There were two strands to contend with, one emotional, one practical. The former revolved around the assumption that Grace loved a man old enough to be her father because her actual father never loved her. It hurt deeply that people said this, not only behind her back but to her face as well. How dare they presume to know anything of the sort? It raised the long since taboo question of why her dad had left, but Ruth stuck to her story: that some things weren't meant to be. Privately she urged Grace not to rush into marriage, while publicly defending her right to do so. *I'm always on your side*, she had told Grace, as if there was ever any doubt.

That having been decided, there was the question of who would walk her down the aisle. Ruth had invited her brother to do the honours – a man Grace barely knew. He had emigrated to Canada in the late Seventies, and she had met him only twice that she could remember – once at her grandad's funeral, and a year later at her grandma's. Ruth had got out the photo albums to refresh Grace's memory. He looked presentable enough, with good posture and her grandad's generous smile.

'But you were OK when I left home,' said Grace. 'Weren't you?'

'Not really,' said Ruth. 'I pretended to be because I didn't want you to worry.'

She drizzled mint sauce on a piece of lamb and chewed thoughtfully.

'It had always been the two of us,' she said, 'and then suddenly it was just me. At least you've got Cal.'

Grace didn't feel like telling her why that wasn't the comfort she thought it was. Her dread of growing old with him, the depressing notion that her best years were behind her, a nagging sense that she was missing out on something important, although she couldn't articulate what. The expiry date for an 'I told you so' had long since passed, but she was still reluctant to prove the naysayers right.

'I only moved a few miles away,' she said. 'I used to drop

by all the time. Josh is in Exeter. I won't see him for months on end.'

'Come on, Gracie,' said Ruth, reaching over to pat her hand. 'You're still young. You have a good job, a nice home, no money worries to speak of, and a husband who loves you.'

'Please don't tell me to count my blessings.'

'Would that be such a terrible thing?'

Grace sighed.

'Ignore me,' she said. 'I've got the winter blues.'

'It's autumn.'

Grace's smile was lukewarm and fleeting.

'Can we change the subject?'

'All right,' said Ruth, in her soothing voice. 'But you know you can talk to me about anything.'

And she would, soon, but not tonight.

The mild weather changed abruptly with the arrival of morning frosts and leaf-swirling winds. Grace and Cal were pleasant and polite, wary of igniting another row. She was relieved to leave the house in the mornings, as if shrugging off an ill-fitting coat. Work was busy and Marty hadn't pried further into her personal life, so that was a blessing. Christina bailed on their Thursday-evening drinks as her entire family had succumbed to the coughs and colds going around. Grace didn't feel great either, but still drove to Chew the following morning, unwilling to miss an opportunity to spend time with David. It seemed the universe was conspiring against them, however, when the heavens opened and their lesson had to be abandoned. He said he would have asked her to the pub for lunch but she had started sneezing and it was clear she was coming down with whatever Christina's lot had. *You should get yourself home to bed*, he told her with that teasing grin of his.

Grace had to wait until the following week to unburden herself about arguing with Cal on his birthday, and being discovered with David by Lydia and her girlfriend.

'Is Lydia gay now?' asked Christina.

'Bi, I think. She doesn't like labels.'

'And you're sure she won't tell Cal about David?'

'She said she wouldn't.'

Christina nodded, as though it was important to garner all the facts.

'What were you really doing with this guy? And please don't repeat the official line that Lydia appears to have fallen for.'

Grace's mouth gaped a little, as if offended.

'What do you mean?'

'Oh, come off it. You can't be that naive, surely. If it's so innocent, why did you beg Lydia not to tell Cal? And why do you think an attractive young man wants to spend time with an unhappily married woman?'

'If you're suggesting he has an ulterior motive –'

'Of course he has an ulterior motive. How can you not see that?'

Grace blushed furiously.

'He's been a perfect gentleman,' she said, now offended for David as well.

'He's playing you, Grace. Let me guess – he's all casual when he suggests you meet: no pressure, your choice. He invites you to confide in him so you see what a good listener he is, how understanding – someone you can trust. You enjoy his company but that's OK because it's all perfectly innocent – he's never made a move. Sound familiar?'

Grace gulped some wine.

'You've been watching too much *Love Island*,' she said testily.

'But I'm not wrong, am I?'

'OK, so why would he be interested in me when there are plenty of girls his own age who would be delighted to be the object of his interest?'

Christina rolled her eyes.

'It's cute that you're oblivious to your own allure. A natural blonde, pretty as a picture, perfect size ten, and that throaty laugh of yours – Harry finds it very sexy.'

'Does he?'

'The point is,' said Christina, 'for David you're a challenge. The thrill of the chase is rather lost on generation Tinder. All they have to do is swipe.'

Could Christina be right and David simply wanted to get her into bed? When Grace allowed herself to fantasise about him, she conjured images of romance and forbidden love. What Christina described was calculated and sleazy.

'Well, I think you're wrong,' said Grace rather prissily. 'But even if you're not, I wouldn't know where to begin with such a liaison.'

'Oh, sweetie,' said Christina, patting Grace's hand. 'You already have.'

She was getting ready for bed when David's text arrived.

Are we on for tomorrow?

Viewed through the lens of Christina's suspicions, he was reeling her in – catch and release. Her fingers hovered, unsure how to reply. Was she playing with fire, like Christina had implied? Grace wasn't a risk-taker – far from it – and yet she wanted to see David, despite Christina's warning and the promise she had made to Lydia. It was only a fishing lesson, after all. Grace pondered this as she brushed her teeth. Christina's parting shot was to suggest that, subconsciously, Grace wanted to get found out. It would bring things to a head with Cal, forcing her to commit to either fixing her marriage or ending it. He was already in bed, dozing. She went downstairs to get some water, her mind dipping and diving through time and space. Back to those early days with Cal, forward to the years ahead. She didn't switch on the light. The ghostly glow of a full moon was more conducive to her mood.

A psychologist once asked her why she married him. It was when she was diagnosed with depression, after Josh started school. Six sessions over as many weeks – her one and only experience of the talking therapies. At first, she resented the intrusion into her innermost thoughts and fears, but the psychologist – *call me Jade* – encouraged her to 'trust the process'. Things got easier once she did. Together they exposed her deep-rooted insecurity – emotional and financial. Her father had left – what was to stop her mother leaving too? And because no one told her why, how did she know it wasn't her fault? She had clung to her mother like a limpet, fearsomely eager to please. When she caught her looking sad or worried, young Grace tried extra hard to make her happy. Happy people didn't leave their children. Jade had slid her a box of tissues at that point, and encouraged her to go on. Grace explained how they never had enough money. She declined party invitations because it meant buying a gift. She hid letters about school trips they couldn't afford, and pretended to love her clothes from the Oxfam shop. On the third session, Grace found herself talking about how safe and secure she felt with Cal. Jade flicked through her notes and asked what it was about this divorced father of three that made her feel that way. *I knew he was a good dad. I knew he wouldn't do to me what his first wife did to him. I knew he wouldn't leave.* Grace remembered Jade's puzzled expression as she asked how she could be so sure. *Because I would never cheat on him.*

Grace unscrewed the bottle of water and took a long drink. According to Christina, she had already embarked on something borderline illicit with David. The fact that she had pleaded with Lydia to keep her secret supported this theory. The sensible course of action was to tell David she didn't want any more lessons. It was one thing to feel dissatisfied in her marriage, quite another to risk her home, her security, her perfectly comfortable life. She stared at his text for a long time before replying.

See you at 12 ☺

TEN

Grace and Cal sipped their morning coffee in bed, watching a windswept young reporter tell of another fatal stabbing. The backdrop was a grim south-London housing estate. On the pavement, propped up against a low wall, was a pile of flowers and teddy bears. A heaviness spread through Grace, thinking of those poor children and their poor, shattered families. The boy and his killer were both fourteen. She wondered if they fully understood the consequences of their actions at that age. Perhaps they were acting out a computer game – pow, punch, shoot, stab – all action and bravado until one of you is bleeding to death. Josh had considered two of the London universities, and Grace was weak with relief when he decided on Exeter in safe, sleepy Devon.

'What's wrong?' said Cal.

'The news is so depressing,' said Grace.

He put his arm around her shoulders and planted a kiss on the top of her head. The limb felt heavy and awkward, but she didn't shrug it off. They were back on an even keel and she wanted to keep it that way. He put down his coffee and slipped her hand under the duvet, guiding it to his stirring penis. He kissed her again, on the forehead this time, and then on her closed mouth. Neither of them had brushed their teeth and his breath smelled thick and sour. Inwardly she recoiled, but rejecting him would fuel more discord in their relationship, so she tried to relax and hoped it would be quick. His erection was harder now, and he pulled down his pyjama bottoms to release it. Grace took him in her hand, but that wasn't what he had in mind. He pulled her hips – a sudden, jerky movement – until she was lying flat. With an urgency that reeked of desperation, he climbed on top of her, but his erection had waned, making penetration difficult. He attempted to push his limp penis into her reluctant vagina, all to no avail. She could have helped him get hard again, but couldn't bring herself to do it. He loved it when she talked dirty, which, considering how prudish he was about bad language, had always rather shocked her. But maybe that was the point, and hearing his pretty, pristine wife begging him to fuck her hard shot a surge of delicious disgust straight to his groin. When eventually he admitted defeat, he rolled off her and exhaled loudly in frustration. They both lay there in silence, staring at the ceiling, until Cal got up and went for a pee. Grace heard him go downstairs and took a long, hot shower to wash away the smell of him. She wasn't sure when it started, but in Cal she had begun to detect a stale, fusty odour that reminded her of her grandmother's care home.

He sat slumped at the kitchen table with a half-drunk cup of coffee and the *Daily Mail*. Grace wanted to pretend it had never happened, but he looked wretched. With his face baggy and unshaven, his pyjamas creased and dishevelled, he seemed old and slightly pathetic.

'Have you had any breakfast?' she said pleasantly.

He shook his head.

'I'll make us some toast then,' she said.

'I'm not hungry.'

He sounded like a sullen child who didn't want to eat his greens.

'It's just toast,' she said. 'You have to have something.'

He sat back in his chair and folded his arms.

'I'm sorry about earlier,' he said.

'It's forgotten,' she said, with an understanding smile.

The muscles in her face felt tight with the effort of all the fake smiling. Things were easier when she was out at work all day, but the weekend stretched ahead of them and she dreaded another fight. They were on a tightrope, and the merest slip could bring them crashing down again. The trepidation she felt was recent, just like his old-man body odour.

'Yeah, it was pretty forgettable,' he said.

'I didn't mean it like that,' she said. 'It's really not a big deal. These things happen.'

'Maybe I should talk to the doctor about Viagra again,' he said.

A chilling prospect. Grace wanted less sex, not more. She ignored his suggestion and asked if he wanted her to top up his coffee.

'Best not,' he said. 'Or I'll be peeing all morning.'

The hypocrisy wasn't lost on Grace. He never showed any sympathy for 'women's problems', expecting her to suffer in silence. And yet here he was, whingeing about his penis and his prostate, and they hadn't even had breakfast yet.

'Why don't you go to the golf club,' she said, keen for a change of subject. 'Get a bit of fresh air.'

'You could come with me,' he said, brightening a little. 'Maybe have some lunch later.'

Only retired people had time to play during the week, so the average age was north of sixty-five. Conversation revolved around sport, cruises and Brexit, none of which interested her one iota.

'I have a fly-fishing lesson at twelve,' she said, sparking a flutter under her breastbone.

She spread a thin layer of Flora on sourdough, reminding herself she was supposed to be making more of an effort.

'But maybe lunch tomorrow or Sunday,' she said.

'OK,' he said, sounding chirpier. 'How about I come to Chew with you – find a nice little pub for lunch afterwards?'

Grace took a sip of coffee and said he would be bored standing around while she practised casting over and over again. She reached for the newspaper and feigned interest in Kate Middleton's new hairstyle, a photo of which took up most of the front page. As far as she could tell, it was indistinguishable from the old hairstyle.

'Seriously, a round of golf will be much more fun,' she said, flicking on a few pages. 'And you can catch up with your friends.'

He didn't argue, but did still look dejected.

'Why don't we get fish and chips tonight?' she said. 'And a nice bottle of wine.'

'If you want,' he said, as though doing her a favour.

Josh calling was just the pick-me-up their morning

needed. Grace propped up her phone on the kitchen island and put him on speaker. She told him his PlayStation games were all boxed up, ready to take to the post office.

'Don't worry,' he said. 'Reading week starts Friday after next. Uni version of half-term. I've arranged to go out with some friends that night so I'll be home on the Saturday.'

Cal and Grace beamed at each other.

'Oh, that's wonderful,' she said. 'It'll be so lovely to see you.'

'I was going to bring someone with me, if that's OK?'

'Of course,' she said, raising her eyebrows at Cal.

As a boy, Josh had never been keen on sleepovers, in his own home or anyone else's. When he stayed at Christina's house, she reported back that he was quiet, well mannered, and eager to leave. Grace told her not to take it personally – he liked his own company and his own space. With friends he preferred quality to quantity, as did Grace. She often wondered if that was why he chose fishing over team sports. Cal encouraged him to play rugby, but Josh wasn't aggressive enough. Privately, Grace was relieved – she considered it a rough, thuggish game. Anglers didn't get concussion or broken bones.

'I'll get Dad to clear out the box room,' she said. 'Make it nice and cosy.'

'No, it's all right,' said Josh. 'Millie can stay in my room.'

Grace and Cal stared at each other, mouths gaping in surprise. Josh had a girlfriend and they were sleeping together. It was a lot to take in. Be cool, she told herself.

'Well, yes, that makes more sense,' she said. 'I can't wait to meet her.'

A few beats of dead air.

'Yeah, but I mean, you won't make a fuss or anything, will you?'

A plea, not a question.

'No, not at all,' she said. 'I just meant it will be nice, you know, to meet your girlfriend.'

Josh groaned.

'We don't do labels, Mum.'

When Grace was a teenager, being introduced to someone's parents, let alone sleeping together under their roof, was the very definition of boyfriend and girlfriend.

'Have you been talking to Lydia?' she said, before remembering Cal knew nothing about that.

'Er, yeah,' said Josh. 'She keeps going on about meeting Millie.'

That made sense. Lydia would be wildly curious, and could be very persuasive.

'Well,' said Cal, once Josh had rung off. 'A girlfriend, eh?'

'I hope she's nice,' said Grace.

'He wouldn't be with her if she wasn't,' said Cal, as if affairs of the heart were ever that straightforward.

The day was bright, if somewhat chilly, and she listened to Heart radio as she drove. Josh coming home was a cheery prospect, albeit with a complete stranger in tow. Grace wondered what she was like, this Millie, her son's first girlfriend/not girlfriend. Christina had once used the term 'fuck-buddy' in reference to a girl Adam was seeing. Grace thought it disgusting and told her so. An image of Cal's screwed-up face flashed into her head, trying to get his flaccid penis inside her. That disgusted her too. It would be better if they were one of those couples who never had sex – preferable even, as there was no pleasure in it anymore. Another thing that had crept up on her, although she had never had much of a sex drive.

Cal was already past his sexual peak when they met, and even in the early days she thought of it as the last job of the day. Before him, she had only had two partners. The first was barely more than a boy – seventeen, both of them virgins, the blind leading the blind – and it was so clumsy she wasn't sure it counted. The other she had dated for a year, but since they both lived with their parents, opportunities for sex were limited, which suited Grace just fine. In her marriage it was always Cal who initiated things, and she considered it her duty to keep him satisfied, even if she wasn't. For her, sex was like having a meal and still being hungry. Orgasms had always eluded her. According to women's magazines it wasn't uncommon, so she decided to accept it rather than fret. Once, when Cal suggested she 'see someone', she flushed scarlet and told him she was fine with things as they were. His attempts to bring her to orgasm made her so tense and self-conscious, she dreaded having sex at all. Over the years they'd settled into a routine of once or twice a month, but after this morning's performance, she would prefer to be celibate. 'Sexual Healing' came on the radio – Marvin Gaye's rich, velvet voice, as sensuous as the song's message of lust and longing. She had never truly experienced either of those things.

David was waiting for her in the office. The last time she saw him was in the windswept pub car park, in the wake of the Lydia incident. Her disapproval joined forces with Christina's suspicions, making Grace wonder why she had come.

'Shall we catch some fish, then?' he said, with a smile that answered her question.

The sun bounced off the lake. They stood side by side on the grass, breathing white wisps into the crisp air. To her delight, Grace got a bite on the line almost immediately, and reeled it in without David's help. He encouraged her to hold the fish as it thrashed, though she was a little unsure at first. It felt slippery and surprisingly firm, its mouth gasping and gaping. David showed her how to remove the hook before she lowered it back into the water. The hour passed too quickly. When he told her it was time to wrap things up, he must have seen her disappointment because he suggested they go to buy some basic fishing tackle. She hadn't thought about buying her own rod and reel. It made sense, though, if she was going to fish with Josh rather than just have lessons, where tackle was supplied as part of the package.

'Aren't you busy?' she said.

That was what he had told her earlier in the week, when he called to confirm her lesson.

'A group cancelled on me,' he said. 'So I have the afternoon free.'

'If you're sure it's not too much trouble,' she said. 'I wouldn't know where to start.'

'I have to swing by the shop anyway,' he said. 'And I get a good discount, so you can buy me lunch to say thank you.'

Christina's warning flashed into her head.

'Lunch?'

'The meal between breakfast and dinner.'

'Are you sure you want to risk it?' she said. 'Last time didn't work out so well.'

'Good point,' he said, cracking a lopsided smile. 'We'd better go somewhere discreet.'

The pub was in a pretty village she hadn't heard of, just outside of Frome. The barman called over to ask David if he wanted his usual, and what would the lady have? Grace wondered if he often brought 'ladies' here. He ordered her a small glass of white without asking. The place was rustic – lots of low beams and horse brasses and framed prints of hunting scenes. He pointed her to a table by the wood burner and went to get their drinks.

The menu was limited to soup, sandwiches and ploughman's. Grace chose the soup and David had a BLT. He took a long drink of beer and wiped his mouth with the back of his hand. This was his local, he said – his house was just down the road. It was the house he grew up in, although he hadn't always lived there. His mother had married a local landowner and they moved to his farm in the middle of nowhere. She kept the house, though, he told Grace, in case the marriage didn't work out.

'And did it?' she said.

'Yeah, it did,' said David. 'Well, for six years, and then she died.'

'Oh God, I'm so sorry,' she said. 'How old were you?'

'Twenty. Old enough to live on my own.'

'You didn't want to stay with your stepdad?'

'No. He was a decent enough bloke, but it was my mum he wanted, not her moody teenage son.'

'You were moody?'

'I didn't think so at the time, but yeah, probably.'

'So he didn't want you?'

'No, well, he wasn't unkind or anything. Actually, he was OK, it's just that it had always been me and my mum.'

'You resented him.'

'A bit, I suppose. And having to live so far from my friends, from civilisation. It's not like I was old enough to drive or anything, at least not for the first few years. And when my mum got sick I didn't want to leave her, so I put off going to uni, then ended up not going at all.'

'That must have been really hard for you.'

David shook his head.

'Shit happens, you deal with it.'

'Do you still see him – your stepdad?'

'We lost touch about ten years ago, after he sold up. It all got too much for him – the house, the land, the livestock. He would have liked a son to take over from him but I wasn't interested, or his son, for that matter.'

'No regrets?' said Grace.

David sunk a mouthful of beer and shook his head.

'I don't believe in regrets,' he said. 'There are things you do and things you don't. Good choices and bad choices. That's it.'

'I suppose it is,' said Grace.

The young woman clearing tables spotted David and her face lit up. She made a beeline for him, her jeans so tight Grace was surprised they allowed movement at all.

'Hi,' she said to David, tossing her mane of dark hair over a scantily clad shoulder.

She was wearing the sort of black lacy vest Grace would have worn as underwear. There was no bra in evidence, though her breasts looked perky enough without one. Grace pulled her cardigan across her chest to deter any unfavourable comparisons.

'Don't normally see you in here at lunchtime,' said the girl, flashing David a flirtatious smile.

He tilted his chin at Grace. 'My friend's treating me.'

The girl glanced at her for a split second, but that was all the acknowledgement Grace warranted. David was the unabashed focus of her attention.

'I don't want to get you in trouble,' he said, nodding over to the barman.

The barman seemed too busy chatting to a couple of customers to notice what David's groupie was up to, so Grace assumed this was his way of getting rid of her.

'Oh, right,' she said, picking up Grace's glass.

She threw David a backwards glance as she walked away, swinging her denim-clad hips from side to side. Grace might as well have been invisible.

'I think you have an admirer,' she said.

'I would have introduced you but I can't remember her name,' he said.

'She would be crushed to know that,' said Grace.

David shrugged.

'My son's coming home from university in a couple of weeks,' said Grace. 'He's bringing a girl with him.'

'You've not met her?'

'No. I'm looking forward to it, it's just ...'

She hesitated, not sure how to express her reservations without sounding prim.

'What?' said David.

'I just worry that it might feel a bit, well, awkward, with them sleeping in the next room.'

'Probably more awkward for them than you. Kids don't want to think of their parents having sex, any more than parents want to think of their kids having sex. I hated that when my mum got married – the thought of them in bed together. Plus, I was a teenager myself, so sex was pretty much the only thing on my mind.'

It was thrilling for Grace to be talking this way with a man. If she and Cal talked about sex, they skirted around the subject using thinly veiled euphemisms to hide their discomfort. And yes, she and Christina joked about sex, but with David it was different. Grace realised she was slightly aroused. They had finished eating and he suggested getting the bill.

'My treat, remember?' said Grace, and went to pay before he could argue.

The second she left David alone, the flirty girl pounced again. Grace couldn't hear what was being said, but whatever it was made the girl laugh riotously. It rang out across the pub, loud and uninhibited. Her body language – a hand on David's shoulder, bending forward when he spoke, putting her face next to his and her breasts in his line of vision – was as subtle as a neon sign. Grace had never been that brazen. Despite his stated indifference, David must see how gorgeous the girl was. Such succulent youthfulness, ripe for the picking, made Grace feel dried up and past it. Recently, she had found herself wrestling with a sense of having missed out. Three men wasn't much of a sexual tally – two, if she discounted the blundering attempt that was her first time. No one-night stands, no quickies in the back of a car, no abandoned al-fresco rolls in the hay. Witnessing how flagrantly this girl was coming on to David, Grace imagined her sexual repertoire would make a stripper blush. Reluctant to stand there like the proverbial gooseberry, she went to the toilets once the bill was sorted. The sight of herself in a full-length mirror was depressing. The girl throwing herself at David wore skin-tight clothes and scarlet lipstick. The woman in the mirror did not.

Walking back towards their table, Grace realised that twice she and David had had lunch together, and both times had been unsettling, although for different reasons. Maybe the universe was trying to tell her something. When he saw her, he stood up and put on his Barbour. The girl gave him a coquettish wave as she sashayed off to collect glasses, drawing admiring glances from men and women alike. Christina's suggestion about an ulterior motive seemed laughable in the circumstances.

'Thanks for that,' said David, handing Grace her own jacket. 'Look, would you mind if we stopped by my place first? I've got a pair of waders I need to return to the shop.'

'Oh?'

'I found out the hard way they have a small tear below the knee.'

'Sure,' said Grace, because an invitation to his home no longer seemed like a ploy to have his wicked way with her.

They walked down the hill, passing terraced houses that opened straight onto the street. The road had double yellow lines all the way along, which was why they left their cars at the pub. His house had a dark-blue front door and an old-fashioned brass knocker. He stood aside for Grace to go in first. The low ceiling and dark wooden beams made her squint for a second, but David flicked on a few lamps that bathed the room in soft light. He told her to make herself at home while he jogged up the open-tread stairs, presumably to fetch the leaky waders. Grace looked around the room, which was longer than it was wide. At one end was a sofa – chestnut leather, worn and cracked – with a scatter of unmatched cushions. At the other end was a dining table and chairs. The floor was quarry-tiled with a large terracotta-coloured rug in the middle. In the centre of the far wall was a fireplace, housing an old-fashioned wood-burning stove and a big basket of logs. On the mantel above were a few trophies and one of those long school photographs that parents feel compelled to buy.

'Bet you couldn't spot which one is me,' said David.

He let the large Orvis bag he was holding drop to the floor. Grace studied the photo, but he was right – it was a sea of unfamiliar faces. He leaned over her and ran his index finger along the top row. He smelled minty, like he had just brushed his teeth.

'There,' he said. 'That's me.'

Grace looked closer and yes – unmistakably David. The same wide grin and dark, unruly hair.

'You haven't changed much,' she said. 'How long ago was that?'

'Um, I was upper sixth, so fifteen, sixteen years.'

A quick calculation made him mid-thirties – ten years younger than Grace. He rested his hand lightly on her shoulder, a confusing gesture. Was it innocently companionable – two people amused by an old photo – or something more? They were both facing forward, quite still. The moment felt charged with heat and possibility. Had she been wrong to dismiss any libidinous intentions? He placed his free hand on her other shoulder and kneaded the taut flesh.

'You're always so tense,' he said. 'You need to relax.'

If there was a time to stop this it was now, but his touch was slow and sensuous, the pressure just right. Her mind emptied of everything, and she surrendered to the pleasure.

ELEVEN

Where are you? I thought your lesson was an hour.

Cal's texts were always grammatically correct – no sloppy abbreviations or silly emojis.

On my way home

It wasn't a lie, but not entirely true either. Grace had started to drive home, but her head was swimming and she'd almost knocked a cyclist off his bike. She pulled over and had been sitting in her parked car for ten minutes – maybe more. Her mind was a wild collage of flashbacks. At first David's lips had barely brushed hers, but the sensation was so unexpectedly exquisite, she yearned for more. Her eyes were closed, heart pounding, face tilted up to his. When his lips touched hers again, lingering this time, something deep inside her stirred. Her breath quickened as she leaned into the kiss, which was slow and soft and deep. It was the most beautiful thing she had ever felt. Pleasure radiated throughout her chest, her belly, her groin, until her whole body was melting into his. She could feel his desire stirring too, and when he pulled back and asked if she was sure, she nodded breathlessly. He waited for a moment as if she might change her mind, and when she didn't, he took her by the hand and led her upstairs.

Another text from Cal jolted her into the here and now.

How long will you be?

She ran her fingers through her hair and groaned. How could she face him? Surely he would notice something was different – that *she* was different. She looked at herself in the rear-view mirror, but could detect no outward sign of what she had done. Get it together, she told herself sternly. A lorry pulled into the lay-by and parked right behind her. The driver climbed down and went over to the bushes for a pee. Right, thought Grace. Time to go home.

Cal was looking out of the sitting-room window when she pulled into the drive. He opened the front door and the interrogation began.

'You've been gone all afternoon,' he said, his arms folded across his chest. 'Where've you been?'

She took a chance that he hadn't phoned around looking for her, and told him she'd been at Christina's – sorry, her battery died.

'How did you answer my texts if your battery died?'

Good question. She hung up her jacket and took off her boots, buying herself time to come up with an answer.

'I charged it at Christina's,' she said. 'Sorry, I thought

you'd be busy playing golf. If I'd known you were home, waiting for me, I'd have called.'

He followed her into the kitchen, where she had been going to fill the kettle but opened a bottle of wine instead.

'Want one?' she said.

Cal shook his head.

'I'll wait for dinner, thanks.'

Grace ignored the snip of judgement in his voice, and drank like she needed it.

'I was worried about you,' he said.

'Sorry,' she said. 'I didn't think.'

The faint froth of alcohol seeping into her veins was most welcome.

'What was the emergency?' he said.

He was trying to catch her out.

'I didn't say there was an emergency.'

'Well, you rushed over there without a word.'

'Like I say, I thought you were at the golf club. Christina asked me to pop round for coffee and I stayed longer than I meant to.'

Her heart pattered like hail on glass. She was a terrible liar.

'I'm going for a bath,' she said, topping up her wine.

'It's five o'clock,' he said, checking his watch.

They weren't the sort of couple who took baths at any old time of day. Showers in the morning, baths at night. Those were the rules.

'Won't be long,' she said, ignoring his disapproval.

She undressed in the bathroom. Her underwear had the unique scent of sex – sharp, sensuous, organic. A squirt of Badedas swirled through the water. She perched her phone and wine glass within arm's reach, and clipped up her hair. Her instinct was to lock the door but with only one loo in the house, and Cal needing to pee every other minute, it was understood that the door should stay unlocked for ablutions such as bathing, tooth-brushing, etcetera. She kept glancing at her phone to see if David had texted, even though she had explicitly asked him not to. It was too risky, she told him. Best if I call you.

When she turned off the tap and slid into the spume of white bubbles, she felt wistful to be washing all traces of him from her body. He had made it do and feel things she never thought possible. Every touch, every kiss, every stroke of his fingers brought her to new heights of pleasure, until spasms of ecstasy made her cry out loud. Thinking about it aroused her all over again. She slipped her hand under the water, teasing her inner thigh with her fingertips, like David had done. With her eyes closed and lips parted, her fingers worked to relieve the desire he had awakened in her. She was almost there – her body arched, chest heaving with each shuddering breath – when Cal walked in.

'What are you doing?'

Grace sat up so fast, bath water sloshed over his Marks & Spencer slippers. She assumed his question was rhetorical, since it was blindingly obvious what she was doing. He looked as mortified as she was. The moment stretched on, millisecond by excruciating millisecond.

'I didn't think you did that,' he said.

His tone was pitched somewhere between shock and censure. She made sure her breasts were hidden under the bubbles.

'Was it because of this morning?' he said.

'Sorry?'

'You're frustrated – is that it?'

Oh God – he thought this was about him. He stood over her with a stony expression, as if he had caught her doing something she shouldn't. It was as if a match had been struck, igniting her indignation. How dare he judge her for what she did with her own body. And how dare he invade her privacy like this.

'If you need to go,' she said, pointing to the toilet, 'then go.'

She reached for her glass and drank. He huffed in annoyance as he unzipped his fly and released a stutter of urine into the toilet bowl. He hadn't bothered to lift the seat, and didn't bother to put the lid down before he flushed. His hand-washing was perfunctory and when he had finished, Grace had to ask him to leave. He seemed to be waiting for her to explain herself, but why should she? When she went downstairs half an hour later, she hoped he wouldn't mention it. She hoped he never mentioned it again. He was watching TV in the sitting room and unless she intended to hide away in the kitchen, she had no choice but to join him. She perched on the sofa and asked what was on. He shrugged moodily and said it was something about lorries on ice.

'*Ice Road Truckers*,' said Grace.

Cal looked at her.

'You know it?'

'Josh likes it,' she said. 'And speaking of Josh, I thought I'd give his room a bit of a spring clean – maybe buy some new bed linen. Make it nice for him and Millie.'

Cal nodded, but it was obvious that Josh's bed linen wasn't high on his list of concerns.

'It surprised me,' he blurted, as if dislodging a fish bone from his throat. 'What you were doing up there.'

Grace felt a stinging heat rise up from her chest. Maybe if she said nothing and kept her eyes fixed on the huge lorries skidding across ice, he might take the hint. He didn't.

'You always told me you didn't like doing that,' he said, his eyes also fixed on the screen. 'Or was it just when I did it – was that what you didn't like?'

The eruption of heat rendered Grace sweaty and stressed, as though a firework had exploded inside her ribcage. She made small puffing sounds and wished he would shut up about it.

'I was just taking a moment to myself,' she said. 'Can't we leave it at that?'

He glared at her and turned up the volume, even though it was already loud. He would rather go stone deaf than wear a hearing aid. They were for old people, he told her stubbornly whenever she pleaded with him to consider it. The noise was too much for Grace – giant juggernauts roaring across ice to a heavy rock soundtrack. She got up and told him she was going to the fish and chip shop to pick up their supper. His response was a grunt, not a thank you, or an offer to go himself. He was sulking but she didn't care. At least she had an excuse to leave.

The queue was always long on a Friday, and Grace seized on the wait as a chance to call David. Her heart hammered with each ring, and catching a glimpse of herself in the window, she realised she was smiling.

'Well, hello,' he said, his voice smooth and seductive.

'Hi,' she said, registering the background hum of voices. 'Sounds like you're out. Is it a bad time?'

'Never,' he said. 'Just having a pint in my local. How about you?'

'Queueing for fish and chips.'

'What glamorous lives we lead,' he said, which made her smile even more. 'Why don't we FaceTime?'

The lighting was harsh and unflattering, and Grace was surrounded by people.

'Not the best time,' she said. 'How about I send you a photo later?'

'Deal,' he said. 'Shall I send you one too?'

'Please,' she said. 'It'll give me something to look at when I'm missing you.'

Instantly she wanted to snatch back the words.

'And speaking of missing me,' he said, apparently unfazed by her eagerness, 'when can I see you again?'

The thought of it incited a sweet ache in her groin. A shriek of laughter in the background sounded like the girl who had been flirting with him at lunch. Jealousy – an emotion totally alien to Grace – pinched her heart.

'You still there?' he said.

'Yes,' she said. 'I'm here.'

'We never did get around to buying you that fishing tackle,' he said. 'Why don't we do it tomorrow?'

A greasy-haired boy cut right across that thought, asking Grace what she wanted.

'Hang on,' she said to David, as the boy stared at her, not even trying to hide his impatience. There must have been half a dozen people behind her in the queue, but all she could think about was David's beautiful body and the beautiful things it had done to hers.

'I have to go,' she said. 'You're distracting me.'

'Miss?' said the boy loudly, as though perhaps the problem was her hearing.

'Sorry,' she said. 'Two cod and chips.'

She watched him shovel thick chips into two boxes and plonk a long piece of battered fish on top. The sprig of parsley was an unnecessary touch – who on earth ate parsley with fish and chips? – and when he handed the boxes to Grace, she thanked him and turned to go.

'Miss,' he called after her.

'Yes?'

'You haven't paid.'

With some tutting from the waiting customers, she tapped her card on the machine and hurried out of the shop. A waning moon hung low in the sky, bright and unobscured. Grace hummed as she walked – Marvin Gaye, 'Sexual Healing'.

The evening dragged on in front of the television. They ate with little conversation, other than how good the chips were. Cal fell asleep around nine, like he did most nights, and the sight of him – jaw slack, mouth gaping – elicited a pang of guilt. He wasn't a bad man. She had wanted steady and reliable and that was what she got. It was Grace who had changed, not him. All he had done was get older.

She went to the kitchen to top up her wine, thinking about the photo she had promised David. With Cal out for the count, and Chardonnay for Dutch courage, she went upstairs to seize the moment. Selfies weren't really her thing, and she didn't know how to filter or Photoshop, but she gave it her best shot. In the flattering light of a bedside lamp, she undid the top few buttons of her blouse, exposing a modest amount of cleavage. She hoped her smile was coquettish, but in the photo it looked sweet rather than alluring. She shifted up a gear, filling her head with lustful thoughts and rearranging her features accordingly. She wet her lips with her tongue, tousled her hair with her fingers and stared daringly into the camera. This second attempt was much more what she had in mind. With only a moment's hesitation, she pinged it over to David and waited anxiously for his response. Seconds passed, then minutes, his silence giving rise to self-doubt. Maybe he was engrossed with the pub waitress. Maybe he collected photos of his married conquests. Maybe Grace had made a fool of herself.

She changed into her sensible pyjamas, wondering what he saw in her in the first place. An afternoon of fun with a frustrated, middle-aged woman – nothing more, nothing less. She wished she could unsend the photo – reach into cyberspace and grab it back. Now that she looked closely, she could see lines around her eyes and frizz around her hairline. She dropped the phone face down on the duvet, cross with herself. After a particularly vigorous tooth-brushing, she realised the only way to stop obsessing about why she hadn't heard from him was to turn off her phone altogether. She stared at it anxiously, her finger hovering over the button, and as if by magic, a text appeared.

You're gorgeous x

Her chest swelled with joy. She pressed the screen to her heart, as if wanting him to hear how fast he made it beat. A second ping followed the first. David's selfie – hair adorably untidy, clear blue eyes gazing straight into hers, his smile teasing and conspiratorial. It was almost obscene how happy she felt at that moment.

TWELVE

Grace slept fitfully, too excited and newly in lust to drift off completely. She was impatient to start the day, having spent much of the night thinking about her date with David and planning her excuses to Cal. The groundwork had been laid the previous evening, when she told him she wanted to buy things for Josh's room – make it seem less boyish. He would be sleeping there with a girl, after all. She could tell Cal she was going shopping, which was true, albeit for fishing stuff, not bedding. Still, she would be gone for hours and if recent evidence was anything to go by, Cal wouldn't be happy about that.

It was Marty Devlin, of all people, who provided the solution to her problem. He called Cal to say a place had become vacant on the golf club committee, and he wanted to put Cal's name forward. Cal was clearly chuffed, as was Grace. This could be just the boost he needed. Better still, he had been invited for lunch with the other committee members, and told Grace he might play nine holes afterwards.

'I'll be out most of the day,' he said. 'And I don't want you to feel neglected.'

If this was an oblique reference to yesterday's mortifying bathroom incident, she refused to be drawn.

'Don't be silly,' she said. 'It'll be good for you. I planned to go shopping anyway, and have a bit of lunch out.'

With that settled, the morning was a blur of activity. Grace usually cooked breakfast at the weekend but since Cal was having a proper lunch, he said toast was fine. While he was showering, she called David and arranged to meet him at the country sports place he had talked about. Best do that first, he said pointedly, or we might get sidetracked like we did yesterday. He texted her the address with a thumbs-up emoji.

Cal left before her, looking smarter and happier than she had seen him in a while. It was unusual for Grace to be in the house alone. Cal always seemed to be skulking around or stuck in front of the telly. She found herself humming as she dressed. No jeans and T-shirt today, she told herself, slipping into a teal silk shirt, slim black trousers and kitten-heeled ankle boots. Her hand trembled slightly as she applied peach lipstick that accentuated her cupid's bow. A kaleidoscope of butterflies swarmed in her stomach, and she had to make herself calm down. Yesterday's near miss with a cyclist had given her a terrible fright. Today when she got behind the wheel, she adhered religiously to the speed limit, much to the annoyance of other motorists, who flashed her or made gestures to express their displeasure.

Forty-five minutes later, when she finally parked as near to the shop as double yellow lines allowed, she spotted

David, sending the butterflies swarming again. It was hard to believe this good-looking millennial was waiting for her. She wasn't an adulterer – the very notion was absurd. No one would believe it – she hardly believed it herself – and yet here she was. He watched her walk towards him, his easy smile dissolving her doubts and the killjoy voice in her head saying no good could come of this. He was worth it, she told herself. She was worth it too.

They embraced chastely – it was a busy street, after all – and he held open the shop door. Inside, it smelled of old wood and leather. The two assistants – one old, one young – greeted him like an old friend.

'This is Grace,' he said. 'One of my fishing protégés. And these fine gentlemen,' he said to Grace, 'are Stanley and his son Will.'

Hearing David describe her as his protégé was odd, but how else could he describe her – his girlfriend, his lover, that awful term Christina used? Stanley outlined the technicalities of reels and rods and related paraphernalia, most of which went over Grace's head. It was half an hour before they left the shop, a hundred pounds poorer and laden with bags. David asked if she fancied some lunch and though she wasn't hungry, she wanted to be agreeable.

'Sure. Do you have somewhere in mind?'

'I do,' he said, 'but it's a surprise. I'm parked just along from you, so why don't you get in your car and follow me.'

They drove through the busy shopping area before David turned off onto a side road, and then into a narrow back street. He squeezed his Land Rover into a space, leaving just enough room for Grace's Nissan.

'Where are we?' she said, looking around for a likely lunch venue.

'You'll see,' he said, taking her hand.

He unlocked a solid wooden gate around the same height as him, and led her into a pretty courtyard.

'Tradesman's entrance,' he said.

She didn't recognise his house from the back.

'I thought I'd cook for you,' he said.

'Really?' she said. 'No one ever cooks for me. Well, except my mum.'

'Then you're in for a treat.'

Walking into his house again flooded Grace with a rip tide of emotions – excitement, desire, apprehension, all swirling in different directions. Food was the last thing on her mind, but he said he was looking forward to cooking a salmon he had caught that summer up in Scotland.

'It's been sitting in my freezer,' he said, 'waiting for a worthy guest.'

Grace was flattered she was considered worthy, but wondered how many other women he entertained. It was unlike her to be suspicious, probably because she was so sure of Cal's fidelity. He understood the pain of being cheated on and would never inflict that on someone he loved. Grace was loath to disappear down that particular rabbit hole of recrimination, and snapped her attention back to David, asking if there was anything she could do.

'Yeah, you can sit and talk to me,' he said, pointing to a pair of high stools tucked under the breakfast bar. She pulled out a stool while he took a whole fish from the fridge – much bigger than anything she had caught in the lake. He poured them both a generous glass of Chablis and told her he was going to use the rest to poach the salmon. She asked him where he had learned to cook.

'Dunno really,' he said, chopping shallots like a trained chef. 'I've lived on my own for so long, I just had to get on with it.'

'Have you never lived with anyone?' she said. 'A girl, I mean.'

He crushed some garlic cloves and put them in a roasting tray with the wine, shallots and a few knobs of butter. The fish was already gutted and the cavity cleaned. He stuffed it with rosemary and parsley, before laying the whole thing in the metal tray.

'Voila,' he said, covering it with foil and sliding it into the oven.

'You didn't answer my question,' said Grace.

'About?'

'Living with someone.'

'Ah, that,' he said, raising his glass to his lips. 'I've had a few near misses, but no.'

She waited, curious to hear more about his love life, but he didn't elaborate. In fact, he had never mentioned anything about girlfriends or relationships, even when she had spoken about her problems with Cal. If she had been braver, she would have asked if he was in the habit of sleeping with married women, but did she really want to know? It was easier to sip her wine and watch him work, rather than torment herself with inconvenient questions.

He put a saucepan on the hob to boil and prepared the vegetables.

'You're a very neat cook,' she said.

'I have to do the clearing up, which is an incentive to

create as little mess as possible. Top-up?' he said, opening a second bottle.

Grace shook her head. She had hardly touched the first glass. When he opened the oven to check the salmon, the intoxicating aromas of fish, garlic and wine wafted through the kitchen, making her think of sunshine and summer holidays in the Med.

'You OK for time?' he said, testing the flesh with a fork.

'Yes,' she said. 'My husband is at his golf club all afternoon.'

David turned off the oven and drained the vegetables.

'Actually, my friend Christina has a theory,' she said, by way of a non sequitur. 'She thinks I want to get caught.'

He looked surprised.

'And do you?'

'The thought of it makes me feel physically sick. When Lydia saw us in the pub, I was terrified she'd tell Cal.'

'But she didn't.'

'No, thank goodness. I managed to talk her round.'

'Good,' said David. 'We don't want to complicate things.'

But things were already complicated for her – surely he knew that? A married woman lying to her husband in order to spend time with her lover – the stakes couldn't be higher. She was the one taking all the risks. She was the one with everything to lose. If their fling, their affair – whatever this turned out to be – was discovered, it wouldn't be David who had tossed a grenade into his life. Grace didn't want to think about the collateral damage to her family.

'Where do you want to eat?' he said.

She looked blank.

'Here or at the dining table?'

'Here,' she said, trying to enjoy the moment, as Lydia would say, and not dwell on the worst-case scenario.

There was no point in all of this if she didn't allow herself to enjoy it. A beautiful man wanted to feed her, make love to her, rescue her from mundanity. He wiped the surface of the breakfast bar with a damp cloth, before laying out two place mats and cutlery. Grace was hugely impressed by his domesticity. He filleted the salmon with expert precision, like a waiter in a smart restaurant. The vegetables he tossed in butter, before giving them a final twist of salt and black pepper. He finished by spooning some of the poaching juices over the fish.

'Bon appetit,' he said, putting Grace's meal in front of her.

'I can't believe you did this for me,' she said. 'Thank you.'

'You should taste it first,' he said, but of course it was as delicious as it looked. The fish was moist and flaky, the broccoli al dente, just how she liked it, and the potatoes were soft and waxy. It meant a lot that he had gone to all this trouble, and she told him again how grateful she was.

'And there was me thinking you were only here for my body.'

It was the first time either of them had alluded to what happened the previous afternoon. Grace wasn't au fait with the etiquette of such things, and was glad it was David who had brought it up, and not her.

'Do you have to rush off afterwards?' he said casually as they were finishing their food.

Was he asking if she wanted a repeat performance? Just the thought of it shot a bolt of desire through her body.

'No,' she said breezily, as though it was a perfectly innocent question. 'Why, what did you have in mind?'

The side of his mouth curled up, as if to suppress a smile.

'I thought you might be tired,' he said. 'Maybe need a lie-down.'

She crossed her legs to quell the sensation building there. He was waiting for her answer.

'That would be nice,' she said coyly.

In a split second he had lifted her from her seat and was running up the stairs, carrying her like a bride over the threshold. She squealed with delight, her arms clasped around his neck. He threw her on the bed, panting with the exertion, and she spread herself out, his for the taking. With his shirt discarded, and the buckle of his belt undone, he straddled and undressed her. There was an urgency about it that hadn't been there the first time. Yesterday it was as if he knew this was momentous for her, and respected that by taking things slowly. Not this time, though. His jeans were barely off when he began working his way down her body, licking and kissing her naked flesh. When he buried his face between her legs, she came so fast and hard she could have sworn she saw stars. He stroked her hair, her face, her belly, waiting for her to catch her breath, and then he was inside her, telling her how wet she was, how beautiful. Her second orgasm built more gradually and he read her body perfectly, so that when she came, he did too. She could have wept with joy. It was a travesty to think she might have gone through her whole life never knowing such exquisite pleasure. She felt utterly and completely content, in spirit, body and mind. They must have fallen asleep, because suddenly it was late and she had to drag herself away from the man she wanted to be with, and go home to the man she didn't. David took a selfie and texted it to her – their heads together on a pillow, faces aglow with satisfaction.

'I'll treasure it forever,' she said lightly, as though being droll.

In truth, she had never been more serious.

THIRTEEN

Grace arrived home around the same time as Cal, who was jaunty and puffed up with self-importance. The meeting had gone well, he told her, and the committee would let him know their decision next week. Over nine holes after lunch, Marty reassured him that the wait was just a formality – all part of the power play. Grace raised her eyes at 'power play' – the sheer pomposity of it – but Cal was uncorking a bottle of red, so didn't notice. He veered into gossip mode then, going on about a guy who sold his roofing business for millions, and another guy in his seventies (always guys, she noticed) getting married for the fifth time.

'Fifth,' said Cal incredulously. 'Must be barking mad.'

'I'm glad it went well,' said Grace, taking a glass from him. She preferred white, but red was better for his heart.

'How was your day?' he said, having exhausted the subject of his own.

A vision of herself spreadeagled across David's bed made her face burn.

'Hot flush?' said Cal.

Did he think he was being funny? As a man who never sympathised with the female predicament, Grace wasn't sure why he was interested in her hormones all of a sudden. Sometimes she wondered if he wanted to remind her that she was getting older too. If he knew that the real reason for her blushes was an afternoon of orgasmic love-making, he wouldn't look so pleased with himself. She swallowed that dangerous thought with a long glug of wine, but the urge to tell someone about David – part confession, part boast – was gathering strength. What had happened with him was so unexpected, so miraculous, she worried the secret would burst out of her in an unguarded moment.

Cal's interest in her day was mercifully short-lived. Without waiting for her to answer his question, he started talking about himself again. She let him ramble on, and breathed a long sigh of relief when the combination of fresh air, exercise and wine made him doze off in front of the TV. That gave Grace the rest of the evening to think about David, talk to David, exchange texts with David, moon over photos of David. It was as if she was a teenager again, but with good sex.

Grace and Cal had no plans for Sunday, so she encouraged him to show his face at the golf club. She knew David was busy at the lake but would have liked the house to herself. The suggestion backfired when Cal agreed that being seen at the club was an excellent move, and insisted they eat there. She couldn't think of a good reason why not, so she dressed demurely and allowed Cal to parade her around like a trophy. Playing the dutiful wife – smiling, making small talk, enduring tedious talk about birdies and handicaps and pars – was her penance for yesterday. Still, she was glad Cal had found a new lease of life. It made her feel less guilty somehow.

Marty and June joined them for lunch and as Grace listened politely to the conversation, she felt like an outsider. Their interests weren't her interests, their concerns far removed from her own. Retirement and pensions featured heavily, along with hip replacements and laser eye surgery. Being forced to consider things that hopefully were years away made Grace fear she was squandering the precious remnants of her youth. She still looked and felt young. David was considerably closer to her in age than the three people she was spending her Sunday with.

This was the first time she thought seriously about leaving Cal. Before, not being in love with him didn't seem reason enough to give up her home and security, particularly as they got on reasonably well most of the time. How many people in long marriages were still in love anyway? It was bound to fade over the years. People settled into a routine, a way of being around each other that worked. This was what Grace had always told herself when she felt dissatisfied with her lot. The lacklustre sex life, the difference in age and interests – for years she had convinced herself they didn't matter. What mattered was that Cal was a good father, a reliable husband, a decent man. But that no longer seemed enough to keep her with him till death do us part. Now she realised there was so much she had missed out on and if she stayed with Cal, hers would be a life half lived.

She began to formulate her exit strategy. They would have one last family Christmas together, and then she would tell him. 2020 – new decade, new life. Just having a plan felt as if a weight had been lifted. As a temporary measure she would move in with her mother, giving Cal a chance to get his head around things. Eventually they would have to sell the house and split the proceeds, so Grace could buy a small flat. As long as it had a spare room for Josh, she would make it work. She even had a brainwave with regard to Cal's living arrangements, and would suggest he move in with Beth. Her cottage had three bedrooms and since Zac lived with his dad, two of them were empty most of the time. The village was conveniently situated between Bristol and Bath, with a lively pub and corner shop. They would be company for each other, Grace told herself, and Cal would never manage on his own. It made her feel better knowing – hoping? – that after the inevitable rows and recriminations, he would be OK. It was impossible, of course, but she didn't want to hurt him.

***

The first person she told was her mother. Ruth had cooked one of her childhood favourites – cottage pie with a cheesy mash topping – but she pushed it around her plate with a fork. When Ruth asked what was wrong, Grace almost lost her nerve before blurting it out.

'I'm going to leave Cal.'

Ruth stared at her, speechless.

'I've been thinking about it for a while. I don't love him, Mum, not the way I should.'

Ruth put down her knife and fork.

'Why didn't you tell me you were unhappy?'

'I tried to, but you told me to count my blessings – remember?'

'Oh Gracie, I thought you were just fed up, you know, missing Josh, working too hard.'

'I do miss Josh, but it's more than that. I feel my life is on hold and if I don't act, it will stay that way.'

Ruth sat back in her chair and sighed.

'And what does Cal have to say about all of this?'

'He doesn't know. I thought we'd have one last family Christmas together and then I'd tell him.'

Ruth shook her head slowly from side to side.

'He'll be devastated. So will Josh and Lydia.'

'I know, but what can I do? Stay in an unhappy marriage to spare their feelings? They've both got their whole lives ahead of them. Mine is more than halfway through.'

Neither of them spoke for a few minutes. Cal's handiwork was evident everywhere in the kitchen. The laminated flooring that had taken him an entire weekend to lay, and the newly tiled splashback over the sink. He wouldn't touch the electrics himself, but had found someone qualified to replace the old ceiling lights with twinkly spotlights and a dimmer switch. This caring, dependable side of her husband wasn't something Grace wanted to think about right now.

'Josh is coming home next Friday,' said Ruth eventually. 'You don't think he'll notice something's wrong?'

'Well, Cal hasn't. I'm good at pretending everything's fine. Goodness knows I've had enough practice.'

'Have you read that book I gave you?' said Ruth. 'About the empty nest?'

'Not yet.'

'You should. It predicts this sort of thing – feeling disappointed, a lack of purpose. How do you know it's not just a phase and that in time it'll pass? I would hate for you to make a huge mistake.'

Grace wondered if the book also predicted torrid affairs. Josh going to Exeter had made her admit the marriage was flat and stale. Her relationship with David had prompted her to do something about it. She wanted to explain this to her mum, but couldn't. If Cal ever found out she had cheated, it would kill him. And what would Josh and Lydia think of her? Grace knew it was cowardly, but she needed to stick to her story that the marriage had simply run its course. No one's fault – these things happen. If they knew about David, they would judge her harshly.

'Look, Mum,' she said. 'I'm not rushing into anything. I've got until Christmas to think about it. You're right – I have to be sure.'

FOURTEEN

One of Grace's co-workers was celebrating her birthday and, as was the tradition, she'd bought a box of assorted doughnuts for everyone. The whip-round had produced enough money for a card and an M&S voucher, which Marty presented to her, along with a few kind and witty words. He had been out of the office at site meetings, so Grace had hardly seen him. She was grateful for that. Mixing business with pleasure made her uncomfortable and after their golf club lunch, Cal had wanted to know why she had been so quiet. She had denied it, but Marty had mentioned it too as he passed her desk on his way out. 'June wondered if you were all right,' he said, which made Grace smile. As if June Devlin cared about her welfare.

The box of doughnuts came her way but Grace declined. She had a headache brewing, the sort that makes your stomach feel off as well. Marty perched on the corner of her desk.

'Not on a diet, surely?'

'No, just feeling a bit under the weather.'

'You do look rather peaky. If it's a bug you should go home before you spread it around.'

Grace was pretty sure it wasn't a bug, but the thought of an unexpected day off was tempting. She could call David – see if he was busy. He had been swamped with back-to-back lessons on Friday, depriving them of any time alone. It felt unnatural being with him yet not being intimate. They managed a discreet kiss when he walked her to the car, but it had only made her want him more.

'Yes, you're probably right,' she said. 'Thanks, Marty.'

Outside, the sky was low and steely. A fine drizzle thickened the air. She shivered as she walked to Starbucks, hoping a coffee might perk her up. At a quiet table in the corner, she phoned David. Just hearing his voice gave her a boost. When she told him she had the rest of the day free, he asked her to come over, make up for last weekend. She agreed with an unseemly degree of keenness, before remembering her car was in the driveway at home. David's keenness matched her own.

'No problem,' he told her. 'I'll pick you up in an hour.'

'I can't be seen getting into a Land Rover with a strange man,' said Grace, thrilled at the thought of it.

'I'll meet you at the drop-off area around the back of the station,' he said.

'It's a date,' she said, astounded that she had just arranged a clandestine rendezvous with her lover.

With an hour to kill, she could buy what she needed for Josh's room. TK Maxx was her go-to place for household purchases. She wondered if the compulsion to search out bargains and discounts was a hangover from her cash-strapped childhood. At the entrance, an assistant offered her a large plastic basket on wheels. Grace carried it down the escalator because she hated being cooped up in the lift. A pale-grey throw caught her eye, which she matched with smart striped bedding and big square cushions. The sight of a brand-new fluffy bath mat made her consider how shabby her old one looked, so she put that in the basket as well. Scented candles were her weakness – anything with cinnamon or vanilla – so she picked up a few of those too. Only when the cashier bagged them all up did Grace realise she had bought too much to carry. Four large carrier bags – bright red plastic, with a vast TK Maxx logo emblazoned on either side – sat on the counter. Grace threw her handbag over her shoulder and struggled to fit two bags in each hand.

As she waddled out of the store, she caught a glimpse of herself in one of the full-length mirrors dotted around under harsh spotlights. Her hair had frizzed at her temples, and her face was blotchy with the effort of holding the overstuffed bags. They were cutting into the palms of her hands, and she hadn't been aware that she was grimacing until confronted by her reflection. She couldn't let David see her like this. She wanted him to think of her as pretty and alluring, not a harassed, sweaty housewife. Unable to hold the bags a second longer, she dropped them where she stood. A man walked right into her, almost knocking her off her feet. He was looking at his phone rather than where he was going, but instead of apologising, he just glared. Grace had never been particularly interested in feminism, but remembered being lectured by Lydia about 'the male gaze'. It meant women were seen by men primarily as objects of their own sexual desire. Not Grace – not by this guy. He scooted around her and the giant bags, huffing impatiently. His attitude to her – a guy around David's age, but nowhere near as attractive – resurrected a question she had tried to bury, namely, what did David really see in her? According to Christina, men were curious about sex with an older woman. But if that was the case, surely he wouldn't keep coming back for more? Her phone pinged.

Be there in five x

He must have driven like a maniac. Grace steeled herself to pick up the bags and hurried to the station. It wasn't far, but she had to keep stopping to rub her hands where the plastic handles had gouged deep red marks. The sensible thing would be to ask David to meet her right there on the street, but Sod's Law dictated she was bound to see someone she knew. She soldiered on, panting with exertion. When David spotted her, he jumped out of the Land Rover and rushed to help.

'Been shopping?' he said with a cheeky grin, relieving her of the bags.

She breathed a long sigh of relief and tried to tidy her hair, but seemed to have lost all feeling in her hands. He put the bags on the back seat and opened the passenger door for her. It was the first time she had been in his car. She expected it to be strewn with fishing stuff, but it was actually quite tidy. Before she had a chance to click her seat belt into place, he planted a kiss on her cheek.

'I look like a bag lady,' she said. 'Literally.'

He laughed.

'You look beautiful. A little hot and bothered maybe, but still beautiful.'

She didn't believe him for a second, but was grateful for the lie. He chatted as he drove, describing the Mexican fish tacos he wanted to cook for her. It was a lovely thought and she told him so, but the headache that had threatened was now a tight band around her skull, and she was starting to feel queasy.

'You're very quiet,' he said.

She looked at his profile – straight nose, generous mouth, strong jaw.

'And you're very handsome.'

'Are the two things related?' he said, with a sexy half-smile.

'Possibly. I'm wondering what you see in me.'

'I'm pretty sure we've already covered that,' he said, which was as reassuring an answer as Grace could have hoped for.

He pulled onto the dual carriageway and put his foot down. Grace watched the speedometer jump from fifty to seventy and then edge towards eighty. Cal was so cautious behind the wheel. She wasn't used to whizzing past other vehicles, but felt safe with David. He wouldn't let anything happen to her.

They arrived at his house in half the time it would have taken if she had been driving, or so it seemed. Christina's voice was in her head – *he can't wait to get you into bed.* David opened the passenger door and led her through the rear courtyard. Last night's rain had made the paving stones slick and slippery. She gripped his forearm for support.

'Can I use your bathroom?' she said, when they got inside.

'You know where it is. I'll get us a drink.'

His house had a masculine smell – musk, woodsmoke, old timber – rather like the country pursuits shop. The stairs were bare and worn, each tread creaking under her feet. She believed a person's bathroom told you a lot about them. David's was neat and clean, with a tiled floor (black and white diamond pattern) and plain white walls. She sat on the toilet and peed, wondering if he kept any paracetamol in his medicine cabinet. When she wiped herself, she saw she was bleeding and that the flow was heavy. No, she thought wretchedly. Not now. She managed to find one flattened tampon at the bottom of her handbag, which looked woefully inadequate but would have to do. The medicine cabinet was over the sink, its doors mirrored, forcing her to admit she didn't look her best. It seemed intrusive, opening the cabinet, but she wasn't being nosy – she had a legitimate reason. She didn't know what she expected to find – Viagra, class A pharmaceuticals? – but the contents were pretty pedestrian. Toothbrush, whitening toothpaste, dental floss (full marks for oral hygiene), shaving foam, disposable razors, non-drowsy antihistamine, an old tube of Ralgex. No paracetamol, though, or any painkillers for that matter.

'Everything all right?' he said, when she joined him in the kitchen.

There was a glass of white wine waiting for her on the breakfast bar. How ironic that the only time she didn't have to drive and could actually enjoy a drink, she didn't really want one.

'Don't suppose you have any paracetamol?' she said.

'Um, sure,' he said, rummaging through a drawer. 'There you go.'

He filled a tumbler with water and put it next to the packet of pills. She swallowed two with the whole glass of water.

'I have my period, and a rotten headache. Sorry. I'm sure this wasn't what you had in mind for this afternoon.'

'You want to lie down?' he said.

If his lustful plans being thwarted was a source of disappointment, he hid it well. She agreed to a quick nap, in the hope that when she woke, she would feel better. She followed him to the bedroom and kicked off her shoes.

'Are you warm enough?' he said, putting his hand on the radiator. 'I can turn the heating up if you're cold.'

'I'll get under the duvet,' she said, climbing into bed fully clothed.

The sheets and pillowcases smelled of David. She burrowed down and curled into the foetal position, fighting a sudden urge to cry. Get a grip, she told herself sternly. The effort of leading what was essentially a double life – wife to Cal, lover to David – was wearing. Her emotions were a volatile mess – highs, lows, and everything in between. When she thought about a future bursting with possibility, she felt briefly euphoric. But then she would look at Cal, blissfully oblivious to the devastation that awaited him, and her heart would ache. She pushed that thought away, allowing sleep to fold around her.

Later, when David woke her with tea and biscuits, she was surprised to see it was already dusk outside.

'How are you feeling?' he said, perching on the side of the bed.

She sat up slowly, her head still heavy with sleep.

'Better,' she said. 'What time is it?'

'Four-thirty. I thought you might have to get back.'

She sipped the tea, scalding and strong, just as she liked it.

'I do,' she said, reaching for a biscuit. 'Thanks for this. Just what I needed.'

'Anything else I can get you?'

'Don't suppose you have any tampons, do you?'

He smiled sheepishly.

'Is that a trick question?'

'A genuine question.'

'No, but I can pop out and get some if you like.'

She drank some more tea, thinking how lovely and thoughtful he was. Cal would never dream of doing a tampon run, but then again, she would never ask him.

'That's OK,' she said.

He tucked a wayward strand of hair behind her ear.

'When can I see you again?' he said.

'You really want to?'

'Of course. Why wouldn't I?'

'Because.'

'Because?'

She didn't want to list all the reasons why not. He got into bed and pulled her close. Her head found its perfect resting place on his chest.

'Here's what's going to happen,' he said. 'I'm going to drive you home, you're going to get a good night's sleep, and we'll talk tomorrow.'

She looked up at him, wishing this was the world – just the two of them, with no one to answer to and no one to hurt.

She didn't mean to say she loved him. The words simply spilled from her mouth.

FIFTEEN

David pulled up in the street next to Grace's and unloaded her bags. He wanted to drop her nearer the house, but she was worried a neighbour might see them. 'Say I'm an Uber driver,' he told her, but she didn't want to risk it. There was a moment before they parted when he leaned over, as if to kiss her, but then didn't. A small thing with a big impact. She felt stung, rejected, unworthy. As she shuffled along the street, laden down with shopping and shame, she prayed he wasn't watching. *Pull yourself together, Grace.* She repeated it like a mantra. When she dropped the bags on her doorstep so she could get her key, Cal was there, waiting. He was still wearing his golf clothes – a garish patterned jumper over a sky-blue polo top. His face looked weathered and jowly.

'What's all this?' he said, lifting the bags into the hallway.

'Stuff for Josh's room,' she said. 'Remember?'

Grace slipped off her coat and shoes and told him she was going up for a shower.

'Now?' he said.

Yes, now. Her clothes smelled of David's bed – a gut-wrenching reminder of the fool she had made of herself.

'My tampon's leaking,' she said, knowing this would shut Cal up.

She locked the bathroom door with a defiant click and undressed. Her belly was swollen, her breasts marbled with blue veins. She had blamed her period for what she said to David – *my hormones go a bit loopy this time of the month* – but it sounded like the lame excuse it was. Her head had been resting against his chest, his heartbeat strong and steady in her ear. It was such a tender moment, Grace gazing up at him adoringly – was it any wonder she got carried away? Her reckless declaration of love had stunned every atom in the room. Time stopped. She hardly dared draw breath. *Um, I wasn't expecting that*, he had said into the juddering awkwardness – a hard, cold blade of a comment. She shifted from her supine position and sat bolt upright, smoothing the duvet with her hands. *Me neither*, she had said, trying to make light of it.

A tap on the door startled her.

'It's locked,' said Cal, rattling the handle.

'Two minutes,' said Grace, stepping into the shower.

She needed a little privacy and it wouldn't kill him to wait just this once.

'Why did you lock it?' he said, when she let him in.

She was wrapped in a bath towel, her hair clipped up.

He hastily unzipped his fly and peed with some urgency. Her headache had returned with a vengeance, and a deep ache dragged at her belly. She got a couple of co-codamol from the medicine cabinet and washed them down with a few handfuls of water.

'Not feeling well?' he said.

'No,' she said. 'Can you sort yourself out a takeaway?'

'I ate at the golf club,' he said. 'And had a few celebratory drinks.'

It took her a second or two to catch up.

'Oh, you got the committee thing,' she said. 'That's great.'

'Thanks,' he said, although he didn't seem particularly happy about it.

'I'm pleased for you,' she said, forcing a smile.

'Yeah, Marty was too, when he called to tell me.'

'Marty?'

'He asked how you were.'

Cal's eyes drilled into her as he waited for a response. Without knowing what Marty had told him, that was tricky.

'I felt dreadful,' she said. 'You know how I get when my period's due.'

'He said he sent you home.'

'That's right,' she said, reddening under his gaze.

If Cal knew she wasn't at work, why hadn't he asked her about it the moment she got home? Perhaps it was a test to see if she would volunteer information about where she had been all day. The fact that she hadn't must have looked suspicious.

'So, where were you?' he said.

She had read somewhere that the most convincing lies were those woven with the truth.

'TK Maxx, to get that stuff for Josh, and I bumped into Christina.'

'Christina shops in TK Maxx?'

'I know – shocking, isn't it?'

As an attempt at levity, it failed. The steamy bathroom

felt claustrophobic, especially with Cal standing between Grace and the door.

'Why didn't you come home afterwards?'

She swallowed, wishing she was a better liar. It felt as if a tiny bird was trapped in her chest.

'She and Harry are having problems,' said Grace. 'She needed to talk.'

'All afternoon?'

'We lost track of time.'

She prayed that would be the end of it. Cal wasn't one for idle gossip.

'What kind of problems?' he said.

His persistence was bemusing. Other couples' marital strife was a subject he would usually avoid. She tried to keep it vague, uninteresting.

'Oh, the usual, you know ...'

'Not really,' he said, staring at her.

She pressed her fingers against the throbbing pain in her head, wishing it would stop – wishing *he* would stop.

'She thinks they're growing apart.'

'Sounds serious,' he said, frowning. 'I've always wondered about those two.'

'Have you?'

'Well, she's got her hands full with all those kids, and chats up other men right there in front of him.'

'All those kids? She's got four, same as you,' said Grace, indignant on her friend's behalf. 'And the other thing is harmless flirting. A bit of fun. I don't know why you take it so seriously.'

'Maybe she's lonely, with him working all the hours God sends. It's a wonder they ever get to spend time together.'

Ah, was that what he was getting at? Perhaps he was hinting that this was their problem too. If so, she would prefer him to just come out and say it. There wasn't enough air in the overheated bathroom – she could hardly breathe. Her armpits were damp with fresh sweat. She couldn't cope with this now.

'I'm sure they'll be fine,' she said with a small shrug, as if that was the end of the matter. 'Now if you don't mind, I'd like to get ready for bed.'

'Now?' he said, checking his watch.

'I just need a good night's sleep.'

When she finally got the bathroom to herself, she slumped onto the loo seat, unable to believe that everything could so easily unravel. She had pulled at the loose thread of her dissatisfaction, and now the whole fabric of her life was threadbare. It was all her own doing, she knew that, but she wasn't hardwired to deal with the fallout. Drama simply wasn't in her DNA. If this was a story in a magazine, Grace would think the woman was mad. Maybe she was.

Cal waiting for her in the bedroom was an unwelcome sight. She assumed he had gone downstairs to watch television.

'Everything OK?' she said.

'I don't know, Gracie – you tell me.'

What did he mean by that? She took a breath and told herself he meant nothing other than the obvious, and it was her guilty conscience that translated an innocent question into a sinister one.

'Just a heavy period,' she said.

In the interests of marital harmony, she pecked him on the cheek. That was what husbands and wives did, after all.

To her relief he stood up to go, but he stopped before he got to the door. He turned to look at her – a lingering stare that made her shrink into herself.

'You should have come home,' he said.

He was right, thought Grace, but for all the wrong reasons.

The co-codamol induced a long, dreamless sleep. She didn't hear Cal come to bed, and he was already up when she woke at eight, an hour later than usual. When she came back from the bathroom, there he was, holding her phone.

'You've got a text,' he said, staring at the screen.

Her heart leaped into her throat. It could only be David. No one else would be texting her first thing in the morning. Cal handed her the phone.

'Beth can't make it on Monday,' he said.

Grace read the message, weak with relief.

'That's a shame,' she said, trying to affect disappointment.

A get-together had been Lydia's idea – a chance for everyone to meet Millie. As it turned out, it was Lydia who had persuaded Josh to bring her home for reading week. Such was her curiosity about her little brother's taste in girls. Grace happily went along with it, inviting the family over for supper and drinks. She had never expected Beth to come, and imagined Julia wouldn't either.

Grace hadn't seen Lydia since that awkward evening in Caffè Nero, when she'd quizzed her about David. They had spoken on the phone about arrangements for Monday and exchanged a few texts, but David's name was never mentioned. Grace had been sincere when she reassured her there was nothing between them, but events had galloped on since then. Could she lie to Lydia's face if she asked her the same question a second time? She hoped it wouldn't come to that.

It was Josh's night, after all, and Lydia adored him. She was twelve when he was born, smitten with his cute chubbiness, his pink angelic face. Each fluttering eye movement, each milky burp and wind-induced smile, was a miracle to Lydia. Julie and Beth had shown little interest, other than thinly veiled resentment for their father's only son. Their sour indifference still stung Grace, eighteen years on. She didn't care that they shunned her, but bristled with resentment that their hostility extended to her kind, blameless boy.

'What about Julia?' said Cal.

'Haven't heard from her yet,' said Grace, getting back into bed.

'Not going to work?' he said.

She certainly didn't feel like it, but neither did she feel like being around Cal all day. Perhaps she could encourage him to go to the golf club, or take the cars to the Polish car wash so they would be all nice and shiny for the weekend. There was always a queue at the Polish car wash – he could be gone for hours.

'No,' she said. 'Marty won't mind. Could you call him for me?'

'If you're sure,' said Cal. 'Does this mean I've got you all to myself?'

He used the same oblique tone he had used last night, when he cornered her in the bathroom.

'I won't be much company,' she said, to lower any expectations he might have.

When he offered to make her some coffee and toast, she accepted with a grateful smile. Her strategy was to be cordial and pleasant so that when Josh got home, an air of harmony would prevail. She told Cal she wouldn't be long and sent him downstairs, needing some time alone to wallow. It was torture, looking at photos of David on her phone, but she couldn't help herself. The one with their heads together on the pillow made her want to cry. *Look how happy we were, with our sleepy, sated smiles.* The memory of that afternoon aroused her, despite the period ache, the wretchedness, the roar of regret. She wanted to call him, text him, but what would she say? Right at the beginning they had agreed she would initiate contact. She was the one who was married, after all. Yesterday, when she'd stupidly said she loved him, she had tried to pass it off as a slip of the tongue – an expression, nothing more. I love Cornwall and carrot cake too, she had said with a fake smile. In truth, she had pieced together a mental collage – the myriad ways he made her feel chosen and cherished – and made them more than the sum of their parts. A middle-aged woman, starved of intimacy, falling for an enigmatic younger man. It was the stuff of love songs and poetry – a story as old as time itself. The novel on her bedside table was a love story too – boy meets girl, boy loses girl, boy fights for girl and they live happily ever after. If only.

Grace followed the smell of toast to the kitchen and found Cal dressed for golf again. He had been asked to make up a four.

'Nice day for it,' she said, glancing out of the window.

The sky was a rare and perfect blue, the sun big and bold. Grace wondered if a dose of fresh air might do her some good too – better, surely, than moping around the house. Once Cal had left, she showered, dressed, and texted Christina. Grace needed to warn her about what she had told Cal. It was unlikely that either she or Harry would bump into him, but she didn't want to take the chance. Christina texted straight back – *Come over*, she said, with a red wine emoji.

The drive gave Grace ten minutes to decide how honest she should be. With full disclosure, she could get a much-needed second opinion on her relationship with David – if she still had one. Grace was out of her depth, hopelessly lacking in experience when it came to men. Christina was older, wiser, more worldly. Her people carrier was in the driveway, a reminder that she still had three children at home. If Grace still had children at home, none of this David business would have happened.

'Why aren't you at work?' said Christina, ushering her into the large, pleasantly cluttered kitchen.

'Just having a few rough days,' said Grace, taking a seat at the refectory table.

The air smelled of garlic and onions.

'You do look a bit peaky,' said Christina. 'Would soup help?'

She stood at the Aga, stirring the contents of a saucepan twice the size of any Grace owned.

'Just tea,' she said. 'But only if you're making some.'

Christina filled the kettle and put it on the hotplate.

'You're not knocked up, are you?' she said, eyeing Grace suspiciously.

Grace laughed.

'Absolutely not,' she said. 'I'm having the period from hell.'

'Ah,' said Christina knowingly. 'Welcome to the perimenopause – a delightful precursor to the actual menopause, when you officially become a dried-up old crone.'

'Great,' said Grace. 'Something to look forward to.'

Christina handed her a mug of strong tea and looked at her quizzically, rather like Cal had last night.

'What?' said Grace.

'Not sure,' said Christina. 'You seem –' She paused, searching for the right word. 'Troubled.'

Grace inhaled sharply.

'I'm having an affair,' she said.

Christina was uncharacteristically silent, her face a portrait of puzzled astonishment.

'With David, the guy from the pub quiz,' said Grace, in case it needed saying.

Christina tilted her head to one side, eyebrows raised.

'Well, aren't you a dark horse,' she said coolly.

This wasn't the reaction Grace expected.

'Does Cal know?' she said.

'I can't imagine how he could, but he was sort of strange last night – asking weird questions.'

'What sort of questions?'

Grace took a moment to try to order her thoughts. Christina wasn't going to be happy about what she had told Cal and she couldn't blame her.

'Right,' she said, for some reason imagining that chronology was what mattered here. 'My boss sent me home yesterday because I was sick, but instead of going home, I went to David's. Only my boss is a friend of Cal's, as you know, and long story short, he knew I wasn't at work.'

'Shit,' said Christina. 'What did you tell him?'

'That I went to TK Maxx and bumped into you.'

'Me?'

'Yes, sorry. It was the first thing that came into my head.'

'And he believed you?'

'He was sceptical at first, but I told him – and please don't be cross with me – I told him you and Harry were having problems and you needed to talk.'

Grace watched with apprehension as Christina stiffened. Her lovely heart-shaped face took on a hardness Grace had never seen before.

'I see,' she said, pressing her lips together.

'I'm sorry,' said Grace. 'I'll tell him I got it wrong – all a silly misunderstanding.'

If there had been a scintilla of doubt about how badly she'd screwed up, Christina's icy stare confirmed it.

'I'd rather you didn't discuss my marriage at all,' she said.

How stupid of Grace to think that Christina – with her big, happy family – would sympathise with an adulterer. Grace was ashamed, sitting there in front of her dearest friend, expecting her to condone what she had done.

'I'm so sorry,' she said again, because what else could she say? 'I should go.'

Grace left her untouched mug of tea and reached for her bag.

'It's just you've rather hit a nerve,' said Christina curtly. 'Harry fucks around. Nothing serious. Recreational, he says. Not really a fan of monogamy.'

Now it was Grace's turn to be astonished.

'I had no idea,' she said. 'I mean, I would never have thought –'

Christina folded her arms across her chest, as if to repel her friend's pity.

'Clearly,' she said. 'So you'll forgive me if discovering that you used my situation to cover up your own recreational fucking is rather galling.'

Grace looked horrified.

'No,' she said. 'It wasn't like that at all. And I didn't know about Harry. I'm so sorry.'

The tears weren't a ploy to soften Christina – they surprised Grace too. She searched in her bag for a tissue but didn't have one. Not a single tissue. God, she was hopeless.

'Here,' said Christina, putting a box of Kleenex in front of her. 'And drink your tea.'

Like a distraught child, grateful to have a sensible adult take control, Grace did as she was told. The tea was stewed now, but comforting nevertheless. She blew her nose and wiped her eyes.

'Do you want to talk about it?' said Christina.

'I was going to ask you the same thing,' said Grace.

They exchanged a small smile – friends again.

'It's not recreational with David. I mean, the sex is incredible, but it's more than that.'

'Please don't say you're in love with him.'

'Too late,' said Grace. 'I already did.'

Christina pulled out a chair and sat opposite her.

'You told him you loved him?'

'I didn't mean to. It just slipped out.'

The memory brought a scorch of humiliation to her cheeks, turning them ruby red.

'I made a joke of the whole thing, said I wasn't being serious, but it was still awkward, to say the least.'

'I can imagine. Did he run for the hills?'

'Well, I haven't heard from him since, if that's what you mean. Although it was only yesterday, and I'm the one who's supposed to contact him, not the other way around.'

'You can't seriously believe you're in love with him.

Infatuation I can understand – he's very easy on the eye. Lust too, if the sex is that good, but love?'

Grace put her head in her hands and sighed.

'You're right,' she said. 'Of course you're right. It's just –'

'What?'

'It's such a cliché, but when I'm with him, it's as if I come to life. Every feeling, every sensation is magnified. The rest of the time I'm just sleepwalking – going through the motions. Nothing interests or excites me. The highlight of my week is our Thursday-evening drinks. I know Cal's a good man, but it's not enough.'

Christina looked sceptical.

'Be very careful, Grace,' she said. 'You have a lot more to lose than lover boy. And whatever you do, don't tell Cal. You think purging yourself of your sins will make you feel better, but it will make him feel like shit.'

Grace suspected she was speaking from experience. She was stoic and dignified, but Grace could sense her anguish. What the hell was Harry thinking, risking his marriage, his family? His wife was a goddess – beautiful, clever, wittily acerbic. Didn't he know how lucky he was to have her? Grace's own situation was completely different.

'Believe me, I have no intention of telling Cal. I have made a decision, though.'

She took a deep breath.

'I've decided to leave him.'

'Not for David, surely?'

'No, for me.'

Christina shook her head.

'I knew you were in a rut, but seriously – ending a twenty-year marriage. It's a bit drastic, isn't it?'

'I don't love him,' said Grace. 'Being with David has made me realise there's so much I'm missing out on.'

'Sex, you mean.'

'Yes, but not just that.'

'Then what?'

'Without Josh to anchor us, we're two ships sailing in different directions.'

Christina reached across the table and covered Grace's hand with her own.

'All very poetic, sweetie, until you're another middle-aged divorcee, adrift in a dating pool full of sharks.'

SIXTEEN

The last time Grace saw Alice Reed was at her fiftieth birthday party, blind drunk and sexually rapacious. She had offered Cal a lap dance and refused to take no for an answer. He feigned amusement, but Grace could tell he was stupefied with embarrassment. Harry had no such qualms. He stuffed a ten-pound note down Alice's cleavage, which everyone thought hilarious at the time. It seemed a lot less funny now, in light of yesterday's revelations about Harry's infidelity. Christina had invited Alice to join them at All Bar One, along with Bella Harrington. They knew Alice and Bella from the boys' school – both divorced, but with very different attitudes to it.

When Alice left her husband, it was with a warrior cry of triumph. He was mean with money throughout their marriage, but in the divorce she got half of everything. No more going cap in hand when she wanted a new coat or the boiler needed a service. He had once bought her a Dustbuster for Christmas and put it, unwrapped, under the tree. Alice embraced the single life with gusto. She joined Weight Watchers, fixed her teeth, dyed her hair blonde and signed up to dating sites.

Bella's was a sadder story. Everyone thought her husband a lovely chap – pillar of the school community. He fund-raised tirelessly so that Josh and the other sixth-formers had a brand-new wing, complete with games room, kitchen and study pods. No one believed the rumours at first. The girl must be making it up – an attention-seeking fantasist – but photos on her phone said otherwise. He hadn't broken the law – she was eighteen, technically an adult – but his reputation and marriage were in ruins. Bella had some sort of breakdown. She bore the stain of his sin as if it were her own, and crumpled under the shame. The divorce was quick but painful, like severing a limb. Alice took her under her wing at first, but Bella's melancholy was a mood-killer on double dates. Both women were cautionary tales, which was why, Grace assumed, Christina had invited them along.

The first bottle of wine was quickly polished off during a catch-up about their respective children. All except Josh were on a gap year, and their mothers proudly shared stories of far-flung adventures. Alice admitted to more than a smidge of envy. Her daughter – a gregarious redhead with strong opinions – was backpacking around Australia. Until her divorce, Alice and her family had holidayed in Wales, and in the two years since, the furthest she had got was Spain. 'That's easily remedied,' Christina said, prompting a toast to new adventures. Grace had to admit that divorce agreed with Alice. She looked ten years younger and considerably more glamorous than in her dowdy married days.

Over the second bottle of wine, Christina gently interrogated Alice and Bella about their love lives.

'The internet has a lot to answer for,' said Bella, slightly looser now that she had had a few drinks.

She looked around the busy bar and declared it exactly the sort of place she would have met someone, back in the day.

'An actual flesh-and-blood person,' she said. 'Not just a face on a screen.'

'But there's so much more choice now,' said Alice. 'Hundreds of men, all at the swipe of a finger.'

'Half of them are married,' said Bella. 'And if you won't sleep with them, you never hear from them again.'

'Or even if you do sleep with them,' said Alice with a shrug. 'But heigh-ho, there's an endless supply. Next one, please.'

She laughed loudly, showing off her white Hollywood teeth.

'You make it sound very seedy,' said Christina.

'Because it is,' said Bella. 'You're expected to be bald down there' – she nodded towards her lap – 'and the things they want you to do.'

She took a swig of Chardonnay.

'What things?' said Grace, beginning to feel uneasy.

Bella looked at Alice, as if passing the baton to her more experienced friend.

'BDSM,' she said. '*Fifty Shades* stuff. And choking. For some reason, that seems to be very popular.'

'Choking?' said Grace. 'As in –?'

Alice put her hand around her throat.

'Exactly,' she said.

Grace couldn't understand how choking someone, or wanting to be choked, was in any way sexual. And she certainly wasn't bald down there, as Bella put it. She couldn't imagine being that exposed.

'I blame porn,' said Christina. 'Young people have a completely unrealistic idea of what sex actually is. Girls shave off their pubic hair' – she nodded at Bella in agreement – 'and think there's something wrong if they don't have a screaming orgasm every time a boy touches them. They don't understand that porn is acting – terrible acting at that.'

'Josh is bringing a girl home this weekend,' said Grace, feeling suddenly anxious about it.

The idea he may have watched porn – worse still, been corrupted by it – sickened her.

'Earplugs,' said Alice. 'That's my advice. Believe me, you don't want to hear what they get up to.'

Grace must have looked as appalled as she felt, because Alice laughed and told her not to worry – she was sure Josh would be discreet.

As the evening wore on, Alice became more tipsy and Bella more morose. Grace stood up to go to the loo and gestured for Christina to go with her.

'So this is your not-very-subtle way of showing me the horrors that await a single woman,' said Grace.

'Is it working?' said Christina, dabbing her lips with gloss.

'David is nothing like those perverts Alice and Bella are talking about. He's lovely.'

'Lucky you, but they won't all be like that, believe me. You'll be double-dating with Alice, fending off lecherous advances.'

Grace felt the colour rise in her cheeks. She didn't understand why Christina was so adamant that staying in a bad marriage was better than leaving it.

'Look,' she said. 'I know you mean well, and I know you're fond of Cal, but my mind is made up. A bit of support would be appreciated.'

Christina went into a cubicle and locked the door. Her haughty abruptness was confusing. Yes, she was upset that Grace had used her as an excuse to cover her tracks with Cal, but they were past that now. She waited until Christina reappeared and asked if she was trying to scare her. Christina didn't reply. She looked down as she washed her hands, avoiding Grace's reflection in the large, mottled mirror. There was a hint of belligerence about her that was puzzling, as though she took Grace's decision personally. It didn't make sense, but there it was. Christina turned off the tap and dried her hands with a paper towel.

'I think you're making a horrible mistake,' she said, lobbing the soggy towel into the bin.

Christina had always been the big sister in their friendship, and that was fine with Grace. But she had overstepped the mark, bringing Alice and Bella along to regale her with tales of porn and choking and meaningless sex.

'Yes, you've made that very clear,' said Grace. 'But it's my life, my decision.'

Christina stood tall and pulled her shoulders back, as if asserting dominance.

'I'm very sorry if my concern has offended you,' she said crisply.

'Are you jealous?' said Grace.

She had never challenged Christina like that – never had

cause to. The accusation landed a blow on her perfectly composed face. She frowned, but only for a millisecond, and then recovered herself. Her expression was as cold as arctic air.

'Why would I be jealous?' she said.

Because I have the courage to leave and you don't. It was obvious, now she thought about it. Christina must be furious with Harry for being casually unfaithful. Hurt too, however flippantly she dismissed his infidelity as 'recreational'. She probably told herself that looking the other way was the sensible and sophisticated thing to do. It was what women had been doing for centuries – a means of preserving their marriage and social status. Why jeopardise her big house, her big family, over something so trivial? This mindset must have worked too, because Grace never suspected there was anything amiss between them. But when Christina learned that her closest friend – conventional, uncomplicated Grace Wheeler – was walking away from an unhappy marriage, she would have been badly shaken. And yes, maybe even a little jealous of Grace's gumption. But she couldn't say any of this. If she did, Christina would lose face, knocking their friendship off its axis. An axis that had served them well for over a dozen years.

'No reason,' said Grace. 'I'm sorry. I don't know why I said that.'

Bella burst in, bleary-eyed and perspiring.

'I'm the search party,' she said. 'Alice sent me. Oh, and a heads-up – we have company.'

'Company?' said Grace.

'Couple of guys on the next table. Alice asked them to join us.'

Grace looked at Christina, ready to follow her lead.

'Delightful though that sounds,' she said, 'I have to get back to my brood.'

'Me too,' said Grace. 'Things to do at home.'

Bella disappeared into a cubicle, unzipping her jeans as she went. Grace trailed Christina to the table so they could get their coats. Alice positively glowed, basking in the attention of two age-appropriate men. They wore suits and wedding rings and predatory smiles.

'Have to dash,' said Christina.

'Not joining us?' said the heavier of the two men.

Christina ignored him and air-kissed Alice.

Grace did the same, and caught up with Christina as she stepped onto the street. The rain was thick and sleety, forming icy puddles where they stood.

'Please don't leave like this,' said Grace. 'We've never fallen out.'

Christina was focused on her phone, presumably trying to get an Uber. Grace decided on a change of tack.

'Look, you know we're having a bit of a family get-together on Monday evening. Everyone's curious to meet this girl – Millie. Why don't you come too? I'd love to get your opinion. Please – say you'll think about it.'

Christina dropped her phone into the expensive leather bag slung over her shoulder.

'I'm not sure I could look Cal in the eye,' she said stiffly, 'knowing what you've been up to.'

'Then let's rewind,' said Grace. 'Pretend you don't know.'

Christina's Uber pulled up. She fixed Grace with a hard stare, as though trying to decide if that was even possible.

When she kissed her lightly on the cheek, Christina looked resigned. She threw Grace a weak smile as she climbed into the car.

'Know what?' she said.

SEVENTEEN

Could Josh have grown? To Grace he seemed taller, broader, older. Her heart squeezed at the sight of her boy – almost a man now, she realised with a surge of pride and sorrow. She threw her arms around his neck and pulled him in for a bone-crushing hug.

'OK, Mum,' he said, extricating himself with a bashful smile.

He had filled the narrow hallway to the extent that Grace hadn't noticed the rather scruffy creature behind him.

'This is Millie,' he said, moving aside so she and Grace could greet each other.

She hid her surprise at Millie's appearance under a warm, welcoming smile. The girl was certainly striking, with almond-shaped eyes and wide, fleshy lips painted pillar-box red. Her hair – thick tendrils tied up in some sort of ragged cloth – was streaked with blue, pink and purple. The oversized woollen jumper she wore had horizontal hoops of colour, and both hands were adorned with a garish assortment of rings. Grace hesitated, unsure of the etiquette, and in that tiny moment of indecision, Millie flung her arms around her, treating Grace to a mulchy, organic odour she hoped wasn't marijuana. Even more alarming was the sharp, oniony whiff of sweat emanating from Millie's armpits.

'So lovely to meet you, Grace,' she said.

The metal bar in her tongue was a surprise, as was the tattoo crawling down her neck. Grace didn't want to gawp, but at first glance thought it some sort of sea creature, with a turgid, snake-like body, tail fin and scales.

'You too,' said Grace, ushering them into the sitting room.

She caught Millie eyeing the beige decor, Cal's leather recliner chair, the embarrassingly large, wall-mounted TV, the dull staidness of it all. For a split second, Grace felt ashamed. When she got her own place, it would sing with colour.

'Where's Dad?' said Josh.

'He had an early round of golf,' said Grace.

His newfound status at the club kept him out of the house for hours on end, which suited them both. They had never been a couple that talked much about their feelings, preferring to skim over them and move on. But recently it was as if their relationship had two distinct dimensions. On the surface they were distant and scrupulously polite, but this strained civility belied the swirl of emotions that lay beneath. Grace was frequently unnerved to catch Cal studying her, as though trying to read her mind. And what would he find if he did? Her plan to leave him, her yearning for another man, her desire to live the second half of her life differently from the first? But now Josh was here – a blessed distraction – with this exotic creature in tow.

Grace was astonished by his choice. It wasn't just the hippy clothes, the tattoos and piercings (she had missed the nose stud, and assumed there were other adornments, hidden from view), or even the rainbow hair. Millie seemed a different species to her quiet, conventional son. Grace imagined her stoned at festivals, chaining herself to railings, experimenting with sex. Josh had never been to a festival, nor a protest march – never had sex before Millie, as far as Grace was aware. And she would have known, she was sure of it. He wouldn't have said anything – that would only have embarrassed them both – but she would have noticed the subtle signs of sexual awakening. Had Cal seen them in her? She chased that thought right out of her head.

'That must be him now,' said Josh, as the front door opened.

Cal blustered in, apologised for not being there when Josh arrived, and smothered him in a bear hug. It pierced Grace's heart to witness their raw affection – a reminder that she wasn't just ending a marriage, she was breaking up a family.

'And you must be Millie,' said Cal, letting go of Josh to kiss her on both cheeks.

If he was surprised by her appearance, he hid it well, and vice versa. Josh must have warned Millie about the age difference, because she didn't baulk at the sight of this deeply lined, silver-haired man, practically old enough to be her grandad. Grace had always looked young for her age – a by-product of being small and fair, and slathering herself with factor 50 in the summer – but Cal had aged rapidly since his heart scare. At the golf club last Sunday, one of his cronies made a joke about it being 'bring your daughter to work' day. Cal had laughed dutifully, but inwardly he was probably squirming, as was Grace.

'Have you had lunch?' he said.

'They've just got here,' she said. 'Are you hungry?' she asked Josh.

'Silly question, Mum,' he said. 'Millie?'

She turned those curious navy-blue eyes on Grace, and said, 'You know I'm vegan, right?'

Wrong. Grace couldn't believe Josh hadn't told her. She wracked her brain, thinking back to the full trolley of food she had bought at Sainsbury's. A large chicken – corn-fed, free-range, organic – eggs, sausages, two packs of smoked bacon, pepperoni pizza (Josh's favourite), lots of milk, cheese and yoghurt.

'She's trying to convert me,' said Josh, grinning adoringly at Millie.

'He's a work in progress,' she said, playfully slapping his arm. 'At least he's stopped eating meat.'

She screwed up her face, suggesting the notion of animals as food was abhorrent. Grace and Cal exchanged a knowing look that implied a shared understanding of their son – his surprising taste in girls, his astounding decision to forgo bacon sandwiches. Cal also seemed to intuit that these unexpected dietary restrictions would ruin Grace's carefully thought-out meal plans. Yesterday, when he was helping her unload the groceries, she had told him the pizza was for when Josh and Millie arrived, the chicken for their Sunday roast, the bacon, eggs and sausages for the weekend full English. So much for planning.

'Why don't you two take your bags upstairs,' said Cal. 'Get settled in.'

As an afterthought he added, 'Mum's done a good job on your room, son.'

Grace threw him a grateful smile. Josh's presence had thrust them back into the role of parents – allies in the common goal of ensuring their son's health and happiness. Josh took Millie's hand and they skipped upstairs like newlyweds, leaving Grace and Cal alone.

'Vegan?' she hissed. 'How am I going to feed her? And I'm sure Josh is still growing – he needs lean protein.'

'Let's not panic,' said Cal calmly. 'Why don't you google some vegan recipes. If you need anything, I'll pop out.'

'Right,' said Grace, for once pleased Cal was there. 'That's a good idea, thanks.'

'We're a team,' he said, in his 'take charge' voice. 'I'll go get changed – be down in five.'

Grace realised he was right. Where Josh was concerned, they were a team. Her phone rang, slicing through that thought. Up until Josh arrived, she had been checking her phone obsessively, longing for a message from David. On Thursday she had texted to cancel their lesson – *Sorry, can't make tomorrow* – but had heard nothing back. And, yes, technically he wasn't supposed to contact her, but it didn't contravene their agreement if it was about fishing. His silence seemed to confirm Christina's assertion that he had run for the hills.

Grace stared at her friend's name on the screen, debating whether or not to answer. It had never occurred to her that Christina would relate more to Cal's position than to hers. How could it have? Until last week, Grace had no idea Harry cheated on her. She felt terrible about that, but ignoring her calls wouldn't solve anything.

'Hi,' she said. 'You OK?'

'Fine,' said Christina. 'Now tell me, what's Josh's girl like?'

To Grace's relief, she sounded as busy and bright as she always did. Grace popped her head around the door to check Josh and Millie were out of earshot, before speaking in a stage whisper.

'Wait for it,' she said. 'A vegan hippy with body piercings, tattoos and multicoloured hair.'

Christina let out a hoot of laughter.

'Oh, and she's wearing those yoga pants with the baggy crotch, and a hairy jumper that looks like she knitted it herself.'

'You're not a fan then,' said Christina.

'No, I didn't mean that – first impressions, that's all. But what on earth am I going to feed her?'

'Something vegan, obviously,' she said. 'I can't wait to tell Adam.'

'Adam?'

'He gets home tomorrow. Some problem with his visa that needs sorting out in London. Either that or risk seeing the inside of a Ugandan prison.'

'Brilliant,' said Grace, giddy with relief that their friendship was intact. 'Not about the visa, obviously, or the Ugandan prison, but does that mean you'll both come on Monday? Josh would love to see him, and I could really use some fellow carnivores to eat the mountain of food in the fridge.'

Cal came in, looking for his reading glasses.

'Christina,' mouthed Grace, pointing to her phone.

She listened carefully as her friend rattled off a list of vegan food.

'Jacket potatoes with baked beans, pasta with tomato sauce – no egg in the pasta, no cheese on the sauce – Marmite on toast or crumpets, Weetabix with almond milk, guacamole, hummus, the whole spectrum of fruit and veg.'

'You're a star,' said Grace. 'Thank you.'

'Good luck,' said Christina. 'See you Monday.'

'Why are you smiling?' said Cal, as Grace put her phone in her pocket.

'Didn't know I was,' she said.

When she headed to the kitchen to prepare lunch, he sat and watched her work. Seeing Josh and Millie together got him reminiscing about their own early courting days. If he wanted to stir up fond memories of what it was like between them in the beginning, an old-fashioned word like 'courting' wasn't the best way to go about it. And it didn't help when he recalled an incident at work, when he had pulled her onto the fire escape for 'a quick kiss and a cuddle'. Grace had no recollection of him doing that, and couldn't imagine allowing it. Rather than contradict him, she busied herself chopping tomatoes. It seemed prudent, in the spirit of domestic accord, to keep her doubts to herself. Undaunted by her silence, Cal continued his dubious meander down memory lane.

'This PC stuff takes all the fun out of office romances,' he said, wistfully nostalgic for the good old days.

'Well, you were my boss,' said Grace.

'And your boyfriend,' he said defensively.

'Things are certainly different now,' she said.

She kept her tone neutral, so it wasn't obvious whether she considered that a good thing or not.

'I imagine Millie's a feminist,' he said, by way of a non sequitur.

Perhaps he believed feminists were responsible for bosses having to refrain from feeling up staff members on fire escapes. He lowered his voice to a loud whisper.

'She seems the Greenham Common type,' he said.

Another stark reminder that he was of an older generation. Grace understood the reference, but only because Greenham Common was a hot topic when she was at primary school. Some of the mothers joined the protesters, and Grace remembered being terrified in case her mum went too. One parent had already abandoned her – why not the other? She must have been around eight or nine and started sleeping in her mum's bed, something she had never done before.

'That's as may be,' said Grace diplomatically. 'But she's Josh's girlfriend, and this is our chance to get to know her.'

She was determined to keep an open mind, but from what she had seen so far, Millie was an independent, assertive young woman, forcing her life choices on their impressionable, eager-to-please son. Cal rolled out his usual comments about Grace being overprotective, but she refused to take the bait. Of course she felt protective towards her only child. It was the most natural thing in the world. She did wonder, however, if she was that cliché of a mother who believed no one was good enough for her precious boy. It was a relief when Josh and Millie came down to eat, and Grace didn't have to examine that possibility too closely.

The four of them settled around the table for a vegan spread of microwaved jacket potatoes filled with baked beans, a lightly dressed tomato and avocado salad, and focaccia with an oil and balsamic dip – no meat or dairy in sight. Millie dominated the conversation with her backpacking stories (amazing), her views on organised religion (bad), climate change (very bad) and Brexit (dire). Josh hung on her every word.

'Are you studying medicine too?' said Cal.

Grace admired his restraint in breezing past the B-word. She expected Millie's dismissal of the referendum result to trigger a robust defence of Leave voters, but his interest in her studies was more conducive to a pleasant lunch. Millie took a drink of wine and shook her head.

'Anthropology,' she said.

'What does an anthropologist do, exactly?' said Cal.

Millie chewed her food thoughtfully before she answered.

'Funny you should ask,' she said, glancing at Josh.

They smiled conspiratorially, hinting at a private joke. Grace felt a hot twinge of envy, seeing him swept up by this boisterous young woman. She had expected him to be with someone sweet, shy, modest, and wasn't prepared for the life force that was Millie.

'I suppose it's about understanding human behaviour across time,' she said, twiddling a loose coil of hair around her fingers. 'You know, cultures, languages, archaeological remains.'

'Sounds fascinating,' said Grace. 'How about you, Josh? Classes going well?'

He glanced at Millie before he answered. It was a small gesture, but to Grace it seemed to convey a need for approval, or, more worryingly, permission.

'Good,' he said.

'Is that it?' said Cal jokily. 'That's all we get?'

Josh shrugged, as if there wasn't much more to say.

'It's a lot of work,' he said, 'but no, it's fine.'

'Not much time for fishing then,' said Cal. 'And speaking of which, Mum's been taking lessons.'

All three of them stared at Grace, her face burning under the scrutiny.

'It's nothing,' she said.

Her dismissive response clearly puzzled Cal.

'What do you mean?' he said. 'She's up at Chew every Friday. Even bought her own rod and stuff.'

Grace's heart raced, thinking what a coward she had been to cancel yesterday's lesson with a brief text.

'Really?' said Josh. 'Why?'

'She wanted to surprise you,' said Cal proudly, as though the whole thing had been his idea.

Josh looked at her with such naked affection, her insides melted. In that one, fleeting moment, he was her boy again.

'I can't believe you did that, Mum,' he said. 'Let's go tomorrow. I want to see you cast.'

This was exactly what she had wanted – the reason she took lessons in the first place. But Chew was David's territory, and the thought of seeing him made her stomach clench with excitement one moment, dread the next. She needed an excuse, without making it too obvious.

'How do you feel about fishing, Millie?' she said, expecting the vegan among them to be anti. 'Cruel, I imagine.'

To her amazement, Millie offered a non-committal shrug.

'As long as you put the fish back unharmed,' she said.

Really? That was her answer? Grace was tempted to point out that having a sharp metal hook in its mouth probably wasn't a pleasant experience, but took a swig of wine instead.

'What about Dad?' she said to Josh, before realising with horror that Cal might see it as a family outing and insist on coming too.

'I've got a round of golf first thing,' he said. 'Tee off at eight.'

Grace took another hit of wine. Josh looked at Millie like he was giving her a gift.

'It's so peaceful at the lake,' he said. 'You'll love it.'

For his parents' benefit he added that Millie was really into nature, conservation, all that stuff.

'Mm,' said Grace, desperate now.

And then a brainwave.

'But isn't your fishing gear at uni?' she said to Josh.

'No problem,' he said. 'I'll rent some at Chew.'

Great. She was officially out of ideas. Ironic that instead of looking forward to her first fishing session with Josh, she was grubbing around for excuses not to go. David had ruined it for her. Not deliberately, but that didn't make it any less ruined.

She found it difficult to concentrate on Millie's protracted tale about how she almost drowned in a fast-flowing river in Cambodia, and the amazing local fisherman who came to her rescue. 'Amazing' appeared to be her favourite word. Josh encouraged her to tell them about her gap year, working on a sustainability project in Brazil. He beamed with pride as she spoke, but Grace's head was whirring with thoughts of David. She wondered if she should text, asking him to stay away. But why should he? Fishing was his livelihood and if he had lessons booked, he could hardly be expected to cancel them to suit her.

'Mum?'

She hadn't realised Josh was speaking to her.

'Sorry,' she said.

'We're going to head off,' he said. 'I promised Millie I'd show her around Bath, and we'll probably have a curry and some drinks later – said we might meet up with Lyd.'

'Good idea,' said Cal, who proceeded to name and review most of the Indian restaurants in the city centre.

Grace declined an offer of help to clear up, and was touched when Cal discreetly took Josh to one side and asked if he needed money. He was a good dad. She should remind herself of that more often.

Once Josh and Millie had gone, Cal joined Grace in the kitchen for a debrief.

'What do you think?' he said. 'Seems a bit of a chatterbox to me.'

Saying anything negative felt disloyal to Josh.

'Probably nervous,' she said diplomatically. 'Although I'm a little surprised she's his type.'

Was that a passive-aggressive way of saying she didn't like her? Cal cut through that thought with a question.

'What is his type, then?'

'I don't know,' she said, loading plates into the dishwasher. 'Someone a little more reserved, perhaps.'

Cal smiled at her with affection – a rarity these days.

'You expected him to be with someone more like you.'

'No,' said Grace indignantly, although now he mentioned it, maybe that was exactly what she expected.

'It's OK,' said Cal. 'I was the same with the girls. It's natural to be more comfortable with people who are like us. Human nature.'

'You need to ask Millie about that,' said Grace tartly. 'She's the expert.'

'Now now,' said Cal, amused.

'I'm only joking,' said Grace, glad they could be like this.

'To be honest,' said Cal, 'I'm impressed with the boy. I wouldn't have thought he had it in him. And he's not going to marry her, is he? She's his first girlfriend. It's good that she's more experienced.'

If he was alluding to what she taught him in the bedroom, Grace wished he hadn't put that picture in her head. Not only could she not stomach the notion of Josh in that context, in referring to the benefits of experience Cal had forced her to think about David, and everything he had taught her.

'Our lad's all grown up now, Gracie,' said Cal, as if it needed saying.

He was right, though. Josh was living his own life, and Grace was no longer at its safe, solid core. He would always love her, but he didn't need her in the same way anymore. She remembered Ruth telling her it was the price mothers paid for having raised their children to be independent. It was necessary and right, but caused a unique kind of grief. Cal must have seen that in her face, because he asked if she was OK.

'Guess I have to be,' she said.

They went to bed around ten-thirty, after agreeing there was no point waiting up for Josh. Instead of lying back to back – their default sleeping position of late – Cal pulled Grace into a stiff embrace. She had wondered if he would try to capitalise on the goodwill that had flourished between them during the day, and this was her answer. He had taken their show of unity and built it into something it wasn't – at least, not for her. His body felt both foreign and familiar, as if he was a stranger she had known all her life.

'It's been nice,' he said, 'having our little family together again. I know you've been struggling.'

She was thinking how unworthy she was of his understanding, when a hand migrated towards her bottom. She didn't want him to feel rejected, but needed to quash any amorous expectations he might have.

'I've still got my period,' she said.

Cal found menstrual blood offensive, and hardly touched her when she was bleeding. Once, when her tampon leaked onto the bed sheets, his revulsion was such you would think he had stumbled upon a particularly grisly crime scene. Without any hope of sleep, she turned on her side and closed her eyes. In no time at all Cal's breathing became a raspy, rhythmic snore that got louder when he rolled onto his back. Grace knew she wouldn't relax until Josh was home safely. It was almost midnight when she heard him and Millie stumbling around, laughing, shushing each other and then laughing some more. Clearly, they were drunk. When Josh used to tell Grace about school friends drinking until they dropped, she counted herself lucky that he had no taste for alcohol. She supposed drinking was to be expected now he was at university – another rite of passage. One of them tripped on the stairs, prompting a stuttering fit of giggles. Grace stared into the darkness, an invisible force pressing down on her. She had so looked forward to Josh coming home, but it wasn't supposed to be like this. Instead of being bouncy with joy, her head was full of David. For the first time in her life, she had made a fool of herself over a man. Look how that turned out, she thought pathetically, dreading what the morning might bring.

EIGHTEEN

Josh ambled into the kitchen in boxers and a T-shirt, purple-grey smudges under his eyes. He yawned so wide Grace saw his wisdom teeth.

'How's the hangover?' she said.

He flopped onto a chair and scratched his stubble.

'What?'

She put a glass of water on the table in front of him.

'I assumed,' she said.

'Sorry, did we wake you last night?'

'I wasn't asleep. Can I get you some breakfast?'

Josh shook his head.

'Coffee's fine,' he said. 'I'll take some up to Millie.'

'No need,' she said, appearing in a flimsy cotton dressing gown.

Her hair was wild and loose – her breasts too. Yesterday's shapeless jumper had concealed their voluptuousness. She hugged Josh from behind, resting her chin on his shoulder. The thin fabric gaped, revealing an indecent amount of tattooed cleavage. Grace's own modest B-cups were hidden under a quilted, ankle-length robe, complete with pockets and a hood. The notion of baring her breasts to a stranger with a tattoo gun was inconceivable. She didn't know what had happened to young women in the last twenty-five years. They seemed so much bolder, determined to wear their sexuality like a badge of honour. When Grace was a young woman, it was all about being demure – a 'nice' girl, as her mum would say. Grace thought back to the waitress in David's local, and how brazenly she had signalled she was up for a bit of no-strings fun. The way she had offered herself to him was so casual, as though sex was a purely recreational activity – Harry's excuse to Christina. Was it really that easy to divorce the physical from the emotional? Not for Grace it wasn't, although she admitted life would be simpler if it was.

'How are you feeling?' she asked Millie, a question that elicited only a groan.

Grace's plan, hatched in the early hours of the morning, was to play up the sympathy, selflessly offering to forgo a morning's fishing so Josh and Millie could stay at home and nurse their hangovers. She had hoped for gales and a downpour, but the sky was stubbornly clear. Bronze autumn sunshine flooded the kitchen, making it a perfect morning for a drive out to Chew. Josh disentangled himself from Millie and made two cups of coal-black coffee, sweetened with heaped teaspoons of sugar. Grace didn't realise he drank coffee now.

'Anything to eat?' she said. 'Something to line your stomach?'

Was it too much to hope this would nudge them into

admitting they couldn't face food, at which point Grace would gently suggest they go back to bed and sleep it off? Yes, unfortunately it was.

'I wouldn't mind some toast,' said Millie, sitting down.

She rearranged her dressing gown, making only a cursory effort to cover her breasts and thighs.

'And Marmite,' she said. 'If you have any.'

Josh loved Marmite, meaning Grace always had at least one jar in the cupboard. 'Coming right up,' he said, dropping a couple of slices of sourdough into the toaster. Grace had scrutinised the ingredients to make sure it was vegan friendly. Millie teased her hair with her fingers, the way femmes fatales do in movies. Grace watched with dismay as she and Josh visibly brightened. As well as coffee, he poured them both a tumbler of orange juice. The first plate of toast was followed by a second, Grace's hopes of them being too hungover to leave the house dashed. She sipped her coffee, too anxious to eat.

'We'll just finish this and have a shower,' said Josh, slathering the third round of toast with Marmite. 'I can't believe we're going to fish together, Mum.'

'Me neither,' she said.

An hour later, as they piled into Grace's little car, she wished she had texted David to warn him she would be at the lake with her son. It wasn't as if she hadn't tried, but each time she lost her nerve. The silence between them had taken on a physical form, becoming more solid with each passing day. It seemed insurmountable now – a line that couldn't be crossed. Loading her rod into the boot, Grace thought back to the afternoon David took her to buy it, the lunch he had cooked for her and the wonderful sex that followed. She should have known it was too good to be true.

Josh and Millie sat cuddled on the back seat, his arm around her shoulder. It felt vaguely voyeuristic to Grace, seeing them each time she checked the rear-view mirror. She tried to avoid doing it, but had no choice when she overtook a lorry on the dual carriageway. They seemed to be asleep. Grace felt a pang of maternal nostalgia, remembering how Josh used to fall asleep in her arms when he was a baby – the warm weight of him, the milky scent of innocence. It was the happiest time of her life. She thought she had found a different kind of happiness with David, but it was all an illusion – now you see it, now you don't. The possibility that she might be driving towards him made her insides curdle.

There was no sign of his Land Rover in the car park – a source of relief and disappointment. Inside, Reggie greeted her with a shaggy-beard smile. Her heart lurched at the familiar smell of instant coffee and wet wool. She expected to turn around and see David, with his flat cap and enticing smile.

'Hello, young lady,' said Reggie. 'You here for a lesson?'

'Not this morning,' she said. 'I'm here with my son. Can I pay you for a few hours on the bank – catch and release?'

'Listen to you with the terminology,' said Josh, grinning.

He turned to Reggie and told him he needed to rent a rod.

'This your boy?' Reggie asked Grace, in his broad West Country burr.

'It is,' she said proudly. 'This is Josh, and his girlfriend – sorry, friend – Millie.'

Josh and Millie exchanged an amused smile when Grace

corrected herself. As she tapped her PIN into the little machine ('It's a bit slow,' said Reggie, waiting for a connection), a desire to ask after David set her heart thumping. She resisted, knowing she couldn't feign nonchalance.

'You're all set,' said Reggie, handing her two passes. 'Lovely day for it.'

It really was. An unblemished sapphire sky, and water that gleamed under the sunlight. Grace let Josh choose a good spot for them to settle, and was touched by his gallantry when he spread his jacket on the grass for Millie. She sat down, cross-legged, and pulled a book from her backpack. Grace asked Josh for help setting up her rod, because she couldn't remember a single thing David had taught her.

'You're making me nervous,' she said, as Josh waited for her to cast.

He laughed – a sound she missed sorely. With Millie engrossed in her book, Grace could almost believe it was just her and Josh by the water again, like it always used to be. She told him to cast first, and watched the effortless way he flicked his line out onto the lake. Her own attempt was pathetic, the slack line landing only a few feet from the bank. Josh stared at her and sighed.

'Don't look so serious, Mum,' he said. 'It's supposed to be fun.'

'I'm trying too hard to impress you,' she said jokily, even though it was true.

'Come on,' he said, encouraging her as if he were the parent and she the child. 'Give it another go, only this time try to relax.'

She shook the tension from her shoulders, and surprised

herself by managing a moderately adequate cast. The line glided straight ahead before plopping onto the water about twelve feet away.

'See, much better,' said Josh, eyes fixed on the fly bobbing on the surface. 'I can't believe you actually took lessons.'

'Part of my cunning plan to spend time with you,' she said.

Millie had abandoned her book and looked like she was sleeping. Her eyes were closed, and her ample bosom rose and fell with each slow breath. Having Josh to herself was the tonic Grace needed. A fat bee hovered lazily between them, tempted out of its slumber by the late autumn sun. She waved it away, unsure if bees still stung at this time of year. Josh had had a bad reaction to a sting when he was ten, and she had been hyper-vigilant ever since. If she shooed the bee too aggressively it might become agitated, so she made a slow, sweeping motion with her hand, encouraging it to fly away. At first she barely noticed a figure in the distance, waving. It was in her peripheral vision, and only when she shielded her eyes from the sun did it come into focus. David. Her heart punched at her chest. He must have thought she was waving at him, and oh God – he was coming over. She fiddled with her reel, trying to look casual and competent and utterly unfazed.

'Grace,' he said, smiling. 'I didn't know you were fishing today.'

'Last-minute thing,' she said, unable to control a disconcerting twitch in her top lip.

David and Josh looked at each other, presumably waiting to be introduced. Grace froze, her brain unable to process this bewildering turn of events. As the silence stretched on,

David took the initiative and offered Josh his hand.

'David Gill,' he said. 'I've been giving your mum fishing lessons.'

Watching her son and her lover shake hands was a surreal experience for Grace. In her mind they existed in separate, hermetically sealed compartments, and seeing them together was perplexing, like hearing your two favourite songs played at the same time. David glanced knowingly at the sleeping girl.

'Heavy night?' he said to Josh, in an affable, man-to-man kind of way.

Josh smiled, as if pleased to have this acknowledged.

'Something like that,' he said. 'Think we're both a bit worse for wear.'

'Fresh air will sort you out,' said David.

They talked fishing for a while – technical stuff Grace didn't understand – their easy rapport bittersweet. In her post-Cal world, she had dared fantasise about David and Josh becoming friends, having a few beers, taking fishing trips together. She knew it was madness, but here they were, getting on better than she could have hoped.

'Caught anything, Grace?' said David.

'Not yet.'

Instinct told her that the less she said, the better.

She feared she might give herself away. Either Josh would sense something between her and David, or David would sense she was shaking inside. Her brevity came across as curt, rude even. Josh threw her a quizzical *what's up with you?* look, but all she could do was bite her lip and wish to God it would stop twitching. She willed David to leave them in peace. Hadn't he wreaked enough havoc in her life without spoiling this too? Wanting him and not wanting him caused her physical pain – a sharp stomach spasm that made her wince. How absurd that she had sailed through adolescence without knowing the anguish of unrequited love, only to experience it now, in middle age.

'Well,' he said. 'Guess I should get on. Great to meet you, Josh, and nice to see you again, Grace.'

She didn't watch him walk away.

'He's cool,' said Josh. 'Why were you weird with him?'

'I wasn't,' she said defensively.

He stared at her.

'Um, you were,' he said. 'You OK, Mum?'

'Caffeine deprived,' she said. 'I'm going to get a coffee. Do you want anything?'

He shook his head.

'No, thanks.'

She picked up her handbag and slung it over her shoulder.

'Oh, and don't forget I've made sandwiches,' she said, pointing to the backpack Millie was using as a pillow.

While Josh and Millie were still in bed, Grace had been pulping avocado with sea salt, olive oil and a squeeze of lemon juice, so it spread like butter.

'Are you sure I can't get you a drink?'

'Actually, yeah, that would be good,' he said. 'Red Bull, Lucozade, something like that.'

'No problem,' she said, forcing herself not to look in David's direction.

She wondered if an energy drink might do her good too. Her limbs felt shaky and weak, probably because she hadn't eaten. As she neared the building, she managed to convince herself that things could have gone worse.

Josh had buffered the awkwardness between her and David, and was none the wiser. *Dodged a bullet there*, she told herself. A tap on the shoulder made her turn around and come face to face with her lover.

'What are you doing?' she said, her blood pressure erupting.

'Hoping to talk,' he said.

She looked back at the lake.

'I don't want Josh to see us.'

David led her to the side of the building, where a thick clump of trees offered them cover. Grace's head swivelled this way and that, checking for prying eyes.

'Relax,' he said.

'That's my son over there,' she said, in case he didn't understand how much was at stake.

'I know. Nice kid.'

Grace took a breath and allowed her eyes to meet his. To deny the attraction would be like denying gravity. Every cell in her body hummed, pulled into his orbit by an invisible force. Even in their so-called honeymoon period, she had never felt anything this intense with Cal. Not even close.

'What do you want, David?'

He looked mildly confused, as if the answer was so obvious, he didn't know why she had to ask.

'To talk to you – find out why you cancelled our lesson, why you haven't called.'

'I –'

She seemed unable to form a coherent sentence.

'I was –'

'What, Grace?'

She looked at the ground. How could he expect her to explain? It was humiliating.

'You could have called me, you know,' she said.

'You told me not to. Your rules, not mine.'

'I know, but after what I said. I was mortified.'

'But we're cool, right? I mean, you weren't serious –'

'God no,' she said. 'Of course not.'

He tucked her hair behind her ear, letting his palm rest on her cheek. She knew he was going to kiss her. She also knew she should stop him, but knowing and doing were different things. His lips were soft and sensual, his tongue warm. Her body remembered and responded, becoming instantly aroused. The sweet ache in her belly told her she needed more, but David stopped.

'Isn't that your son's girlfriend?' he said.

Millie was walking in their direction, looking slightly dazed.

'Oh God, it is,' said Grace.

Millie had spotted them and came over, her rainbow hair spilling out from its wooden clip.

'I'm looking for the loo,' she said.

'Oh, it's right there,' said Grace. 'Actually, I'll come with you. I was on my way to get some coffee.'

'Great,' said Millie, looking at David.

He offered his hand.

'David Gill,' he said. 'Grace introduced me to Josh when you were having a kip.'

Millie stared at his outstretched hand, as if unsure what to do with it. Far too formal a gesture for someone as bohemian as Millie, Grace imagined. She took it nevertheless.

'Millie Khan-Reeves,' she said.

Panic swarmed around Grace as she agonised over what, if anything, Millie had seen. There was nothing in her manner to suggest she had caught her boyfriend's mother kissing this strange man. A close call, though. They would have to be more careful next time.

NINETEEN

It was a perfectly innocent remark. They were having a drink together before Josh and Millie headed out for the evening, when Josh mentioned to Cal that he'd met Mum's fishing instructor. Grace blushed rose-pink, remembering the taste of coffee on his tongue.

'You were asleep,' Josh told Millie. 'David something.'

'Yeah, your mum introduced me when I went to find the loo,' said Millie.

Rose-pink became hot red. Cal used his 'I'm-only-joking' voice to ask if he had anything to worry about.

'She seems very keen on fishing all of a sudden,' he said, winking at the teenagers.

It was too close to home for Grace – first Lydia had met David, now Josh and Millie – and too laden with truth. Grace's abrupt change of subject warranted nothing more than a raised eyebrow from Josh. She asked about the place they were eating tonight – a new vegan burger bar she had never heard of. It hadn't escaped her notice that he was hungrily chomping his way through a large bowl of salt and vinegar crisps, and that was after two rounds of sandwiches by the lake and a heaped plate of pasta when they got home. Grace wished he didn't have to fill up on carbs. It went against every maternal instinct to watch in silence as her boy, in his final few years of growth, eschewed entire food groups to please a girl. She wanted to say that if Millie really liked him, she wouldn't try to change him, but Cal had warned her not to interfere. He took the view that Josh's vegan phase would last as long as his Millie phase, so don't worry about it. But Grace did worry. Josh had been raised to think for himself, not blindly follow others. She and Christina had often bemoaned the perils of peer pressure, and how easy it was for even the best and brightest to succumb.

In their early teens, Josh and Adam had started hanging out at Warleigh Weir during the summer holidays. Grace wasn't happy about it, but their school friends were allowed and since Christina didn't object, Grace felt she couldn't either. The area was a well-known local beauty spot, its clean shallow water making it popular with families. But the closer you got to the weir itself, the deeper and more unpredictable the water became. This was where Josh's crowd congregated. They would dare each other to jump from a rocky ridge into the fast-flowing river below. There was no lifeguard, and teenage boys weren't exactly known for their common sense and caution. The inevitable happened during an August heatwave, when a boy in Josh's class smashed into the rocks, breaking a leg and three ribs. He would have drowned if a couple of older boys hadn't managed to drag him onto the riverbank. Neither Josh nor Adam mentioned it when they got home – probably scared they would be banned from going back. Christina saw it on the local news and immediately called Grace, telling her to switch on the television. They watched in dismay as an air ambulance landed in the field to whisk the injured boy to hospital. Josh played the whole thing down, insisting the boy had tried to do a backflip to impress some girl. *I'd never be that stupid*, he had told her, but wasn't he trying to impress Millie, albeit in a less dramatic fashion?

Grace brought up the incident, hoping Josh might make the connection, but there was no sign that he did. Once they had left, Cal opened another bottle of wine and suggested they settle down for the evening. He patted the space next to him, inviting Grace to sit. He usually watched television from the comfort of his recliner chair, but tonight he was on the sofa. There was a BBC drama he wanted to watch – something about the coughing major who won a million pounds. When Grace sat down with her wine, Cal took her hand in his and rested it on his lap. He looked so happy with his lot, as if all was right in the world again. This was how things were before Josh went to Exeter. Him being home had pulled them back to that earlier version of themselves, but for Grace it wasn't real. She felt such a fraud, allowing him to believe in the fiction of their mutual happiness. A more honourable person would be honest – rid him of any false hope. But this wasn't the time, she told herself. Not with Josh and Millie here. She thought about it a lot, though, and rehearsed the conversation that would end her marriage. In her mind they were civilised and grown-up about it, her tone gentle but firm. She would always care about him, but didn't love him the way a woman should love her husband. No one's fault, they had simply grown apart. She would talk in terms of a trial separation, which seemed kinder than asking outright for a divorce. Until then, she was marooned in a marital no man's land – neither in nor out. She glanced down at his hand, as familiar as her own, and felt a jolt of doubt. Josh had breathed life into their home again, rekindling the embers of their dying marriage. In fixating on Cal's shortcomings as a husband, Grace had muted his qualities as a father. Seeing him with Josh brought them to the fore, stirring feelings of gratitude and affection. It was simpler when they were emotionally estranged – more definitive and clear-cut.

'You all right, love?' he said, giving her hand a squeeze.

She answered with a smile – another small deceit.

'Mind if I put this on pause for a sec?' he said, reaching for the remote. 'I need the little boy's room.'

It was the first time Grace had been alone all day. Four adults in a modest terraced house didn't allow for much privacy. She was itching to call David, but hadn't had the chance. Millie interrupting their interlude by the lake had left them with unfinished business. She glanced at her phone and wondered if she dare. Her finger hovered over his name, but she heard Cal on the stairs so that was that. He returned with the bottle of wine and said they might as well finish it. His face was ruddy and relaxed – a picture of contentment.

'That Millie is a bright spark,' he said.

'Oh?'

'I asked her what she liked to drink, you know, given her

self-imposed dietary restrictions, and she told me spirits were vegan, except for things like Baileys that add cream.'

'I've never thought about it,' said Grace.

'Neither had I,' said Cal. 'We had quite a fascinating chat, as a matter of fact.'

'What about?'

'Oh, the meaning of life – nothing too heavy.'

'Very amusing,' said Grace. 'Hope you steered clear of politics and religion.'

'Not at all,' said Cal. 'Some of her ideas are a bit naive, but that's because she's young. What she said about countries getting bogged down in their party systems, that struck a chord, though. You only have to look at America – richest country in the world, and they're more interested in guns than healthcare.'

Grace looked at him askance.

'You've voted Tory your whole life,' she said.

'So far,' he said. 'But it's good to keep an open mind.'

Open-mindedness wasn't something she associated with Cal. Seeing Millie head out tonight in silver Dr. Martens, ripped jeans and a pink fluffy coat, Grace expected him to be as bemused as she was. Yet he seemed to have taken to her quirkiness, and was genuinely interested in getting to know her better. It made Grace question if she was the stuffy, strait-laced one, not him. Perhaps she was deliberately blind to his good points because seeing the worst in him helped justify her actions. Only that afternoon he had promised to take Ruth's car for its MOT. He wouldn't risk her being ripped off by some unscrupulous mechanic. *Family looks out for each other*, was his stock response whenever Ruth expressed gratitude for his many kindnesses. *You've got a good man there,* she would tell Grace. Little wonder she had cautioned her against leaving him.

After the ten o'clock news, Grace and Cal went to bed, leaving the hall light on so Josh and Millie wouldn't have to stumble around in the dark like they did last night.

'Try not to let them wake you again,' said Cal, turning on his side in an effort not to snore.

Grace tried to read, but her attention kept turning to her phone, charging on the bedside table. She wondered what David was doing, and if he was thinking about her too. She checked that Cal was asleep, knowing she would text David even as she told herself not to.

Good to see you today Mr Gill – we must do it again xx

He texted straight back, as if he had been waiting for her message.

Soon I hope Mrs Wheeler xx

TWENTY

Grace had booked Monday off work. She wanted to treat Josh and Millie to lunch at the Pump Room, but it turned out they already had plans. He asked if Millie could borrow her bike so they could cycle along the canal to Bradford-on-Avon. It was something they used to do as a family. Grace remembered having to pedal furiously to keep up with Cal as he thundered along the towpath, calves thick with muscle. All she could see of Josh, strapped into his child seat, was the back of his head, encased in a silver helmet that he said made him look like a spaceman. It seemed like yesterday and a lifetime ago. How was that possible? She watched from the window as they headed off, her chest heavy with love.

'Penny for them?' said Cal.

Grace shook her head. She didn't want to share her trip down memory lane. Her new resolution was to look forward, not back.

'Right, I'm off,' he said. 'Be back mid-afternoon to help get ready for our little soirée.'

He said 'soirée' with a French accent and twirled an imaginary moustache. She smiled, wishing she could love him again. Maybe she would have found her way back to him if she hadn't met David, but he was the one in her head and her heart. She called him once Cal had driven away, ostensibly to confirm next Friday's lesson, but really just to hear his voice. Their conversation was short but satisfying, like scratching a hard-to-reach itch. When he hung up she called Lydia, trying to persuade her to bring Kiara tonight. 'Neither the time nor place to leap out of that particular closet,' was her reply. Grace had an hour or two to kill before she needed to start getting everything prepared. The food was already bought and Cal had said he would take care of the drinks.

In lieu of their usual Monday supper, Grace decided to drop in on her mum for an impromptu visit. She stopped at the garage to fill up with petrol and got a small bunch of flowers. When she let herself in, she called 'Only me!' from the hallway.

'Grace?' said her mum, appearing from the kitchen. 'Why aren't you at work?'

'Day off,' she said, surprised to see Ruth wearing make-up and a dress that flattered her trim figure.

'You look nice,' said Grace.

The kitchen door was ajar and she could just make out a leg. A man's leg.

'You have company?' she said.

'This is Charles,' said Ruth, introducing the silver-haired gentleman sitting at the table.

He stood up and shook Grace's hand, which seemed very formal under the circumstances. She noticed he was nicely dressed too. His navy sports jacket had silver buttons and his shoes were polished to a shine. Grace couldn't remember the last time she had seen a man in her mum's kitchen, other than Cal.

'We're going to a talk at the Holburne,' said Ruth. 'Charles is interested in ceramics, and then we're having lunch at that nice pub by the river.'

It took a minute for the penny to drop and realise her mum was on a date.

'Oh, sorry,' she said. 'I should have called.'

When she handed Ruth the flowers, Grace spotted a much nicer bouquet by the sink, waiting to be arranged in a vase. She thought of those old films where men with impeccable manners romanced women with flowers and compliments.

'Don't be silly,' said Ruth. 'We've got a few minutes before we need to leave. Let's have a cup of tea.'

'No, Mum, really. It was just a flying visit. I've got lots to do at home.'

'My grandson is home from university,' Ruth told Charles. 'We're having a bit of a family get-together.'

'Why don't you come?' said Grace.

Charles glanced at Ruth, as if gauging her reaction.

'It's up to you,' she said, with a smile that lit up her eyes.

'Well, if you're sure I won't be intruding,' he said.

'Not at all,' said Grace, feeling as though she was the one intruding.

She made her excuses, telling Ruth she had to swing by Christina's to pick up some serving platters and extra wine glasses. Ruth followed her into the hallway.

'You've never mentioned a Charles,' said Grace, *sotto voce*.

'I'm sure I have,' said Ruth. 'He's the widower from across the street. You remember – his wife was bedbound after a stroke. He insisted on caring for her himself. Couldn't bear the thought of her going into a home. She died earlier this year.'

Grace vaguely remembered Ruth telling her she dropped in on a sick neighbour from time to time, but nothing about a suave husband.

'Are you two an item, then?' she said, with a conspiratorial smile.

'I wouldn't say that, exactly. He's just a bit lonely, like me.'

Grace's smile vanished. It was the first time Ruth had admitted to being lonely. In the forty years since her divorce, she had never had a significant other. Whenever Grace suggested she should meet someone, Ruth insisted she was happy as she was. Her days were filled with part-time jobs and voluntary work, and she used to help out with Josh whenever Grace needed her to. Being busy wasn't the same as being happy, though – a lesson Grace had learned too. Maybe Ruth had quietly ventured into the sleazy dating world Alice and Bella described, and decided she was better off single.

'Oh, Mum,' said Grace.

'I'm fine,' said Ruth, waving away her concern. 'But it's nice to have a bit of company.'

A gentlemanly neighbour did seem a much better prospect than some random guy matched by a computer algorithm.

'Well, I think it's lovely,' said Grace.

'Me too,' said Ruth. 'And speaking of which, how are things with Cal?'

'A bit better with Josh home. And he's getting on famously with Millie, which is rather surprising.'

'Why?'

'You'll see for yourself tonight.'

'Intriguing,' said Ruth. 'Can't wait.'

Seeing her mother framed in the doorway as Grace drove away stirred up the oddest feelings. She certainly didn't begrudge her a bit of happiness – far from it. She was delighted for her, but at the same time found herself trying to dispel a nagging fear that things might change. She had never had to share Ruth with anyone.

'Am I a selfish person?'

It was the first thing she said when Christina opened the front door.

'I can't possibly answer that without context.'

'I've just interrupted my mother on a date.'

Christina's eyes widened.

'Go Ruth,' she said, evidently impressed. 'Tell me more.'

'Charles – seems nice. Very dapper. A widower from across the road. She said she was lonely.'

'Oh, that's sad.'

'I know. I mean, she's always rushing around doing things for people, and she's got plenty of friends, as well as me and Josh and Lydia. It just never occurred to me that wasn't enough.'

'And you think that makes you selfish?'

'Yes. As does having an affair, leaving my pensioner husband, breaking up a family.'

That seemed enough to be going on with. Grace didn't feel the need to bring up her tryst by the lake as well. Christina didn't contradict anything she had said. Her silence was unnerving.

'Say something,' pleaded Grace.

'It sounds like you've had an epiphany,' said Christina. 'Dare I ask what brought it on?'

Grace slumped onto a chair, still wearing her winter coat.

'The nicer Cal is, the worse I feel.'

'I think that's called guilt,' said Christina.

'It's Josh being home. Cal's such a good dad, and he's really made an effort with Millie.'

'Is that a bad thing?'

'It's hard to explain.'

Christina put Grace's tea in front of her.

'Try.'

Grace shrugged off her coat, only now noticing how much heat the Aga was throwing out.

'I've always thought of myself as a good person.'

'So what's changed?'

'Me,' said Grace. 'I've changed. How can I be having an affair? It's just not who I am.'

She took a slurp of tea.

'And I'm almost too ashamed to admit it, but you know what I thought when I saw my mum with this Charles?'

'I assume that's rhetorical.'

'For a split second, I thought, how inconvenient.'

'Inconvenient?'

'Yes. My cunning plan was to move in with Ruth when I leave Cal, but if Charles is around, I'll just be in the way.'

'You may be jumping the gun a tad.'

'I know, but how selfish am I that it even crossed my mind?'

'So you're still determined to leave? No second thoughts?'

'I did waver a bit the other night. We were watching telly, holding hands, drinking wine, and I thought, this isn't so terrible, is it? Does a marriage have to be terrible before you walk away? I just don't know.'

A shadow crossed Christina's face.

'I didn't mean you,' said Grace. 'I realise it's complicated.'

Christina stirred her tea, even though she didn't take sugar. When she looked at Grace again, it was as if she was appraising her.

'I think you're suffering from cognitive dissonance,' she said.

Grace stared at her blankly.

'I've no idea what that is.'

'It's anguish caused when you believe yourself to be one thing, but behave as though you're another.'

'I don't understand.'

'You've always thought of yourself as a good person.'

Grace nodded.

'But a good person doesn't cheat and lie and deceive those close to them, or think, however fleetingly, that their saintly mother having a suitor is an inconvenience.'

'Make me feel worse, why don't you.'

'So there's an internal contradiction that you're finding difficult to reconcile.'

Grace nodded again, more emphatically this time.

'You're right,' she said. 'I thought that the other night when Cal was singing Millie's praises. I've always considered myself to be the broad-minded one –'

Christina spluttered on a mouthful of tea.

'What?' said Grace indignantly.

'You are many wonderful things,' said Christina, 'but broad-minded might be a bit of a stretch.'

Grace bristled slightly but pressed on.

'Compared to Cal, though,' she said.

'Politically, yes. He's a bit Brexity, but then so are over seventeen million other people.'

'Another example of this dissonance thing,' said Grace. 'I really don't know myself at all, do I?'

'Do any of us?' said Christina, checking her watch. 'I hate to open this Pandora's box of self-loathing only to slam it shut again, but I have to pick the twins up early from school. They're going to the orthodontist to get braces fitted.'

'Oh, right,' said Grace, genuinely disappointed.

Christina's insights were highly enlightening, and she wished they had time to dig deeper.

'But I will say this,' said Christina. 'Human nature is multi-faceted, and it's very rare for someone to be completely good or completely bad. We're all a complex mix of both – me, you, Cal, Harry. Even the Kray twins loved their old mum.'

Grace stood up and put on her coat.

'I feel I should be lying on a couch, paying you by the hour,' she said.

Christina had laid the platters and glassware in a cardboard box lined with newspaper.

'Thanks so much for this,' said Grace, picking up the box. 'I'll get everything back to you tomorrow.'

'No rush,' said Christina. 'Can I bring anything tonight, apart from a few bottles of fizz?'

'Just Harry and Adam,' said Grace. 'Although there is something.'

'What?'

'I hate Josh being so ravenous that he eats his own body weight in carbs. I told you Millie's press-ganged him into her vegan crusade.'

'You did. Also, wow – you really don't like her, do you?'

'No, I do. Well, I'm trying to, but that's beside the point.'

'Which is?'

'Could you use your exceptional powers of persuasion to punch a few holes in her "vegans save the planet" stance? At least you might give Josh food for thought.'

'Nicely done,' said Christina, grinning.

'Seriously, though,' said Grace. 'Think about it?'

'I will,' said Christina. 'Should be an interesting night.'

TWENTY-ONE

Cal had pushed a trestle table up against the wall, and Grace dressed it with a white linen tablecloth and some candles. The food was laid out on Christina's large platters – cold chicken with potato salad, a thick slab of Brussels pâté, crudités with vegan dips, a cheese plate and bread – and Cal had made a bowl of punch. It was reddish-amber in colour, but when she asked what was in it, he tapped the side of his nose mysteriously.

'If I told you I'd have to kill you,' he said, handing her a small amount to taste.

It burned her throat as she swallowed.

'Too strong,' she said, coughing.

He tasted it himself and agreed it was a bit heavy on the alcohol.

'Needs more grenadine,' he said, heading to the kitchen.

The doorbell signalled the arrival of their first guests, Ruth and Charles. He looked very formal in a suit and tie.

Grace introduced him to Cal, who handed them both a glass of his punch.

'What do you think?' he said. 'Be honest.'

Charles nodded approvingly but Ruth agreed with Grace – too much alcohol. The two men struck up a conversation, and Ruth asked Grace where the lovebirds were.

'Upstairs, having a shower,' she said. 'They've been out cycling all day.'

'I'm very curious to meet her,' said Ruth. 'And can't wait to see Josh.'

'You called?' he said, sidling up beside her.

His hair was clean and damp, but his shirt looked like it had been dragged from the bottom of his holdall.

'Come here, you,' said Ruth, hugging him hard.

The sight was bittersweet for Grace – her son so big and her mum so small. It felt like five minutes ago that Ruth first cradled her newborn grandchild, the only one she would ever have.

'Let me look at you,' she said, sandwiching Josh's cheeks between her palms. 'More handsome than ever.'

Millie was in the doorway, wearing a floaty tie-dye dress and an elaborate hairband. Josh moved to one side.

'This is Millie,' he said, proudly presenting his girlfriend. 'And this is my grandmother, Ruth.'

Grace had never heard him refer to her mother by her Christian name. She wasn't sure how she felt about it, but the doorbell rang again before she had time to think.

'It's freezing out there,' said Lydia, thrusting a bottle of wine into Grace's hand. They embraced warmly, any unease between them forgotten. Lydia hung up her coat and joined the others in the sitting room. Grace was about to put the wine in the fridge when the doorbell rang for the third time. Christina and Adam – no sign of Harry. Grace looked along the street in case he was parking.

'He's not coming,' said Christina.

She took off her coat and told Adam to go find Josh. He pecked Grace's cheek on the way, exuding a whiff of fresh laundry and aftershave. How smart and preppy he looked, in a crisp blue shirt and navy chinos. Much smarter than Josh.

'Had to work late, apparently,' said Christina.

Her skin looked fiercely pale against an ink-black blouse. The slash of red lipstick made her seem hard and stern.

'Oh well,' said Grace. 'I'm sure it couldn't be helped.'

Christina looked at her coldly before sweeping into the kitchen with a bottle of Moët in each hand. Grace didn't know what to say. Under normal circumstances she would have encouraged Christina to get it off her chest, but this was a family occasion, not conducive to a rant about Harry. Christina put one bottle of champagne in the fridge and opened the other one. Grace held out two flutes for her to fill.

'I'm sorry,' she said. 'That's rotten.'

Christina shrugged.

'One way of putting it,' she said. 'He knew I was looking forward to tonight.'

Grace needed to cheer her up – take her mind off her errant husband.

'Come on, I want you to meet Millie,' she said. 'Oh, and my mum's brought Charles. I'll introduce you.'

Christina followed Grace into the sitting room, taking the open bottle of Moët with her.

'I'd stick to that if I were you,' said Grace. 'Cal's punch is lethal.'

She left Christina chatting with Ruth and Charles, hoping she would get into the swing of things and not spend the evening being cross about Harry. Josh and Millie were with Adam and Lydia – chatting, drinking, laughing. Grace thought it wonderful to have her nearest and dearest all together like this. Even Christina was smiling now. Cal came up behind Grace and slid his arm around her waist. He nuzzled her ear, his breath warm and boozy.

'I forgot to tell you how lovely you look,' he whispered.

The doubts she'd had the other night reared up again. It wasn't too late to change her mind. She had told her mum she was unhappy, but all marriages had their ups and downs. Christina was the only person who knew about David, and in her book, infidelity didn't seem to be a deal-breaker. Grace glanced around her home, filled with love and laughter, wondering if that was enough to make her stay.

'Get a room,' Josh called over, with mock revulsion.

A burst of raucous laughter suggested they had been drinking Cal's punch. Grace fetched some plates from the trestle table.

'Eat something,' she said, handing them each a plate. 'If only to soak up all that alcohol.'

Josh looked on enviously as Adam helped himself to roast chicken, pâté and a thick wedge of runny Brie. Josh chose crudités, dips and bread.

'Is that all you're having?' said Christina, looking at his meagre rations. 'Adam eats me out of house and home.'

Josh chuckled politely and looked at Millie.

'Yeah, well, I'm vegan now.'

'Vegan?' said Christina, as though this was news to her. 'Why?'

Grace waited to hear his answer. 'Because my girlfriend told me' didn't seem a likely option.

'It's healthier, for a start,' he said, although without a great deal of conviction. 'And better for the environment.'

Christina tilted her head to one side, as if considering both these points on their merits.

'Mm,' she said. 'I would have thought the healthiest thing was a balanced diet.'

'A plant-based diet can be balanced too,' said Millie, inserting herself into the conversation.

'You must be Josh's girlfriend,' said Christina. 'I don't think we've been introduced.'

'Millie,' she said. 'And you're Adam's mum, right?'

'That's right,' said Christina. 'An unapologetic carnivore, I'm afraid.'

'So was this one when we met,' said Millie, smiling at Josh. 'Until I explained how meat isn't just murdering animals, it's murdering the planet too.'

She was slurring her words slightly.

'Oh, I don't know,' said Christina. 'Surely grass-fed lamb from a Welsh farm just down the M4 is better for the environment than a mango that's travelled halfway around the world?'

Even though Grace had encouraged this debate, suddenly it didn't feel like a fair fight. Millie's youthful conviction was no match for Christina's flinty intelligence, especially as the girl was clearly a bit worse for wear. Adam must have had the same thought because he asked his mother when she became an expert on all this stuff.

'I'm not an *expert*,' she said. 'I helped Rupert and Lucy with a school project for Earth Day, and found it all rather interesting.'

'Evidently,' said Adam.

Grace took Christina to one side and topped up her champagne.

'Thanks for trying,' she said quietly. 'But I don't think Josh is going to change his mind anytime soon.'

Lydia put her hand on Grace's shoulder.

'Sorry to interrupt,' she said. 'Can I have your phone? Your playlist needs a bit of livening up. Dad's punch has got us in the mood for dancing.'

Grace meekly handed Lydia the phone.

'Passcode?' she said.

'1505,' said Grace.

'Josh's birthday,' said Lydia. 'How sweet and predictable.'

She went back to the others, swinging her hips and shoulders to an imaginary beat.

'Are you OK?' said Grace.

'No, not really,' said Christina. 'Charles was telling me how he cared for his invalid wife. He didn't see it as some great sacrifice, just being true to his marriage vows.'

'In sickness and in health,' said Grace.

'Till death do us part,' said Christina.

'It's quite a big ask, though, isn't it?'

'For some people,' said Christina.

Grace must have looked wounded because she added, 'I mean Harry. He can't even drag himself home when he promised he would.'

'Why don't I come over tomorrow?' said Grace, uncomfortable with the topic. 'We can talk about this properly.'

Christina nodded, but her attention had veered towards Cal.

'He looks so happy,' she said, a note of sadness in her voice. 'Ignorance is bliss, I suppose.'

Another swipe at Grace.

'Can we not?' she said.

Christina nodded again, more curtly this time.

'You're right,' she said. 'I'm off to powder my nose and when I come back, I might risk some of the punch that's got the kids so merry.'

They were huddled around Grace's phone, selecting music for a more party atmosphere. Most of the food had been eaten, and Grace commandeered Cal to help her clear the table so she could lay out dessert. They scraped plates into the bin and put them in the sink to soak. It was only when she got the pavlova and chocolate fudge cake out of the fridge that she realised neither were vegan. There was a bowl of cut fruit but nothing to go with it.

'What?' said Cal, seeing her look perplexed.

'I need vegan ice cream,' she said. 'I forgot to put it on the list.'

'Does it matter?' he said.

'Yes,' she said. 'I'm sorry. Have you had too much to drink to nip to Sainsbury's? It's open until ten.'

'The things I do for you,' he said.

He kissed her on the mouth, light and fleeting.

'I'll be back before you know it.'

Peals of laughter spilled out from the sitting room. The music was louder now, with a faster beat. Lydia's voice was almost a shriek – *oh my God, you look hilarious!* Christina popped her head into the kitchen and asked if Grace needed a hand. She looked brighter now – hair brushed, lipstick reapplied.

'Let's get a drink,' said Grace.

The youngsters were crowded around her phone. When Josh saw her, he shouted over, 'I want to show the girls those Christmas jumpers you made me and Adam wear.'

She smiled fondly, remembering how adorable they looked. It took a second to realise Josh must be scrolling through her photos, and another to be gripped by horror at what he might find. She felt hollow and weak, as if all the blood had drained from her body.

'I'll find it,' she called back, forcing the panic from her voice.

She tried to push her way to Josh so she could grab her phone, but the kids kept blocking her, as if it was a game.

'Text it to me, Josh,' said Christina, joining in the fun. 'Something to embarrass my firstborn with.'

Everyone was crowded together, trying to see this incriminating photo.

'I knitted those jumpers, if you don't mind,' said Ruth, pretending to take offence.

Josh added to the hilarity by holding the phone above his head, making it harder for the others to wrestle it from him. Grace tried again to breach the wall of bodies, but it was hopeless. Josh was scrolling and laughing, scrolling and laughing, and then he suddenly stopped. She watched the joy leach from his face. He had found the incriminating photo – not two boys in silly jumpers, but two lovers in bed. His withering look sliced through her chest, straight to the heart that loved him without condition. His hand dropped to his side, allowing Millie to take the phone. She stared at it, and then at Grace. The laughter died away, replaced by an air of confusion. Lydia's eyes widened in horror as she looked over Millie's shoulder. She grabbed the phone and shoved it in Grace's face. She and David filled the screen, their heads next to each other on a pillow.

'You swore you were just friends,' said Lydia, eyes blazing.

What could Grace say? There was no point denying it when the evidence was literally staring her in the face. Everyone was looking, silent now and horribly sober. Josh was pale with shock, or maybe disbelief – how could Grace tell when she had never seen that expression before?

'Come on, Adam,' said Christina. 'We should go.'

She swept past Grace without a word. The front door opened and closed – Christina and Adam leaving – and then heavy footsteps in the hall.

'Got the ice cream,' called Cal, en route to the kitchen.

It was as if all the air had been sucked out of the room.

'Please don't say anything,' implored Grace. 'Not tonight. Not like this.'

Lydia slapped the phone into her hand.

'I'm out of here,' she said, and was gone before Grace could think of a single thing that might make this moment marginally less awful.

She heard Cal go upstairs, presumably to the bathroom.

'I'm so sorry you found that photo,' she said to Josh, 'and I understand how confused and upset you must be, but please, let me tell Dad in my own time.'

'That's why you were weird with him,' said Josh.

'What?' said Grace.

'At the lake. I asked you why you were weird with that guy – David – and you denied it.'

She heard Cal on the stairs.

'Please, Josh, not now. We can talk about it later –'

Cal came into the sitting room and headed straight for the drinks. He poured himself a glass of red and joined the now depleted group of guests.

'Cheers,' he said, raising his glass. 'So, what did I miss?'

TWENTY-TWO

Lady Gaga was singing 'Bad Romance' – a favourite of Lydia's. Cal tapped his foot to the beat, oblivious to the prevailing mood. Everyone avoided eye contact as the song pleaded for love and revenge. They were in a state of suspended animation, trying to process a disturbing new reality. In a matter of minutes, Grace had gone from being a trusted wife to a cheating wife, exposed in front of those she loved most in the world. Cal looked around as though he'd lost something.

'Where's Lydia?' he said. 'And why did Christina and Adam leave so early?'

Josh glared at Grace for one long, piercing moment before he shook his head and walked out. Millie followed him, leaving just four of them: Grace and Cal, Ruth and Charles.

'What's going on?' said Cal.

There was no good answer to that question. All Grace could think was that it wasn't supposed to be like this. She had planned how she would tell Cal the marriage was over

– the words she would use to soften the blow. And that was if she went through with it at all.

'It's nothing really,' said Ruth. 'The boys had a bit too much to drink – a silly squabble, that's all.'

'Josh and Adam?' said Cal. 'They had an argument?'

Ruth shook her head emphatically.

'No,' she said. 'Not an argument. Just a bit of teasing – you know how boys are.'

Cal's confused expression suggested otherwise.

'That's not like them,' he said. 'And what about Lydia? She didn't even say goodbye.'

'She asked me to say it for her,' said Grace, swallowing hard. 'She has an early start tomorrow, so –'

Cal still seemed unconvinced and had opened his mouth to speak when Ruth said it was about time she was leaving too.

'What about dessert?' said Cal. 'Grace sent me out for vegan ice cream.'

Ruth was already gathering up her bag and coat. Charles shook Cal's hand, the poor man seeming quite bemused.

'Thank you for a lovely evening,' he said.

'I'll see you out,' said Grace.

The night air was still and drizzly, with a thready grey mist. A siren wailed, sending the neighbour's dogs into a barking frenzy. Grace shivered in her short-sleeved dress. Charles told Ruth he would wait for her in the car. He doffed an imaginary hat to Grace and left them to talk.

'Do you want to tell me what that was about?' said Ruth.

'Not really,' said Grace.

The siren sounded more urgent as it got closer, like a warning.

'Who was that man in the photo?' said Ruth.

'Someone I met.'

'Are you having an affair?'

It was a 'yes/no' question – no room for prevarication. The siren and the barking stopped simultaneously, as if they had been performing an unmelodious duet.

'Yes.'

Ruth looked at Grace as though seeing her for the first time.

'How long?'

'Not long,' said Grace. 'Hardly any time at all really, but it's changed everything. It's changed me.'

For a moment, Ruth seemed lost for words. Her brief silence was as opaque as the night air.

'You said things were strained between you and Cal,' she said. 'But you seemed happy enough tonight.'

'It's complicated,' said Grace.

Ruth inhaled sharply.

'Well, your secret's out now,' she said. 'You have to tell Cal. It's the very least he deserves. And you can't expect Josh and Lydia to keep this from their dad. It's too much.'

'I know,' said Grace. 'I'll talk to him tomorrow. I will.'

Ruth nodded.

'I don't envy you,' she said. 'Or Cal, for that matter.'

Grace felt sick at the thought of it. Before, it was a hypothetical conversation to be broached sometime in the future. But now it was here and all too real. She had never been the bad guy. It wasn't a role she was suited to.

'Are you disappointed in me, Mum?'

Even as the words left her mouth, Grace knew she was being pathetic. Ruth's feelings on the subject weren't really the issue here. Her mum looked at her, as if deciding how to answer. She took a breath – decision made.

'Your father left me for another woman.'

Grace put her hand to her mouth.

'Why did you never tell me?'

'I was ashamed,' said Ruth. 'Humiliated that I wasn't enough for him. He emigrated to New Zealand and forgot about us – never paid maintenance or anything.'

'Oh, Mum,' said Grace, tears stinging her eyes. 'That's awful.'

Ruth shrugged stoically, as if to say, *What's done is done.* She looked along the street.

'I'd better go,' she said. 'Charles is waiting.'

Grace hugged her tightly, remembering all the years she had scrimped and scraped and done her very best.

'Call me tomorrow,' said Ruth. 'Or before, if you need to talk.'

Grace stood shivering on the doorstep, her warm breath a ribbon of mist, gobbled up by the night. She dreaded going back inside, but had no choice. Pharrell Williams was singing his 'Happy' song, so incongruous it was almost funny. She hovered in the hallway, unsure what to do. Josh might have already decided that his loyalties lay with his poor deceived father, not his lying, unfaithful mother. Pharrell's pitch-perfect voice urged her to clap if happiness is the truth. Josh appeared at the top of the stairs and stopped dead when he saw her. Neither of them spoke. There was a distance between them now, and she had put it there. He carried on down the stairs and she followed him into the kitchen. When she tried to talk, he cut her off.

'I've just come down for some water,' he said, getting two bottles from the fridge.

Cal came looking for them and stood in the doorway behind Grace, trapping her between him and Josh.

'What's this about you and Adam falling out?' he said.

Josh looked understandably confused by the question. He wouldn't know that was the excuse Ruth had used to explain Adam's sudden departure.

'It doesn't matter, Cal,' said Grace.

Obviously he disagreed.

'Your mum went to a lot of trouble for you tonight,' he said. 'The least you can do is help her clear up.'

'It's fine,' said Grace, desperate to keep the pin in that particular grenade. 'Honestly, it won't take long. Go on, Josh, take that up to Millie.'

Josh looked at the water bottles in his hand, and the phone in Grace's.

'Excuse me,' he mumbled to Cal, who reluctantly stepped aside to let him pass.

'What on earth's got into him?' said Cal, as Josh stomped upstairs.

Grace shrugged.

'He's a teenager,' she said, a lame excuse that put the blame on her son's hormones, rather than her own. 'Anyway, let's not make a big deal out of it. Why don't you have a drink while I make a start on this.'

Grace let out a sigh of relief when Cal did as she suggested. A temporary respite, but at least it had bought her some time. The kitchen was cluttered with leftover food and dirty dishes. There were no pockets in her dress, so she put her phone on the windowsill and started to tackle the mess. If she kept herself busy, she might be able to pause the nightmare of Josh finding that photo, currently whirring around her head. She worked on autopilot, wrapping food in cling film, rinsing plates and loading the dishwasher, trying not to dwell on how desperately upset Josh must be. A text from her mum said to call if she needed her. It was heart-wrenching to think of Ruth as a young mother, abandoned to raise her child alone. Grace messaged back.

What would I do without you x

The sound of voices and heavy footsteps brought her and Cal into the hallway. Josh and Millie were heading to the front door with their bags packed.

'We're going,' he said.

'Going where?' said Cal, flabbergasted.

He looked at Grace askance, as if confounded by her lack of intervention. Josh dropped his holdall and hugged him. Grace couldn't be sure because he wouldn't look at her, but she thought his eyes were wet. Millie rubbed his back like Grace used to do when he was small. *There, there, darling – it's all OK.*

'I'm sorry, Dad,' he said.

'Wait,' said Cal. 'You can't leave now – it's late. What's going on?'

'Ask Mum,' said Josh, the words catching in his throat.

Cal held up his hands in frustration.

'Ask Mum what?'

Millie opened the front door, inviting a gasp of frigid air into their home.

'Our Uber's here,' she said.

Josh picked up his bag and scowled at Grace. He had never looked at her that way.

'Ask Mum what?' Cal said again.

Josh stopped suddenly and swiped the phone from her hand. It was so quick and unexpected she didn't have a chance to stop him.

'About what's on here,' he said, thrusting it at Cal.

He stared at it, his face furrowed with confusion. Before he could say anything, Josh was out the door. Grace stood cold and motionless, as if she had turned to stone. She knew she should warn him, that it would be better – well, infinitesimally less appalling – than him finding out the same way Josh had. She tried to summon the courage, but couldn't.

'Grace?' said Cal.

A barely whispered 'I'm sorry' was all she could manage.

There was a dawning realisation on his face, as though he had made the connection between her phone and Josh leaving. Cal put in the passcode and searched. She closed her eyes so she didn't have to watch. He gasped, and she braced herself.

'What the fuck?'

He said it quietly, as if talking to himself. He must have forgotten he didn't swear. The second time he said it louder, and she forced herself to look at him. His face was a violent shade of red, his brow shiny with sweat. He stared at her with a conflation of horror and disbelief.

'Who is he?'

Grace couldn't find the breath to answer. She felt winded, as though gut-punched. He read out David's midnight text, Grace cringing at how perverse her lover's words sounded when repeated by her husband.

'He calls you Mrs Wheeler,' said Cal incredulously. 'So he knows you're married?'

He framed it as a question, clinging to the hope that there might be another explanation, and the whole thing was a stupid misunderstanding. Grace's barely perceptible nod robbed him of that hope.

'I asked you who he is,' said Cal, raising his voice several decibels. 'Tell me!'

'My fishing instructor,' she said, because silence was no longer an option.

Cal screwed up his face in pain, as though he had been hit. She didn't know if she should comfort him, or what the etiquette was in this situation.

'I'm sorry you found out like this,' she said. 'I planned to tell you ...'

Her voice trailed off to nothing, because seriously, what could she say? Apologies were useless – an Elastoplast on a gaping wound.

'Is it still going on?' he said.

His voice was quieter now, and somehow more menacing. She lowered her eyes and nodded. Cal took a few moments to swallow that jagged boulder of truth, and wiped his sweaty brow with the back of his hand. He shoved the phone in her face, like Lydia had done earlier.

'And our son has seen these?'

Clearly the question was redundant, because why else would Josh have stormed off into the night? Cal's face darkened as another terrible truth dawned.

'Oh God,' he said. 'Who else has seen them? Lydia, Ruth – not Adam and Christina?'

He reeled slightly, as though dizzy with humiliation, and had to steady himself against the wall. Grace reached out to him, genuinely concerned for his well-being, but he slapped her hand away and resumed his forensic scrutiny of her phone. She started to cry, but her tears didn't move him. When he hung his head and covered his face, she knew he had found the photo of her and David in bed. She tried to cry quietly, because the wanton destruction of her family was all her own doing. Cal and Josh were the victims here, not her. She was the perpetrator – the villain of the piece. He slammed her phone against the wall, smashing it to pieces. A shard of glass nicked the skin above her eyebrow, drawing a trickle of blood. He towered over her, so close she could feel the scorch of his fury on her skin. He called her a whore – spat the word in her face. His breath was stale and hot, with a back note of something foetid.

'You made out you weren't interested in sex!' he shouted. 'But you just weren't interested in it with me.'

He erupted like a volcano, spitting and spewing rage with every syllable. He kept yelling – *bitch, whore, frigid, slut* – words she had never heard him say. She could smell his sweat, feel his spittle on her face. No one had ever lost their temper with her. It was terrifying. She didn't know what this version of Cal was capable of. How many times had she heard of wronged husbands losing control in the heat of the moment? This was that moment. Fear sparked a flare of adrenaline, priming her to fight or take flight. Her keys were on the console table by the front door, but in order to make a run for it, she had to get past Cal. The adrenaline was like electricity, zapping energy through her limbs. She pushed him to one side, grabbed her keys and slammed the door behind her. Unlocking the car with trembling hands was difficult, but she did it. She kept looking at the front door, expecting a furious Cal to emerge and drag her back inside. When she got the engine started, she reversed out of the drive with no seat belt on, and without checking if the road was clear. Her whole body was shaking now, with cold and shock and dazed disbelief. Calm down, she told herself, as if that was even remotely possible.

She stopped at the end of the street and checked her rear-view mirror. No sign of Cal, thank God. She put on her seat belt and pulled out of the side street, straight into the path of an oncoming van. The headlights blinded her before she had time to react. The driver honked his horn like he was punching it with his fist. Grace pulled over into a bus stop, her nerves jangling. She was freezing in her thin, short-sleeved dress, and flicked the heater to max, waiting for the promised blast of warm air. She wished she had her phone. Instinctively, she touched the small cut above her eyebrow, where the blood was starting to dry. Cal's loss of control had really scared her. Tears washed down her face, and once she began to cry, she didn't want to stop. It felt cleansing, cathartic, necessary. Giving in to the wretchedness was a form of release, which she would have indulged longer if a bus driver hadn't tooted at her. She wiped her face with the back of her hands and indicated to join the traffic, before realising she didn't know where she was going. Her mum's house was the obvious choice, but that was the first place Cal would look. It would be wrong to put Ruth in the middle of this, and the thought of being confronted by an enraged Cal sickened her. No, she couldn't face him, or contemplate another ugly scene. Christina's place wasn't an option either. The look she had shot Grace as she left the party spoke volumes. A wronged wife sympathising with a wronged husband. Christina wouldn't want to see her right now, however extenuating the circumstances. The only other option was David. It was a long drive, and she was probably over the limit, but she headed in the direction of Frome anyway. She drove as if taking her test again – checked her mirrors, remembered to indicate, made sure not to exceed the speed limit. Each time tears smeared her vision, she wiped them away and told herself to get a grip.

The earlier drizzle became wiper-at-full-speed rain, making the unlit road treacherous. When at last she turned into the narrow alley behind David's house, she managed to squeeze her car into the tight space next to his. At first she was grateful he was home, but then she remembered the pub was within walking distance so he wouldn't have driven anyway. It seemed wrong to turn up without warning late at night, but without her phone, she didn't have a choice. The night was dark and starless, with only a thin sliver of moon. She turned off the engine and stepped out into the freezing rain. Even before she opened the gate to the courtyard, she was soaked through and shaking. The stone path that led to the back door was slippery and precarious, especially in high heels. A beam of light shone out from the kitchen, and when she saw David at the sink, she could have wept with relief. She raised her hand, but he had already turned his head to speak to someone. The girl came up behind him, both of them laughing as if sharing a joke. Grace stood and stared, her whole body shivering in uncontrollable spasms. The girl looked vaguely familiar – lustrous hair, pillow-plump lips painted a deep, sensual red. Of course – the flirty waitress from the pub. The one David had claimed he barely knew.

TWENTY-THREE

In the months after her father's disappearance, Grace would dream about him. She had forgotten this until her mother mentioned him earlier tonight. These dreams had a central theme – Grace outside in the dark, watching her father through a window, doing ordinary things like drinking tea or reading a newspaper. She would call him but he never heard, wave to him but he never saw. Her subconscious was grieving a loss her conscious mind wasn't willing to acknowledge. She concocted excuses for his absence, convinced he would come home as suddenly as he had left, but her dream was stubbornly consistent. It kept her alone and invisible on the wrong side of the window.

David raised a wine glass to his lips. The girl did too. Grace had seen enough. To keep watching would be masochistic, and she had endured enough tonight. She would leave them to their wine and laughter, and whatever else they had in mind. Slinking away unnoticed would at least spare her the embarrassment of David seeing her in this state. The girl exuded youthful sex appeal, bolstered by an effortless confidence Grace had never possessed. She bent down to take off the ridiculous high heels. Her feet were soaked anyway so what difference did it make? Better to be barefoot than risk tripping on the slippery paving stones. Imagine if David found her in a drowned heap in the middle of the night, spying on him like some crazed stalker. Thick strands of hair were plastered to her face, and as she pushed them back, something moved over her shoulder. An ear-splitting screech pierced the night, and an animal – dark, agile, most likely feline – sprang out of a tree and landed in front of her. She stumbled backwards and stepped on something sharp, crying out in pain and fright. The animal shot off towards the house, activating a security light that caught her in its arc. David looked straight at her, but it took him a few seconds to react. He craned his neck closer to the window and screwed up his eyes as if to get a better look. She thought he mouthed her name, but couldn't be sure. Her foot throbbed, and the slanting rain felt like it was seeping through her skin and into her bones. The door opened and he ran to her.

'Grace, what's happened? What are you doing here?'

Her teeth were chattering so hard she couldn't answer. He put his arm around her and ushered her into the house. The girl stared, as though wondering how this bedraggled creature had materialised out of nowhere to gatecrash her evening.

'You're freezing,' said David. 'You need to get out of these wet clothes.'

As he led her towards the stairs, the girl said, 'She's bleeding,' and pointed to a red smear on the quarry tiles.

David examined the underside of Grace's foot while she held on to his shoulder, shaking as if zapped by a series of small electric shocks.

'It's not deep,' he said. 'Why aren't you wearing shoes?'

It was a reasonable question, but her jaw was too frozen to answer. He looked bewildered, as well he might. Grace realised what a terrible idea it had been to turn up like this. She tried to say 'I should go' but her chattering teeth rendered the words unintelligible.

'I'll run her a bath,' David told the girl as he headed for the stairs. 'There's brandy in the cupboard. Can you pour her some?'

This clearly wasn't how the girl had envisaged her evening panning out, but she did as she was asked. Grace took the tumbler from her with both hands and sipped. She had never tasted brandy before. Its sharp aromas made her flinch.

'It's medicinal,' said the girl.

Grace wasn't prepared for the intense hit of alcohol, or the fire it lit at the back of her throat. She managed a 'thank you' and sipped some more. When David joined them again, he took a moment to observe the scene in front of him, as if trying to make sense of it. He was holding a large blue bath towel, which he draped around Grace's shoulders. His thoughtfulness threatened to reduce her to a sobbing mess. She couldn't imagine how awful she must look.

'I think maybe you should go,' he said to the girl.

She nodded reluctantly, and David walked her out. Grace could hear them talking on the other side of the door, but not what they were saying. He was back a minute later, and locked the door behind him.

'You should probably have that bath,' he said.

'I'm so sorry,' said Grace, but he was already halfway up the stairs.

She followed him in her bare feet, still clutching the brandy. He left her alone in the bathroom to undress, which, considering his intimate knowledge of her body, seemed unduly coy. One look in the steamed-up mirror confirmed the worst. Her face had black streaks of mascara, and the small cut above her eyebrow looked livid and sore. Her eyes were pink and puffy, her hair plastered to her scalp. No wonder he didn't stick around. Slowly, carefully, she lowered herself into the hot water. The brandy was making her sleepy. Her body felt soft and limp. David knocked before he came in, holding his own glass of brandy, much larger than Grace's. He sat down on the wooden toilet seat.

'How are you feeling?' he said.

'Thawing out,' she said. 'And this is helping.'

She took another sip.

'Has something happened?' he said.

'You could say that.'

'Why didn't you call?'

'My husband smashed my phone.'

David drank deep from his glass and swallowed. His Adam's apple bobbed up and down and Grace thought, that's how men drink liquor in films.

'Why did your husband smash your phone?'

She laid her glass on the side of the bath and rested her head back against the wall.

'He found our texts and photos. Well, strictly speaking it was my son who found them during a family party, so it's common knowledge now. My husband says I'm a whore.'

David stared at her for a moment, as if needing time for this to sink in.

'Did he hurt you, Grace?'

She shook her head.

'Not deliberately – at least, I don't think it was deliberate. He scared me, though – that was definitely deliberate – so I ran.'

'And you came here.'

She looked at him properly for the first time since she had arrived in such a dramatic fashion. He was looking at her too, but not the way he usually did. No teasing smile. No glint in his eyes.

'I'm sorry I spoiled your night.'

He shrugged, as if it was nothing.

'I left my card behind the bar at the pub. Summer dropped it off.'

A girl called Summer, thought Grace. Her parents were probably hippies.

'You don't owe me an explanation,' she said. 'You don't owe me anything.'

He swirled the brandy around his glass.

'I like you, Grace. I like talking to you, kissing you, fucking you ...'

She raised her hand for him to stop.

'I get it,' she said. 'A bit of fun – no harm done.'

'In my case,' he said. 'Not yours.'

Her head was starting to swim with alcohol, heat and exhaustion.

'True,' she said, her tongue feeling slow and thick. 'But don't worry, you didn't ruin my marriage. I did that. You were a symptom, not the cause.'

He finished the rest of his drink and nodded in agreement.

'Right,' he said. 'You're welcome to stay here tonight.'

Where else would she go? She was in no fit state to drive.

'Thanks,' she said.

He went to leave but she called him back.

'I'm embarrassed to ask,' she said, 'but could you help me out of the bath? That brandy has gone straight to my head.'

'Of course,' he said, getting a dry towel.

When he offered his hand, she leaned on it and pulled herself up. He helped her balance as she stepped onto the mat, and wrapped the towel around her. His indifference to her nakedness was vaguely insulting.

'There's a spare toothbrush in the medicine cabinet,' he said. 'Can I get you anything?'

'Just some water,' she said.

The toothbrush was still in its plastic packaging. She opened it and cleaned her teeth, wondering if Summer would be doing exactly the same thing if Grace hadn't turned up. David was on the landing with her glass of water.

'The spare bed's made up,' he said. 'Or you could sleep in mine, whichever you prefer.'

His tone was casual. My bed or the spare bed? Grace or Summer? Tea or coffee? Christina had been right. It was just sex to him – the who, when or where were minor, interchangeable details.

'Spare bed's fine,' she said.

They smiled at each other, as though an understanding had been reached. She didn't tell him that if he hadn't referred to sex with her as 'fucking', it was his bed she would have chosen.

Despite everything, she slept well. Waking alone in a strange room was disconcerting, but not as disconcerting as remembering why she was there. She covered her face and groaned. Her head ached, more so when she sat up. There was a dressing gown on the end of the bed that she hadn't noticed last night. She slipped it on – several sizes too big – and went downstairs. David was in the kitchen, cooking eggs. Her dress was on a hanger by the Aga, and her shoes had been stuffed with newspaper and left to dry. He must have rescued them from the garden. The suede was ruined – blotchy and stained.

'Morning,' he said. 'Sleep OK?'

He was in jeans and a T-shirt, his feet beautiful and bare.

'Not bad, considering. My head hurts, though – do you have any paracetamol?'

A bolt of déjà vu splintered in her brain: the afternoon she had asked for painkillers and tampons and made a fool of herself by declaring her love.

'These do?' he said, putting a pack of Nurofen on the breakfast bar.

She took two and sat down.

'You didn't have to cook breakfast for me,' she said.

He put a cup of coffee in front of her.

'I always cook breakfast,' he said.

She didn't know that. She didn't know him. Had she really upended her entire life for a taste of great sex after twenty years of the other kind? She excised that thought from her head. There would be a time to reflect on this madness, but not now. Her emotions were at saturation point. Any more and she would drown.

'I don't think I can eat,' she said, her stomach tight with anxiety.

He dropped two slices of bread into the toaster. She massaged her temples with her fingertips, unable to comprehend the damage that was done last night. She blinked hard to blur the look on Josh's face when he found the photo of her and David in bed.

'I really need to speak to my son,' she said. 'Although God knows what I'm going to say to him.'

'Do you want to use my phone?'

She shook her head.

'I don't think that's a good idea. I need to buy a new one this morning.'

He slathered the toast with glossy yellow butter.

'Here,' he said, handing her a slice. 'Have this.'

She took a bite and chewed, amazed she could still execute small but necessary tasks like eating and breathing. Her marriage and affair were over – maybe her relationship with Josh too. It was as if everything had been tossed into the air and had landed in the wrong place – the wrong order.

David put a plate of scrambled eggs in front of her and sat down to eat his own.

'Thanks,' she said, pushing the eggs around with a fork.

She glanced over at her dress, wrinkled and limp with a mysterious rip along one shoulder. Did Cal try to grab her as she ran away? She couldn't remember. The idea of wearing that dress again, or putting her feet into those ruined shoes, made her feel sick, but she had no choice. David may very sensibly keep a spare toothbrush for women who stayed over, but he probably drew the line at spare clothes. She caught him staring at the scab above her eye.

'It's not really any of my business,' he said, 'but what are you going to do?'

The subtext wasn't lost on Grace. For the avoidance of doubt, he had told her he was out of her life without actually having to say it. She washed down the eggs with a mouthful of strong coffee.

'Go home, pack a bag, hope to get out of there in one piece.'

Her little laugh was hollow.

'Have you got somewhere to go?'

'My mum's.'

They ate in silence for a few minutes, until, to Grace's astonishment, David offered to come with her.

'To my mum's?'

'To your house, if you don't feel safe.'

She almost laughed again.

'Are you serious? It's bad enough that I have to go back there, but you? Cal would probably keel over, or try to kill you.'

'I can take care of myself,' said David. 'And anyway, isn't he, like, an old man or something?'

She didn't answer. It seemed disrespectful, David talking about him like that. Small fry compared to all the other ways they had disrespected him, but still.

'I didn't mean I'd actually come in with you, just park outside in case he loses it again.'

The thought of facing Cal intensified her anxiety. He might be even angrier now that he'd had all night to think about what she had done.

'Are you sure you don't mind?' she said.

David put his empty plate in the sink.

'I've got to go into Bath anyway,' he said. 'Promised a favour for a friend.'

He didn't explain and it didn't matter. They were done.

'I'd better get dressed then,' she said, eyeing the limp dress.

Slipping it on again made her shiver. It was like one of those *Crimewatch* reconstructions you see on TV, except in reverse – the victim returning to the scene of the crime. The shoes hadn't completely dried out, and were cold and damp against her feet. There was an Elastoplast over the cut on her heel, but she couldn't remember how it got there. When they were ready to leave, she looked around one last time. Her life had changed course in this house, and would never be the same again.

At least the rain had stopped, but it was blowy outside, the wind bitter and sharp. November was a malicious month – the precursor to a long dark winter. David slipped one of his thick zip-up fleeces around her shoulders, and locked the back door behind them. He said he would follow her in the Land Rover and park a little way from her house. Cal didn't know what car David drove anyway, and he was wearing a baseball cap, so even if Cal did spot him, he wouldn't necessarily recognise him from the photos on her phone.

Grace drove with the heater on, making a mental list of what she needed to pack: clothes, shoes, a coat and jacket, her iPad, some toiletries. Grab only the basics for now, she told herself, and go back for the rest when things have settled down. She didn't switch on the radio because music seemed frivolous under the circumstances. David's fleece smelled slightly of perfume, something Grace chose not to dwell on. All things considered, it was good of him to come with her this morning. An act of chivalry, perhaps, to assuage his conscience. But then, what did he have to feel guilty about? He wasn't the one who had broken hearts and vows. She kept checking the rear-view mirror to make sure he was there, and when she turned into her street, he followed right behind.

Seeing Cal's car in the driveway twisted her insides into knots. The whole way home she kept telling herself he might not even be there. He could have gone to Beth's, or the golf club, or maybe to look for her at her mum's. Instead of pulling into the drive, Grace parked in the road. She felt less trapped there, more able to execute a quick getaway if required. Was she being dramatic? She hoped so. Reluctantly, she slipped off David's fleece, and declined to lock the car for the same reason she didn't park on the drive. David had stopped about ten feet behind her, and nodded by way of encouragement. She shivered on the doorstep, not brave enough to go in. You haven't murdered anyone, she told herself sternly. You had an affair. It happens. Cal didn't own her. She wasn't his property. Another quick glance at the Land Rover to make sure David was still there, and she let herself in. Despite the inclement weather, she left the front door open. She hovered on the threshold, assessing the lie of the land before venturing further. Silence – no sign of life at all. That was unexpected. Unsure if it was the right thing or not, she called Cal's name, and then held her breath in case he answered. She waited, but got no response. It didn't make sense that his car was there but he wasn't. Cautiously, she made her way along the hall, heart pounding. The sitting-room door was open, last night's cleaning up unfinished, the trestle table still dressed in its virgin white cloth. The kitchen door was ajar too, the smell of stale, possibly rotting food staining the air.

Grace headed upstairs to the bedroom, determined to focus on the task at hand. Still no sign of Cal, thank goodness. Maybe he went to the golf club to drown his sorrows and very sensibly left the car at home. She remembered she hadn't called Marty, who would wonder why she wasn't at work. He would have called her mobile and when he couldn't get through probably called Cal. She didn't want to contemplate how that conversation might have gone. Concentrate, she told herself as she pulled a suitcase from under the bed. She went through her wardrobe and drawers, piling in jeans, jumpers, underwear, shoes. She took what she needed from the bathroom – toothbrush and toothpaste, face cream, make-up bag – zipped up the suitcase and dragged it downstairs. It was heavy and bumped awkwardly on each tread, but it seemed indecent to ask David to help. At the bottom of the stairs, she had to stop and catch her breath. The central heating must have been on all night, because the house was suffocatingly hot. Instinct told her not to linger for a second longer than necessary, but she was thirsty and went to the kitchen for some water.

She heard him before she saw him. A low, dislocated moan, more animal than human. He was lying face down at an unnatural angle, wedged between the island and the floor units. Grace cried out, letting the water bottle slip from her hands. For a moment she was too shocked to move, but then she dropped to her knees beside him and felt for a pulse. It was what people did on television, although if she had stopped to think about it, if he was moaning, he wasn't dead, so obviously he had a pulse. She knew she should call 999 but didn't have her phone, and in the horror of the moment, she forgot they had a landline. She ran from the house, shouting for David to come quickly. He reacted in an instant and followed her to where Cal was lying. Oh God, she thought – he could have been there all night.

'Have you called an ambulance?' said David.

Grace shook her head. This was her fault. She had given him a heart attack and then fled to her lover. David was speaking to someone – the emergency services, she assumed. He moved Cal into the recovery position, allowing Grace a glimpse of his face. It was damp and ashen, and seemed to have collapsed on one side. David had put his phone on speaker so that both his hands were free. He was loosening Cal's shirt collar now, tapping him on the cheek and saying his name. Grace heard the word 'stroke' – a verb and a noun. Lovely in one context, lethal in the other.

TWENTY-FOUR

Grace felt like a fraud, travelling in the ambulance with Cal. The paramedics – one young, one not – treated her with care and kindness, mistaking her, no doubt, for a loving and devoted wife. She listened to the wail of sirens, and remembered the siren she had heard when talking with Ruth after the disastrous party. Had that been a warning? Cal had raged at her, his face savage and sweaty, as if his whole being was engorged with anger. She should have known that could bring on a heart attack or stroke. How different he looked now, all shrunken and helpless. He was hooked up to medical paraphernalia and being monitored by the young paramedic. She did her best to reassure Grace, saying it was to keep him stable – standard procedure. The girl looked a bit like Millie, only tidier. She suggested Grace call someone – a friend or relative.

'I don't have a phone,' she said.

The paramedic seemed puzzled, as if such a thing wasn't possible. Grace assumed there would be payphones at the hospital. She would call her mum on the landline – the number etched in her memory from childhood. Her addled brain couldn't remember anyone's mobile number.

'It's probably best if I wait until I know more about my husband's condition, don't you think?' she said.

The paramedic looked dubious, as though it was obvious that her husband's condition was perilous, and his loved ones would want to be there for what were possibly his final hours. Grace could barely swallow. It felt as if all the guilt and dread had solidified in her throat. Josh and Lydia would blame her. Everyone would blame her.

Once the ambulance came to a stop, things happened with a worrying degree of urgency. Cal was wheeled into A&E, still attached to the IV drip, the young paramedic rattling off words and phrases familiar to Grace from hospital dramas. *Grey's Anatomy* was her favourite. This was nothing like *Grey's Anatomy*. A huddle of staff was waiting to whisk Cal one way and Grace another. She was shown to a side room, where a woman with a clipboard asked her lots of questions and jotted down the answers.

'Is there someone you would like to call?' she said, once the formalities were completed.

'Where can I find a payphone?'

'Follow the signs for Reception. The phones are by the side of Costa Coffee.'

Grace made her way along the harshly lit corridor, wondering why people were looking at her curiously. Then she remembered her dress was torn, her shoes ruined, and she had a scabby cut on her face. Perhaps they thought she had been attacked, or in an accident. She kept her eyes forward, forcing herself to put one foot in front of the other.

The reception area was big, bright and busy. She spotted the promised payphones, but then remembered she didn't have her purse. A sudden urge to cry stopped her in her tracks, and then she saw David.

'How is he?' he said.

Grace shrugged.

'I don't know – the doctors are with him.'

He handed her Cal's phone.

'This was in the kitchen,' he said. 'I thought you might need it.'

'Thank you,' she said, breathless with gratitude. 'And thank you for what you did. I was absolutely hopeless.'

'You were in shock,' he said. 'Is there anything you need before I shoot off?'

'A coffee?' she said. 'I don't have any money on me.'

David went into Costa while Grace unlocked Cal's phone. No passcode – a picture of her as his screensaver. There were four unread messages from Josh. *Sorry Dad*, at 22.15, an hour or so after he and Millie had left. *You OK?* at 23.05, when he hadn't received a reply, and again forty minutes later. The final message, at 00.13, had an edge of desperation. *I'm worried I did the wrong thing. Mum's not answering her phone either. Please will one of you call me!*

'Here you go,' said David, handing her a styrofoam cup.

He hadn't bought one for himself.

'Thank you,' she said. 'For this, and for everything.'

He put his hands on her shoulders – a moment of tenderness among the chaos.

'Take care of yourself, Grace,' he said, before heading for the exit.

She watched him walk out of the hospital, and out of her

life. The phone in her hand played the *Dam Busters* theme – Cal's ringtone. It brought to mind acts of bravery, personal sacrifice, a sense of doing the right thing, no matter the cost. The name on the screen was Josh.

'Dad?' he said, when she answered.

'Darling, it's Mum. Please don't hang up.'

Her plea was met with silence.

'Dad's in hospital,' she said.

'Why? What happened?'

'I'm not sure,' she said, squeezing her eyes shut to try to expunge an image of Cal's livid face, the pulsating blue vein in the middle of his forehead. 'He collapsed. I'm waiting to speak to the doctor.'

She could hear Josh breathe.

'I think you should be here,' she said, implying the seriousness of the situation without having to spell it out. 'Where are you?'

'At Millie's sister's place,' he said. 'Near Watford.'

Grace couldn't picture where that was. Somewhere north of London?

'Hang on,' he said.

He must have pressed the phone to his chest because everything sounded muffled. Grace waited, grateful he hadn't asked too many questions. She knew it was just a reprieve, that the whole sordid story would come out soon enough, but still.

'Millie's sister's going to lend us her car,' said Josh.

'You don't have a licence,' said Grace.

'Millie's driving,' he said, which filled Grace with a whole new medley of anxieties. Motorway pile-ups, a breakdown pinning them on the hard shoulder with lorries roaring by.

How old was this car? Did her sister belong to the AA? How good a driver was Millie?

'Mum?'

'Yes?'

'We'll be there as soon as we can.'

'Please tell Millie to drive safe,' said Grace, trying to dampen the panic fizzing in her gut, but he had already hung up.

She retraced her steps and found the woman with the clipboard, who showed her to a family room. It was white, sterile and windowless. There were plastic moulded chairs and a low wooden coffee table, scattered with a few old magazines. The woman told her that a doctor would be along when there was any news. Grace sat down and drank some coffee, steeling herself to call Lydia. Unusually, she answered straight away. Cal moaned about the number of times she let his calls go to voicemail, and how it often took days before she called him back. 'Good thing I'm not at death's door,' he would say jokingly. Grace was direct and succinct, just as she had been with Josh. The less said the better, right now. There would be plenty of time for recrimination later. She asked Lydia to let Beth and Julia know, blaming low battery on Cal's phone. In truth, she just didn't want to speak to them. She needed to conserve her emotional reserves for what lay ahead, not deplete them on Cal's disapproving daughters.

When a white-coated medic approached her, she braced herself. He moved one of the moulded plastic chairs so that he was facing her. The poor man looked pale and beleaguered, as if he was running on empty. One side of his spectacles was held together by sticky tape, and his hair was wispy and thin. He introduced himself as Doctor

Rudge, and asked her to confirm she was the family of Cal Wheeler. Grace nodded.

'Your father has had a stroke,' he said. 'But we're doing our best to stabilise him.'

'He's my husband,' she said.

'Oh, I'm sorry,' he said, checking his notes. 'Yes, it's right here. Apologies.'

He proceeded to explain Cal's condition and prognosis.

'Essentially, there are two types of stroke – a clot and a bleed. Your husband's stroke is haemorrhagic – a bleed on the brain.'

Grace found herself nodding, as if to say, *Yes, I suspected as much. Thank you for confirming.*

'The bleed is severe, I'm afraid, located in the right hemisphere, which has caused paralysis along his left side.'

'He's paralysed?' said Grace, horrified by the word. 'Permanently?'

Doctor Rudge removed his spectacles and pinched the bridge of his nose. He gave the lenses a cursory wipe with a crisp white handkerchief, before putting them back on.

'It's difficult to offer a definitive prognosis,' he said, leaning forward slightly, as if to confide something important. 'But a newly damaged brain is vulnerable to further strokes or epileptic fits, which is why the next forty-eight hours are crucial. Your husband's condition is very serious, Mrs Wheeler.'

'So he might die?' she said.

'You need to prepare yourself for that possibility, but as I say, if we can get him stable and keep him that way, his chances will improve.'

Doctor Rudge's words buzzed around Grace like malevolent wasps.

'I realise this is a lot to take in,' he said. 'And you'll have questions going forward, but is there anything you want to ask me now?'

'Why did this happen?' she said.

'Well, there are a variety of factors. Age, general health –'

He checked his notes again.

'I believe your husband has a heart condition? There may of course be a genetic component, and lifestyle can play a part.'

He stopped for a moment, allowing the information to sink in.

'Unfortunately, strokes are very common,' he continued. 'But your husband is receiving the best care, and we will do everything we can to help him.'

In order to do that, it seemed imperative to Grace that Doctor Rudge had all the facts.

'We had an argument,' she said. 'And he lost his temper. Could that have caused a stroke?'

Even as she asked the question, the answer seemed obvious. His blood pressure would have sky-rocketed, causing a blood vessel in his brain to burst.

'Like I say, Mrs Wheeler, strokes happen for all sorts of reasons, but in your husband's case, I suspect the culprits were a combination of age and heart disease.'

It was kind of him to try to let her off the hook, but she didn't deserve absolution.

'I wasn't there when it happened,' she said. 'If I had found him sooner –?'

Dr Rudge sighed, Grace not knowing if this signified sympathy or irritation. He probably had a dozen other patients to see, families to deal with.

'It's impossible to say, Mrs Wheeler, but again, he's receiving the best care.'

He stood to leave and said he would update her when he could. Her coffee was cold but she drank it, just for something to do. She imagined there would be a lot of waiting around in her immediate future – something she had to get used to. A good wife would pray for her husband to pull through, but Grace wasn't a good wife. If it was a choice between death and paralysis, Cal would prefer the former. He had said as much when a colleague was paralysed in a motorbike accident. No, if the prognosis was dire, it would be kinder if he didn't pull through. This was what she was thinking when Lydia blustered in, her face crumpled with concern. Grace tried to hug her, but was instantly rebuffed.

'Where's Dad?' she said. 'How is he?'

'I've just spoken to his doctor. He's had a bleed on the brain. That's all I know right now.'

Lydia flopped onto a chair as if her legs couldn't support her. She put her head in her hands, and it hurt Grace that she couldn't offer comfort. When Lydia had been told Cal needed heart surgery, she was wretched with worry. She was used to her mum being sick, but not her big strong dad. It must have roused memories of Marilyn's long illness and her cruel, drawn-out death. Grace rubbed Lydia's shoulder, but she pushed her hand away and looked at her with cold, judgemental eyes.

'I saw your boyfriend,' she said. 'He was at the traffic lights next to my Uber. Green Land Rover – that was him, wasn't it?'

Not this. Not now.

'Can we just focus on your dad?' said Grace.

'Dad? Does he know?'

She sounded spiteful and bitter, like her sisters in those early days.

'Lydia, please. Let's try to get through the next few hours.'

'Does he know?'

She enunciated each word with icy precision. There was no point lying. If Grace didn't tell her, Josh would.

'Yes,' she said.

Lydia inhaled sharply.

'I don't have to ask how he took it,' she said. 'The evidence speaks for itself.'

Grace thought about quoting Doctor Rudge – age, heart disease, genetic factors – but decided against it.

'What happened?' said Lydia.

When Grace didn't immediately answer, Lydia said, 'Tell me.'

'He found out about David,' said Grace. 'We argued. It got heated and I left.'

'Left?' said Lydia. 'What do you mean, left?'

Grace's heart felt as if it was crushing her lungs and swelling upwards into her throat. She could see the truth dawning on Lydia's face.

'You went to him,' she said, as if she almost couldn't believe it.

The realisation made her physically reel, and she planted a palm on each thigh, as if to stop herself folding in two.

'When?' she said.

Grace knew that what she said next would sever their relationship, and the girl she had loved and mothered would despise her.

'Last night.'

Lydia looked confused, as though trying to solve a puzzle.

'Last night?' she said. 'So, wait. Dad found out you'd been cheating on him, you had a row, and you spent the night with –'

She couldn't bring herself to say David's name.

'I didn't spend the night with him,' said Grace. 'Not in that sense. I just needed a place to stay.'

'Oh, don't try to justify yourself,' said Lydia. 'When did he have the stroke?'

What could Grace say? He hadn't answered Josh's calls, which meant it could have happened soon after she bolted from the house. But she didn't know for sure. Maybe he hadn't wanted to talk to anyone, and that's why he didn't pick up.

'I honestly don't know,' she said.

'Honest?'

Lydia's voice had risen in pitch and volume.

'You *dare* use that word after everything you've done?'

Angry tears welled up, but Lydia tried to swallow them.

'He could have been lying there all night,' she said, clutching the last piece of the puzzle. 'You left him to die.'

'That's not true,' said Grace. 'He was fine when I left him.'

'How could he have been fine? He had just discovered you were fucking another man.'

'Yes, and he was very angry. Look,' said Grace, pointing to the tear in her dress and the cut above her eye. 'He scared me and I ran.'

Lydia shook her head, as if refusing to believe it. And she was right, Cal wasn't an angry man – certainly not an abusive one. It was when Lydia wiped her eyes that

Grace realised she hadn't cried at all. Not when she found Cal moaning on the floor, nor in the ambulance, when he looked more dead than alive. Not even when Doctor Rudge told her he might not survive and if he did he would likely be paralysed. Maybe she was in shock too, or maybe she was heartless.

'I want you to go,' said Lydia, with a contemptuous stare.

'What?'

'Leave. Go see your boyfriend. I really don't care, but you don't get to be here, pretending you give a fuck.'

She was lashing out, understandably, but Grace wasn't in a position to concede. Whatever Lydia's opinion on the subject, Grace was still Cal's wife. Given her recent behaviour it seemed insensitive to point this out, so she used the term 'next of kin', explaining that, as such, she had to be there. Lydia had no comeback, except to regard her with pure scorn. This was how it would be, thought Grace, as a frigid silence descended. She was a pariah, the enemy, a wife in name alone.

TWENTY-FIVE

Cal's older daughters arrived at the hospital in quick succession. Beth got there first, looking hot and flustered.

'What's she doing here?' she asked Lydia, glaring venomously at Grace.

So she knew what had happened at the party. Grace knew Lydia would tell her, but felt a pinch of disappointment nevertheless.

'I told her to go but she won't,' Lydia said to her sister.

'The doctor asked me to stay,' said Grace.

'Where is he?' said Beth. 'The doctor?'

'With your dad,' said Grace. 'He said he'll talk to us once they've managed to get him stable.'

Beth sank into a chair. The resentment imprinted on her face melted into distress. She turned her back on Grace and spoke only to Lydia.

'How bad is he?'

Lydia shook her head.

'I don't know. The doctor had already been and gone before I got here.'

It must have galled Beth that she had to speak to Grace after all. She demanded to know what the doctor had said, and Grace didn't see the point of sugar-coating it.

'He had a bleed on his brain – a serious one,' she said.

'Is there any other kind?' snapped Beth.

'It's all her fault,' said Lydia, scowling at Grace.

She laid the blame firmly and unforgivingly at Grace's feet. The feet that took her from their sick, possibly dying father, straight to her lover's bed. Grace wanted to say that wasn't what happened, but why bother? The bones of the story were accurate enough to condemn her, even without Lydia's half-truths and embellishments. Beth stared at Grace with blatant loathing. She hurled insults and accusations she had probably bottled up for years. The tirade was in full flow when Julia arrived.

'Shh,' she told Beth. 'I could hear you down the corridor.'

'Have you any idea what she's done?' said Beth, jabbing an accusatory finger at Grace.

She proceeded to repeat what Lydia had told her but, as with Chinese whispers, repetition distorted the facts. Grace had to at least try to put the record straight.

'That's not true,' she said. 'He was fine when I left him. Furious, but not unwell.'

'Do you blame him?' said Julia.

'No,' said Grace. 'I don't. But I wouldn't have left at all if I hadn't been scared of what he might do.'

'Liar,' said Beth.

'Who do you think did this?' said Grace, pointing to the torn fabric and the cut on her face.

'He would never ...' said Julia.

'He was out of control,' said Grace. 'I had to get out of there – give him time to cool down.'

'I'm sure running off to your boyfriend didn't help the situation,' said Lydia. 'I caught them having Sunday lunch together,' she told her sisters.

'And you didn't tell Dad?' said Beth.

'She begged me not to – promised there was nothing going on.'

'There wasn't,' said Grace. 'And he isn't my boyfriend.'

Julia was flushed now too. She removed her expensive coat and threw it over a chair. Cal had been so proud when she was made partner at a prestigious law firm. He didn't play favourites, but since neither Lydia nor Beth were particularly career driven, Julia was the one he boasted about.

They told Grace to get out, to wait somewhere else, anywhere away from *their* family. It was easier to comply than argue, and she didn't want to be around them anyway. She dragged a plastic chair into the corridor, and let them get on with the serious business of despising her. It felt like she had been consigned to an adult version of the naughty step. She used the time to think about what she would say to Josh. It was important she intercepted him before the girls could spew their poison. According to them, she had stepped over Cal's dying body en route to a night of passion with her lover. He needed to know that was not what happened.

The stab of joy she felt when he finally showed up quickly turned to heartache. He looked pale and forlorn, his eyes dark with worry. She stood, hoping he would allow a hug, but, like Lydia, he stiffened at the sight of her.

'How's Dad?'

'The doctors are with him,' said Grace. 'They'll let us know more when they can. Is Millie not with you?'

'She's finding somewhere to park. Who else is here?'

'Beth, Julia, Lydia.'

She pointed to the door that led into the family room.

'Why are you out here?' said Josh.

'I've been banished,' she said. 'And I wanted to talk to you alone.'

'Is it my fault?' he said.

'What?' said Grace. 'Of course not. How could it –?'

'Because I was the one who gave him your phone. If I hadn't done that –'

He looked like he might cry, which made Grace want to cry too.

'Listen to me,' she said, gently touching his arm. 'This is not your fault – don't think that for a second. The doctor said strokes are very common, especially in a man of Dad's age with a heart condition.'

Josh looked unconvinced, spurring Grace to take her fair share of righteous guilt.

'If anyone is to blame, it's me,' she said. 'We had an argument and I left. I shouldn't have done that. It was wrong of me. And it was wrong of me to see David behind Dad's back. I should have told him the truth straight away, and not put you in an impossible position. I will never forgive myself for that.'

She dared hold his arm a little firmer, encouraged that he didn't pull away. Perhaps he was considering her apology – weighing it up in his mind. She clung to the possibility of forgiveness, the hope they'd get through this, bruised but not broken. Over his shoulder she spotted Millie jogging towards them, and the moment of conciliation passed. It was his supportive girlfriend he wanted, not his duplicitous mother. She hadn't had the chance to warn him that it didn't happen like Lydia said. The sight of him clinging to Millie pierced Grace's heart. She should be the one comforting him, not a girl he had known for all of five minutes.

'Josh,' said Grace.

She hoped she sounded measured and discreet, but could hear the desperation in her voice. He let go of Millie and turned to her.

'What?'

'Your sisters are very upset,' she said. 'They'll tell you things that aren't true. It's important you understand that. I would never have left your father if I'd known something like this could happen –'

'Stop,' said Josh. 'Seriously, Mum, it's Dad I'm worried about, not you. He might die, and all you care about is what people are saying.'

'No,' she said. 'That's not it. I just wanted you to know –'

He turned to Millie, ignoring Grace.

'Will you wait here?' he said. 'Until I've had a chance to talk to Lyd.'

Millie didn't look too pleased about being stuck in the corridor with Grace.

'Thanks for getting him here in one piece,' she said, after a brief but awkward silence. 'It was kind of your sister to lend you her car.'

'It was an emergency,' said Millie.

'How is he?' said Grace. 'Josh, I mean.'

Millie's free-flowing confidence wasn't in evidence. She seemed quiet, almost reticent.

'Worried,' she said. 'And feeling like he's to blame.'

'I told him it's not his fault.'

'I told him too, but, well, you feel how you feel, don't you?'

Grace couldn't argue with that.

'Would you like to sit down?' she said, offering Millie her chair.

'No, thanks,' she said. 'I might go and get some coffee and sandwiches. We haven't really eaten.'

'Good idea,' said Grace. 'I'm afraid I don't have my purse, otherwise I'd buy them for you.'

'It's OK,' said Millie. 'Can I get you anything?'

'That's very kind,' said Grace. 'But I'm fine.'

Millie slung her cloth bag over her shoulder, looking relieved to have a reason to go. Grace didn't blame her. It can't be much fun, hanging around a hospital with your boyfriend's disgraced mother. At least she hadn't frozen Grace out like the others had. She tried her mum's landline before remembering it was Tuesday, one of Ruth's volunteering days. She found her mobile number in Cal's contacts.

'I've been trying to get hold of you,' said Ruth. 'Haven't you got my messages?'

Grace explained about the argument, the smashed phone, Cal's stroke, the dire prognosis. Ruth gasped at each shocking revelation, before she gathered herself and went into saviour mode. She said she would be there in thirty minutes, and though Grace desperately needed her mum, she didn't want her subjected to the girls' invective. Ruth would defend her, inflaming an already heated situation.

But Grace did need money and a change of clothes. She asked Ruth to go to the house, fetch her handbag, a tracksuit and trainers – anything she could easily slip into – and meet her in Costa at the main reception. They could talk there without hostile interruptions.

The sight of Doctor Rudge approaching shot a burst of panic through Grace. His body language was inscrutable. There was no way to tell if he was the bearer of good news or bad. He opened the door to the family room and stood aside for her to enter. Everyone got to their feet but he addressed himself primarily to Grace, since she was the only one he had met.

'Your husband is stable in intensive care,' he said.

'Can we see him?' asked Lydia.

'He's sedated, so probably won't know you're there.'

'But we'll know,' said Josh.

Doctor Rudge nodded.

'No more than two at a time,' he said.

Beth immediately nominated herself and Julia, invoking sibling seniority. All three sisters glared defiantly at Grace, as if daring her to object. It was Doctor Rudge who said, 'Mrs Wheeler?' as if assuming she would sit with her husband. Before she had a chance to demur, Beth said she had no right to be anywhere near him, since it was her fault he was at death's door in the first place. Grace didn't dignify that with a response, but was firm that Josh should be allowed to sit with his dad. Beth and Julia strenuously disagreed, and what started as a squabble quickly descended into a proxy feud for all the petty jealousies that had festered over the years. Doctor Rudge interrupted, insisting he had neither the time nor patience for this, so it was begrudgingly agreed that Beth and Josh would keep vigil first, Julia and Lydia after that.

'An hour is probably enough for today,' said Doctor Rudge, as his pager beeped.

Beth and Josh followed him out, leaving Grace alone with Julia and Lydia. Despite a ceasefire in snide comments and name-calling, the atmosphere seethed with tension. Millie was back from Costa, and Grace wondered if it was her presence that tempered the vitriol. Maybe having a relative stranger in the room skewed the family dynamic, or maybe the Wheeler sisters didn't want to reveal their inner malice to Josh's pretty girlfriend. The truce came to an abrupt end when the *Dam Busters* theme startled them all. Julia demanded to know why Grace had her dad's phone, but Lydia spoke over her, saying, 'If that's the boyfriend, tell him to fuck right off.' Grace saw the caller was Marty, and remembered she was supposed to be at work.

'It's Marty Devlin,' she said, stepping outside to talk.

Concerned she hadn't turned up for a meeting, he had made several calls to her own phone before finally calling Cal's. She told him about the stroke, the hospital, the seriousness of the situation. He sounded winded by the news, a reminder that he and Cal had been friends for over thirty years. Everyone was more upset than she was. No, that wasn't quite right. She was upset – of course she was – but everything seemed blurry and once removed. Under normal circumstances, being attacked by the girls would have shaken her to the core, but strangely, she felt nothing much at all. Perhaps it was a coping mechanism, and if so, thank God. Without it she would have buckled. Instead, she marvelled at her own fortitude. She promised to keep

Marty updated, and he told her not to worry about work – to take as much time as she needed. That was when it dawned on her that this situation was open-ended and, for now at least, wholly unpredictable.

She had no desire to rejoin the others, so went to Costa to wait for Ruth. The maze of long, fluorescent-lit corridors all looked and smelled the same. The reception area was even busier now. It had the buzz and bustle of a shopping mall, rather than the solemnity of a hospital. Grace looked around and spotted Doctor Rudge sitting alone.

'May I join you?' she said, with a weak smile.

He hesitated.

'I'm off the clock,' he said. 'Just waiting for my wife.'

Under normal circumstances, good manners would have made Grace retreat, but these weren't normal circumstances.

'I wanted to apologise,' she said, pulling out a chair. 'For that scene earlier. It's a difficult time.'

'I've seen worse,' he said. 'At least there wasn't any bloodshed.'

'You're very kind,' she said. 'And with that in mind, can I ask you something?'

'If I say "no", you're going to ask anyway, aren't you?'

She looked enviously at his latte and hoped her mum wouldn't be long.

'What should I prepare for, as far as my husband is concerned?'

'How do you mean?'

'I need to know what to expect.'

Doctor Rudge sat back in his seat and gave her a long, studied look.

'It would be unprofessional of me to discuss a patient over coffee,' he said.

'Off the record, then,' she said. 'You must have seen lots of people in similar situations. What sort of quality of life do they have afterwards?'

It took him a few moments to answer.

'I can only speak in general terms, not about your husband specifically,' he said. 'There are a multitude of factors at play – the size and site of the stroke, age, general health, motivation, luck. Everyone's different. It would be impossible to predict any outcome at this stage.'

He looked relieved when a pretty Chinese woman waved at him.

'That's my wife,' he said, standing to go.

He gathered up his belongings – phone, wallet, keys – and hesitated before he said, 'Look, there's obviously a lot of bad feeling around, but for your husband's sake, I urge you to sort it out. He's going to need his family.'

Easier said than done, thought Grace, although she promised to do her best. Seeing Doctor Rudge greet his wife made Grace feel very alone. Cal had always been good in a crisis. Now he was the crisis. How stupid she had been, believing she could have a fresh start. And how selfish to even think in those terms with Cal hooked up to machines. So much for plans, she told herself, her throat too tight to swallow. It was as if all her hopes for the future were stuck there, and nothing could get past.

TWENTY-SIX

Grace waved frantically when she spotted her mum, who rushed over and hugged her like they hadn't seen each other in years.

'I brought these,' said Ruth, when they untangled themselves.

She handed over a carrier bag with all the things Grace had asked her to bring from home.

'You're a lifesaver,' she said. 'Sorry, unfortunate choice of words.'

Ruth made a small sound Grace couldn't quite decipher.

'I'll get us a hot drink,' she said, 'and you can tell me all about it.'

Grace felt bolstered to have her mum there – someone on her side, irrespective of her transgressions. Ruth came back with milky coffees and carrot cake.

'Sugar's good for shock,' she said. 'Any news on Cal?'

'He's stable but sedated. Josh and Beth are with him.'

'Well, that's promising,' said Ruth.

She seemed reluctant to bombard Grace with questions, so left it at that for now. Grace picked at the carrot cake, barely tasting it at all. She washed it down with coffee, relieved she could actually swallow. When she caught her mum staring at the cut above her eye, she told her it happened when Cal smashed her phone. Ruth shook her head in disbelief.

'I know it must have been a shock, but it sounds as if you're talking about a completely different person.'

'He was out of control,' said Grace.

'And where does this other man fit into the scheme of things?'

'He doesn't.'

'But you said you were having an affair.'

'More of a fling really, and it's over.'

'You threw away your marriage for a fling?'

'The marriage was already done, as far as I was concerned. I just hadn't got around to telling Cal.'

Ruth's face hardened a little.

'Sorry,' said Grace. 'I don't mean to sound callous. I did warn you things weren't good between us.'

'Yes, but "not good" is a long way from "done", as you put it. And I assumed it was serious with this man, that you were in love.'

'I was infatuated. It felt like love but it wasn't real, like those mirages you see on a scorching-hot day. The closer you get, the more they fade, until you realise there's nothing there at all.'

Ruth pressed her lips together, as if working through the analogy.

'I can't imagine what Charles must think,' said Grace,

wanting to shift the focus away from herself. 'I hope I haven't spoiled things for you.'

'Well, if he's going to baulk at the first sign of trouble, he probably wasn't worth bothering with in the first place,' said Ruth.

Their coffees were finished, and Grace had eaten as much of the cake as she could force down.

'I'd better go,' she said. 'I want to be there when Josh gets back from seeing Cal.'

'How is Josh?' said Ruth.

'Devastated,' said Grace. 'I just hope he doesn't resent me as much as his sisters do.'

'Even Lydia?'

'Especially Lydia.'

Ruth dabbed the corners of her mouth with a napkin.

'It's bound to be raw right now,' she said. 'They'll come around.'

Grace didn't share her mother's optimism. She took the bag of clothes and got changed in the toilets, stuffing the ruined dress and shoes into a bin. Ruth wanted to go with her to the family room – moral support, she said – but Grace was adamant.

'I couldn't face another scene, Mum,' she said. 'I'll call if I need you.'

Her trainers squeaked on the shiny linoleum floor as she made her way back to the others. Julia was outside, talking on the phone. She didn't acknowledge Grace, and neither did Lydia, who was sitting alone, staring blankly at the wall. When Grace asked where Millie was, she ignored her. They sat in strained silence, until Josh and Beth returned.

'He looks terrible,' said Beth, wiping her eyes with a screwed-up tissue. 'I just want him to wake up.'

Lydia and Julia exchanged an uneasy look, as if dreading seeing their father in that state. Julia took her sister's hand and they headed off in silence. Grace hadn't seen them hold hands before, not even when Lydia was a little girl. It was always Beth she had gravitated to, the oldest sister and mother substitute, at least until Grace came along. Beth stepped outside to make a call, allowing Grace and Josh a moment alone.

'I'm not sure what's happened to Millie,' she said, hoping neutral territory might get him talking.

'She's gone home,' he said. 'No point her waiting around.'

Grace thought she might have stayed to support Josh, but was relieved she hadn't. It would be easier at home with just the two of them.

'How was it, seeing Dad?'

Josh hung his head, utterly bereft.

'Is he going to die?' he said.

His candour took Grace by surprise. She moved to the seat next to his.

'I hope not,' she said.

He looked her in the eye.

'Do you?'

'Of course I do.'

Grace could only imagine what awful things the girls had said to put that idea in his head. He needed to know the truth.

'Look, your dad and I argued, it got a bit heated and I thought it best to give him some space. And yes, I did drive to David's house, but only because I couldn't think where else to go. I didn't have my purse, so a hotel wasn't an option –'

'Why didn't you have your purse?'

She squeezed her eyes shut, trying to erase a flashback of Cal shouting obscenities in her face. It was difficult to know how much to tell Josh. The truth would justify her running from the house, but she didn't want him to think badly of his father, especially now.

'Like I said, things got heated.'

She realised she was twisting her wedding ring. How could she convey the urgency, the fear she had felt, without telling Josh the whole sordid story?

'I left in a hurry,' was all she said, and let his imagination do the rest.

They clammed up when Beth returned. She flopped down in a chair and let out a long, despairing sigh. It summed up the mood perfectly. And when Julia and Lydia got back from Cal's bedside, they seemed despairing too. No one asked how he was because they all knew the answer.

There was a polite tap on the door, even though it was ajar. The woman who spoke with Grace when she first arrived told them they should go home and get some rest.

'Someone will call if there's any change in your husband's condition,' she said to Grace.

Beth was the first to object, insisting she had no intention of going anywhere. Lydia nodded furiously, tears trickling down her face.

'I understand,' said the woman. 'But you won't be able to see him again this evening, and you'll need all your strength in the days ahead.'

It seemed sound advice to Grace.

'She's right,' said Julia, picking up her coat and bag. 'There's no point hanging around here for the sake of it.'

Beth and Lydia exchanged a look of reluctant acquiescence – decision made. They didn't say goodbye to Grace, but Lydia gave Josh a quick hug on her way out. He called an Uber, and though Grace couldn't wait to get home, she remembered the pile of dirty dishes and rancid smell of leftover food waiting for her there.

What a relief to find her mother had taken care of it all. She had even folded the trestle table and put the tablecloth in the wash. Grace sent her a quick text to say thanks, and promised she would call later. She had forgotten about her packed suitcase, still sitting in the hallway. Josh looked at it, and then at her. His silence was damning.

For supper they ate pepperoni pizza in front of the television, both too dazed to talk. Josh went to his room as soon as he had finished, and stayed there until morning.

When Grace got into bed, bone-tired and aching, she stared at the empty space beside her, unable to believe how everything could change in the space of one day. Tears came at last – for Cal, Josh, the girls, for the terrible hurt she had caused. It felt good to let go – wash herself clean of guilt and remorse. Such a thing wasn't remotely possible, but she wore herself out trying, and slept fitfully until dawn.

Cal's phone was on the bedside table, mercifully silent. No news is good news, she told herself, putting on a dressing gown to go downstairs and make coffee. She didn't want to wake Josh but heard him moving around too. Without Millie there to police him, he had eaten cheese, ham and chorizo. Cal had predicted as much. Grace smiled sadly, wishing she could have shared that with him. She would sit with him today – tell him she was sorry. He probably wouldn't hear her, or even register her presence, but she needed to say it anyway.

The girls seemed less combative than yesterday, as if maybe all their hostility had been spent and they had nothing left to throw at her. She went to see Cal on her own and barely recognised the man lying in the bed. His face had a waxy, greyish pallor, and seemed to have shrunk in on itself. There was a hollowness to his eyes and cheeks that was worryingly cadaver-like. Tubes went in and out of his body, hooked up to IV bags and blinking machines. An oxygen mask covered his mouth and nose. The woman at the next bed talked quietly to its unfortunate occupant, stroking a hand and forearm. Grace didn't want to touch Cal. She was ashamed of that, but couldn't help how she felt. No wonder Josh and the girls had been upset. He didn't look like himself anymore.

'I'm sorry,' she whispered. 'I truly am.'

She didn't stay long. Doctor Rudge was at the nurses' station and beckoned to her as she passed.

'Can we talk?' he said. 'In my office.'

She swallowed hard and followed him. It must be difficult breaking bad news, thought Grace. He spoke clearly and without obvious emotion, but his eyes conveyed compassion. She listened, but heard maybe one word in every four or five. Paralysis on his left side. Difficulty controlling thoughts or emotions. Speech problems. Frustration, anger, despair. It was too much. She looked away and scanned the small, untidy room, stacked with files, books and journals. The dominant colour was a bland, institutional grey – neither light nor dark, matt nor gloss. A framed photo of his wife, resplendent in a vivid peacock-blue dress, provided the only splash of colour.

'Mrs Wheeler?' he said, perhaps realising she had withdrawn into herself.

A reaction he'd seen many times before, she assumed. He stopped talking and folded his hands on the desk, allowing Grace a few moments to process the catalogue of horrors he had described. Her eyes fixed on the peacock-blue dress, the flute of champagne in his wife's delicate hand, the look of pure happiness on her face. It was obscene to taunt patients' nearest and dearest with a scene of such overt joy. Joy denied to them because fate had delivered a hammer blow and nothing would ever be the same again.

When Doctor Rudge resumed his prognosis, it was to dangle a small morsel of hope. No two brains were the same, he said, making it notoriously difficult to predict a patient's recovery. All he could say with confidence was that rehabilitation would help Cal reach his recovery *potential*. This was vague enough to imply both optimism and pessimism, or perhaps neither. When he asked Grace if she had any questions, she shook her head. Afterwards, she thought of several, but the grey walls had begun to close in and the air to feel thin and stale. Even Doctor Rudge's voice sounded smaller and further away, making her wonder if she was losing her mind. She stood up too quickly, causing her head to swim. He tried to get her to sit down again, but she needed to breathe, to think, and she couldn't do that with his pretty wife smiling at her.

Grace walked around for a while before going back to the waiting room. It would doubtlessly give the girls some satisfaction to see her wretched with guilt and grief, and she wished she could oblige. But all she felt was detached, as if everything was happening at a remove. The man in the bed couldn't possibly be Cal. Cal was big and brawny with a cheesy sense of humour and a taste for jokey put-downs. The man in the bed was gaunt and mute.

'How is he?' said Josh.

Grace shrugged.

'Not good,' she said. 'Doctor Rudge called me into his office to talk things through.'

Julia stopped scrolling through her phone for a second and glared at her.

'He should be talking to all of us together,' she said.

'Can you blame him, after yesterday?' said Josh.

Was he actually defending her? Grace chose to believe he was.

'Go on, Mum,' he said. 'What did the doctor say?'

Her scrambled brain struggled to remember. She told them about partial paralysis, personality changes, maybe some difficulties with speech. They looked as dumbfounded as she had. Lydia put her head in her hands before Grace remembered the few crumbs of comfort.

'But if he works hard on his recovery,' she said, 'he could surprise us all.'

She didn't believe that and suspected they didn't either, but some hope was better than none at all.

A pattern was established as the week wore on. The girls let Grace share information about Cal, but apart from that, she was ignored. If she offered Lydia a tissue (she cried a lot), she replied with a curt shake of the head. Josh was neutral, like Switzerland. He seemed distant and withdrawn, but not openly hostile. In the evenings they ate supper on trays in front of the television. Cal's empty recliner chair taunted them cruelly.

Ruth popped around each day to put food in the fridge so Grace didn't have to worry about shopping. Josh watched endless episodes of *The Big Bang Theory*, even smiling occasionally at something the nerdy scientists said. He wouldn't open up to her, but neither had he deserted her. Lydia said he could sleep on her sofa, as if the idea of being under the same roof as Grace was abhorrent. So far, he had declined.

Christina turned up one evening with home-made lasagne and a beef stew. Grace thanked her profusely and invited her in for a glass of wine. She noticed a moment's hesitation before Christina accepted.

'This really is very kind of you,' said Grace, uncorking a bottle of Chardonnay. 'I'm sorry I haven't been in touch.'

'I imagine you've had other things on your mind,' said Christina. 'Ruth called – said you were using Cal's phone.'

Grace drank deeply from her glass.

'Did she tell you why?'

Christina stiffened, as if this was territory she would rather avoid.

'Yes,' she said. 'How is he?'

'I want to say he looks worse than he is, but I don't think that's true.'

'Poor Cal,' said Christina. 'What an awful thing to happen.'

Her phrasing struck Grace as ambiguous. Was she talking about the stroke, or finding photos of her and David? Both maybe, or perhaps Grace was just tired and touchy and finding offence where none existed. She veered the conversation towards the boys.

'Has Adam been in touch with Josh? Millie's gone home. I'm sure he could do with a friend.'

'I suggested it,' said Christina. 'But I think he's rather embarrassed.'

If she was trying to make Grace feel worse, she had succeeded. It was a friend she needed, not food, and certainly not to be reminded of that disastrous party. She understood Harry's infidelity made it difficult for Christina to empathise, but they had been friends for years. She was an extrovert – the bold, flirtatious one – Grace happy to be carried along in her magnificent wake. That was their dynamic, and it worked. It hurt to be judged so harshly by her closest confidante. Josh and the girls, she could understand – they loved Cal and she had betrayed him – but not Christina. Clearly she was disappointed in Grace, but Grace was disappointed in her too.

TWENTY-SEVEN

Six days after Cal's stroke, the swelling in his brain had subsided enough to put him out of immediate danger and be moved from the ICU.

'But what if it's too soon and he gets worse?' asked Beth, her face tight with worry.

'He'll be closely monitored,' said Doctor Rudge.

'But not as closely as in intensive care,' said Julia.

Her tone was combative, as if cross-examining a witness.

'I'm sorry,' he said. 'There are other patients who need the bed more than your father does.'

'So this is a step in the right direction,' said Grace, feeling at least one of them should say something positive.

He nodded and urged them to go home. The process of transferring Cal from the ICU and getting him settled in the Stroke Unit would take much of the afternoon. Julia didn't need asking twice, and the other two weren't far behind her.

'Well, that's good,' Grace said to Josh, as they walked towards the exit.

He should have been going back to university, but was adamant he wouldn't leave until his dad was OK. During those first few days, when he feared Cal might die, Grace didn't try to assuage his pessimism. It seemed entirely reasonable, and she was proud that he was mature enough to face up to reality. As the week went on, however, he became increasingly optimistic, to the point where he was in denial about how seriously ill his father was. She assumed it was his way of coping, but it didn't alter the fact that if Cal did recover, he wouldn't be the same person. Being 'OK', as Josh put it, wasn't even on the list of likely outcomes. Each time she tried to have this conversation, it ended in a stalemate. She tackled the problem again on the drive home from the hospital, feeling she had more leverage now that Cal was out of danger.

'Dad's so proud that you're going to be a doctor,' she said. 'He'd hate you to throw that away when there really isn't much you can do here.'

'I'm not throwing it away. It just doesn't feel right leaving when he's so sick.'

'I know,' she said. 'But the girls and I are here, and you can come home at weekends. I'll even give you a daily progress report – how about that?'

She parked on the drive and followed him into the house, which smelled of fresh laundry. Ruth had washed and ironed his clothes, which were folded in a neat pile, ready to be packed. There was a card too – a bucolic watercolour with trees and hills and a wash of pale sky.

'Your idea?' he said to Grace.

'No,' she said, smiling at the message.

Take care Joshy, love Nan x

'I told her you were going back to Exeter, but the card was her idea.'

He put it on the windowsill next to a straggly spider plant.

'And you must be looking forward to seeing Millie again,' said Grace.

He didn't respond to that, but did pick up his clothes.

'You promise you'll let me know how Dad's doing – like really, not just saying he's OK if he isn't.'

'Absolutely,' she said. 'I'll be there every day.'

He hovered uncertainly, as if deciding whether he should say what was on his mind. He took a couple of steps, but then stopped.

'Lydia said Dad wouldn't want you there.'

Hardly news, but it cut deeper hearing it from him.

'She could be right, but if that's the case, he can tell me himself.'

'How? He can't speak.'

Grace offered a hopeful smile.

'He will,' she said. 'He just needs time.'

Josh went to his room and didn't reappear until Grace called him for supper. She had reheated Christina's lasagne and opened a bottle of wine. *The Big Bang Theory*, even with its canned laughter and endless adverts, was a welcome backdrop. It masked the distance between them.

He got the train to Exeter the next morning. Grace dropped him at the station en route to the hospital, hoping for a hug but settling for a cursory wave. She watched him walk away, backpack slung over his shoulder. Was it only a week ago he'd been brimming with excitement, keen to show off his girlfriend – his new-found status in the world? When Grace compared that version of her son to this one, tears stung her eyes.

TWENTY-EIGHT

Unlike the ICU, the Stroke Unit had set visiting times. Patients were six to a room, all at different stages of recovery. There was noise and activity, patients being hoisted in and out of bed, or wheeled off for physio sessions. Grace discerned a brusque sense of purpose, as if the more committed someone was to rehab, the more progress they would make.

Cal was by far the worst off in his ward. As Doctor Rudge had predicted, his left side was badly affected, especially his face, which looked as if it had melted. He had no sight in his left eye, so anyone on his right was effectively invisible. He was unable to move his arm and leg, which were cold and numb and must have felt alien to him. To everyone's distress, he cried easily. None of his children had ever seen him cry. Grace had caught him shedding a few manly tears at his mother's funeral, but nothing like this. He was a man who kept his emotions under control, and it devastated the girls to see their strong, dependable father reduced to a blubbing wreck. Not knowing what, specifically, was upsetting him (every single thing, Grace imagined) made it more unbearable. He was suffering from mixed aphasia – difficulty understanding what was being said, and a corresponding difficulty speaking. This frustrated him to the point where he would flail his working arm around, lashing out when anyone tried to calm him down.

It wasn't clear whether he recognised his family, since he treated everyone with the same degree of animosity. The first time he looked at Grace, her blood pumped hot and fast. If he knew who she was, would he remember what she did? He stared at her blankly for what felt like a long time, and then closed his eyes. When he wasn't actively angry, he withdrew into himself, something Doctor Rudge said was to be expected. If things didn't improve of their own accord, he would prescribe a course of antidepressants.

The girls insisted he knew who they were, but Grace wasn't convinced. Beth would grip his good hand, put her face close to his and speak as if he were a hard-of-hearing simpleton. 'It's all right, Dad,' she would say. 'You're going to get better, I promise.' When Grace caught her crying in the Ladies, she felt a surge of sympathy.

'I'd give you a hug,' she said, 'but I doubt you'd let me.'

Beth managed a small, tragic smile.

'I keep telling him he'll get better,' she said, dabbing her eyes with toilet paper. 'But I'm not sure that's true.'

'I know,' said Grace. 'But it's still early days. He's bound to improve over time.'

Beth nodded.

'I hope so,' she said.

It was the most civil exchange they had had since this whole nightmare began. Grace wondered if Beth found that resenting her took up too much energy – energy that could be focused on supporting Cal.

'I was on the phone to Josh last night,' said Grace, as they walked back to the ward, 'and he said it takes a hundred muscles to speak.'

'Really?' said Beth.

'Yes, and Ahmed –'

'Which one is Ahmed?' said Beth.

'The young male nurse.'

Grace was going to say 'with beautiful brown eyes and perfect teeth', but thought better of it. She didn't want to encourage the idea that she noticed such things.

'He explained that because language is controlled by the left side of the brain, and Cal's bleed was on the right, his ability to communicate should definitely get better.'

Beth seemed buoyed by this, as if desperate to believe anything other than what she saw with her own eyes.

Back on the ward, Ahmed was attempting to feed Cal his lunch. Muscle weakness had impaired his ability not only to speak, but also to swallow. It was pitiful to see a man who had always been so particular about table manners being spoon-fed, wearing a plastic bib. He railed at the indignity, pushing the spoon away and making a horrible growling sound. Ahmed took Grace and the girls to one side, explaining that if Cal continued to refuse food, he might need to be fed through a tube.

'But what can we do?' asked Lydia.

'Encourage him not to give up,' said Ahmed.

Grace wondered if that was exactly what Cal was doing.

Perhaps he had glimpsed his future and decided he couldn't face it. If so, who could blame him? But it wasn't just Cal who was struggling to cope – they all were. Grace found herself missing the quiet solemnity of the ICU, and though she would never say so, a heavily sedated Cal had been infinitely easier to deal with than this volatile, obstinate invalid. He emptied his bladder and bowels into incontinence pads, which Ahmed or one of the other nurses had to change. Cal expressed his shame in grunts and hand gestures, as if shooing them away. Like every other cruel impairment, Ahmed said they could expect improvement over time, but only if Cal cooperated. He had always been a stubborn man, but this aspect of his character had been exacerbated by the stroke. Perhaps he felt the power to say 'no' was the only control he had left in life. They all cajoled him, encouraged him, pleaded with him, but he refused to give an inch.

Julia was the first to announce she had been summoned back to work. Given that she was a senior partner, Grace wasn't sure she believed her, but understood her desire to escape. Lydia bailed too, saying she had used all her compassionate leave and was working through her annual leave now. Even Beth – arguably Cal's most devoted daughter – said that if she didn't get back to work, she wouldn't be able to pay her rent. As a temp, she only got paid for the hours she worked – no holiday pay, no sick pay, and certainly no pay for sitting by her father's bedside. Grace didn't judge any of them for wanting to get back to their lives, but for her, the disgusting smells and cacophony of not-quite-human sounds *were* her life.

Marty visited a few times, clearly shocked at the sight

of his old friend – brawny Cal Wheeler, with his barrel chest and thick, muscled legs – shrunken and broken in a hospital bed. He conducted one-sided conversations about the golf club, mutual friends, politics. 'It's as if he's not there anymore,' he told Grace after his third and last visit. She didn't blame him for not coming back. Ruth, on the other hand, showed up at the hospital several times a week – moral support for Grace.

They were in the coffee shop when Ruth asked how much weight she had lost.

'No idea,' said Grace.

'Too much,' said Ruth, watching over her as she picked at a cheese and tomato panini.

She kept trying to get Grace round for supper, but by the time visiting hours were over, she just wanted to go home. The sour smell of sickness seemed to cling to her. A long soak in the bath with a large glass of wine was her reward for having got through another dreadful day.

'I'm worried about you, Gracie,' Ruth said. 'You look so thin and tired.'

'I'm a whole lot better off than Cal.'

'It's not a contest,' said Ruth. 'And I notice his daughters are conspicuous by their absence.'

Grace had noticed too. As the weeks stretched on, their visits had dwindled to the occasional half-hour in the evening and a rota system at weekends. Cal's lack of progress had worn them all down, and the stark truth – that his quality of life was horribly diminished – was as obvious as it was unsaid. Josh was the only stalwart, taking the train home from Exeter every Friday to visit his dad. Grace didn't ask about Millie, who never accompanied him. She didn't want to pry. He would tell her when he was ready, or not – his decision. They spoke about practical things, Grace putting the best possible spin on Cal's meagre achievements. *He took a few steps with a walking frame. His swallowing is a lot better. He's using a commode now.* After one particularly upsetting scene – Cal, frustrated at not making himself understood, howled in despair – Josh retreated to the corridor. Grace followed him a few minutes later, and found him sitting with his head in his hands. He let her put her arm around him for a few moments before he straightened up and gathered himself.

Scenes like this were all Grace could think about. Even now, sitting in a busy café with her mum, her head was filled with Cal and Josh and the hopelessness of not knowing where it would end.

'You were like a mother to Lydia,' said Ruth, 'and look how she's treated you.'

'If this is you trying to cheer me up,' said Grace, 'you're not doing a very good job.'

'Fair enough,' said Ruth testily. 'I'm just pointing out that the girls' cries of defiance about not wanting you there have gone strangely silent. Funny that.'

'They all have jobs,' said Grace, unsure why she was defending them.

Her mother was right about Lydia, though. Beth seemed to have softened towards Grace since their conversation in the loo. They would never be friends, but at least they no longer felt like enemies. Julia interacted with Grace in a businesslike manner – asking for updates, discussing Cal's progress, sharing information she had found on Google. There was no warmth in the relationship, but then there never had been. It was Lydia who remained frosty. Lydia who shunned her. Lydia who looked at her with contempt. Last week, when she visited Cal after work, she sat down next to Grace without so much as a 'hello'. He was the one with a blind side, but to all intents and purposes it was Lydia to whom Grace was invisible. Ahmed's shift had been about to finish, but he took the time to check on her – ask if she was OK. Earlier, Cal had lashed out, catching her with the back of his hand. It had left a red mark on her cheekbone. She assured Ahmed she was fine, and thanked him for his concern. He said Mr Wheeler was fortunate to have such a good wife, which made Lydia snort with derision.

Grace needed to talk about something other than Cal or the girls.

'How's Charles?' she said brightly.

Ruth smiled.

'He's very well.'

'And?'

'And what?'

'Is it serious?'

'Oh, I don't know. We enjoy each other's company and have lots in common – that's enough for now.'

'I keep thinking about his wife,' said Grace.

'Do you?'

'You said she had a stroke, and he looked after her himself.'

She rubbed her eyes with the heels of her hands.

'I'm dreading looking after Cal. Does that make me a terrible person?'

'It makes you human,' said Ruth.

TWENTY-NINE

The plan was to get Cal home for Christmas. Susan, his newly assigned social worker, informed Grace of this in the same room where the family had congregated in those early days of life or death. Life had won, but not as they knew it. Six weeks after his stroke, Cal could take half a dozen faltering steps with a Zimmer frame (Susan preferred 'mobility aid'), but mostly he was confined to a wheelchair. He wasn't eligible for a motorised scooter because of his left-side blindness, and the fact that his coordination was haphazard. Susan was brisk and smiley, a woman who got things done, whether you wanted her to or not. Grace guessed she was around fifty, pleasantly plump and with a penchant for bold patterns: stripes, polka dots, flowers and checks. Today's outfit consisted of brown check trousers and a mustard-coloured blouse sporting a big floppy bow at the neck. It was a subdued ensemble by Susan's standards. Grace found it preferable to focus on banalities like Susan's quirky fashion sense rather than her own imminent role as Cal's carer.

She had assumed he would stay in hospital until he was more able, or transfer to a rehabilitation centre where he would continue to receive expert nursing, but Susan had doused that faint glimmer of hope. Health and social care funding for the elderly (Grace hated that word) was threadbare, and since Cal had a young, able-bodied wife who could look after him at home, he wasn't a priority for scarce public resources. Incredibly, he had fulfilled the assessment criteria for being discharged from hospital. With assistance, he could get out of bed and into a chair, walk a (very) short distance with a frame, and swallow soft food. An occupational therapist had visited their home, and despite it being blatantly unsuitable for a man in Cal's condition (no ground-floor toilet, a steep flight of stairs), she assured Grace they could make it work. 'How?' Grace had asked, and then wished she hadn't. A stairlift was strongly recommended, as well as bathroom adaptations such as a walk-in shower with grab rails and a seat, and a raised toilet, also with grab rails. Their current arrangement was a shower above the bath and a normal-height toilet, so all that would have to be ripped out and replaced. The occupational therapist said they needed a ramp at the front door for when Grace took Cal out in his wheelchair, a daunting prospect. She constantly berated herself for being a terrible person, one who had to fight a sense of revulsion when she thought of pushing her elderly husband around town in a wheelchair. It would have been easier if she had loved him. Everything she did was out of duty, sympathy and guilt, and to show Josh she was truly sorry. Loving Cal wasn't part of the equation.

When she voiced her concerns about how she would manage, Susan responded with much earnest nodding and reassurances about external support. She referenced the Community Stroke Team, an army of health professionals tasked with continuing Cal's rehabilitation once he was home. He would be discharged with a care plan, she told Grace, and urged her to organise the adaptations as soon as possible. 'They will make everyone's life easier,' said Susan – a wildly optimistic pronouncement in Grace's opinion. Apparently, she could apply for a Disabled Facilities Grant, but it was means tested and involved an arduous and time-consuming application process. Given that she and Cal had savings, and he had a reasonable private pension, Susan thought it unlikely they would be eligible for financial support anyway. In happier times, Grace and Cal had talked about building a sunroom overlooking the garden, or converting the loft for when grandchildren arrived. Instead, an army of builders was turning their house into an old people's home. Grace knew it was wrong to feel aggrieved, and frequently reminded herself that Cal was the victim here, not her.

A few days before his discharge, she was sitting in Costa when Doctor Rudge walked in. They often bumped into each other and exchanged a knowing smile or the occasional pleasantries. Once, he quipped that she spent more time in the hospital than he did. This particular day, she was tucked away at a small corner table, but it was a busy lunchtime and after Doctor Rudge got his sandwich and coffee, he looked around for somewhere to sit. When he saw Grace, he came over and asked if he could join her. Every time she saw him, he appeared harassed and untidy. His white coat looked too big for his slight frame, and his hair, though sparse and thinning, needed a good cut. The taped-up spectacles still hadn't been repaired, and his trainers had seen better days. She expected he wanted a break from patients and their demanding relatives, beseeching him for assurances and certainties he couldn't give. This was why she didn't attempt to strike up a conversation, and was surprised that he did. When he enquired how she was, she told him Cal was coming home this weekend. The doctor poured two packs of sugar into his coffee.

'That wasn't what I asked,' he said, stirring it with one of those thin wooden sticks.

'I didn't realise you wanted an actual answer,' she said.

'And what is the actual answer?' he said, pulling the cellophane off his sandwich. 'I assume the social worker has explained everything?'

'Yes, and the house is being adapted as we speak,' she said. 'My mother's busy plying the builders with endless tea and biscuits.'

Her tone was flat and resigned, which was pretty much how she felt. He took a hefty bite of his sandwich – egg and cress, from what Grace could see. She had developed a morbid fascination with what people stuffed in their mouths. Muffins, cakes, sandwiches, pastries. Comfort calories. For Grace, there was no comfort. Sometimes she found it difficult to swallow, and had nightmares about choking. Ahmed had got her feeding Cal his meals – practice for when he came home. Everything was mashed or puréed, so had the consistency of baby food. When it dribbled out of the droopy side of his mouth, she had to wipe his chin. Grace used to love feeding Josh in his high chair, however messy mealtimes got. Cal's mealtimes were an abomination. Once, she had to run from the ward and gag. Ahmed had followed her out and rubbed her back, turning her nausea to despair. His kindness was heartbreaking, because it reminded her of love.

'It will certainly be an adjustment,' said Doctor Rudge, chewing. 'But you won't be on your own. There's plenty of professional support, and make sure you get the family to do their bit.'

'His daughters all have full-time jobs,' she said. 'And my son's studying medicine at Exeter.'

'Poor sod,' he said, with a wry smile.

He carried on eating and drinking his coffee – soot dark and steaming. Grace sipped hers too, even though it was cold. She must have been sitting there longer than she thought.

'You need to look after yourself,' he said with his mouth full. 'You won't be much use to your husband if you get sick.'

'Have you been talking to my mother?' said Grace.

He smiled.

'Maybe you should listen to her.'

His table manners left something to be desired, but then doctors were probably used to eating on the go. He did have a point, though. She felt tired and run-down, and Cal wasn't even home yet.

'Can I ask you something?' she said. 'Will my husband remember what happened before his stroke?'

The doctor hesitated. Grace wondered if he was weighing up whether to be kind or honest.

'Possible, but not probable,' he said. 'Why?'

'We argued and I left. I can't help thinking that if I'd been there, got help straight away, he wouldn't be in this state.'

Doctor Rudge swallowed the last of his sandwich.

'I remember you asking something similar when we first spoke.'

'You thought I was his daughter.'

'Sorry about that.'

'Don't be. He's old enough.'

That day was the last time she saw David. How ironic that her lover had saved her husband's life. It was David who had spoken to the emergency services, checked Cal's airway, put him in the recovery position. She had kept that a secret from all of them. Sometimes she wanted to blurt it out – let them know they owed him a debt of gratitude. It was laughable to imagine they would see it like that. All it would do was reignite their smouldering resentment, so she kept her mouth shut.

'Seriously, take care of yourself,' said Doctor Rudge, getting up to go. 'And reach out if you need help.'

Cal left hospital the same way he had arrived – in an ambulance. Grace had brought in a Christmas hamper for the staff, to thank them for all their hard work and patience. God knows they had earned it. A porter took him down to the ambulance bay in his wheelchair, to be loaded into the vehicle like cargo. Grace followed in her car, a sick trepidation churning up her stomach. Josh must have been waiting by the window, because he came outside as soon as the ambulance pulled up. He watched the wheelchair being lowered, his expression difficult to read. Relief at having his dad home, or maybe shock at being faced with the stark reality of what lay ahead. Josh pushed him up the newly installed ramp and into the hallway, Grace following behind with his holdall. She had gone to M&S and bought him a couple of tracksuits (buttons and flies required dexterity Cal no longer possessed) in a Medium instead of his usual Large. The stroke had diminished him in every conceivable way.

'Welcome home, Dad,' said Josh, laying a firm hand on his shoulder.

Cal reached across and covered it with his own, his gaze fixed firmly on the stairlift. He said something neither of them understood, so he repeated it, louder but still no clearer. Josh looked at Grace, who shrugged.

'Let's get you settled,' she said, her tone artificially bright.

Cal pointed at the stairlift and wailed. This, Grace understood. The stairlift was an incontrovertible symbol of his infirmity, proof positive that he would never be the man he once was. His wife was now his carer, and he couldn't even say how shit it all was, because that too was beyond him. He made a fist with his good hand, and punched the arm of his wheelchair repeatedly, before Josh intervened.

'Stop it, Dad,' he said, restraining him. 'You'll hurt yourself.'

Cal almost laughed at this – ironically, the clearest of all his verbal expressions. Josh looked at Grace imploringly, as if to say, *What do we do?*

'Take him into the sitting room,' she said. 'I'll make us some lunch.'

Alone in the kitchen, she braced herself against a torrent of despair. Susan had warned her this might happen, and told her not to fight it, but to wait calmly until it passed. Grace counted to twenty-five before the feeling subsided, and then forced herself into carer mode. She took one of the many Tupperware containers from the fridge and placed it in the microwave. Mashed potato, mince, peas and gravy. It smelled so much like the stroke ward, nausea rose in her throat. She had a drink of water to help swallow it back down. Her mum had cooked an assortment of pulped and blended food, much of it stacked in the freezer. *Just until he gets his strength back*, she had told Grace unconvincingly. Everyone was determined to put on a brave face, but really it was denial.

She made a pot of tea and allowed Cal's to cool, before pouring it into an adult sippy cup. Susan had recommended a website that sold aids for the disabled: thecompletecarer.com – something like that. Grace felt demonstrably *incomplete*. She missed her son (physically present, emotionally absent), her friends (no time), her job (Cal's stroke had spurred Marty to sell the company), her freedom. Most of all, she missed David. Last week she'd thought she saw him walking along the street. The man was about twenty feet in front of her, the same height and build, the same dark thatch of hair, the same well-worn Barbour. Her heart kicked hard as she hurried to catch him up. It wasn't David – she saw that as she got closer – but for those fleeting seconds she had felt exhilarated and excited again.

The one person she wanted to tell was Christina, but their friendship had changed. Ruth said it was based on all the things they had in common – twenty-year marriages, children the same age, a tribe of mutual friends – but those things had changed too. Her mother was nothing if not perceptive. Grace's relationship with David, and her decision to leave Cal, had forced Christina to examine her own relationship with Harry, something she was loath to do. Her solution was to stay away – out of sight, out of mind. No one likes to be around sickness and misery. It was unfair, though, Grace felt, to be punished for Harry's infidelity.

The microwave pinged, bringing her back to the task at hand. She spooned the gloopy concoction onto a plastic plate, which came with a matching plastic spoon. Both were a jaunty sky blue, making the entire meal look like it was meant for a young child. Not a happy meal, that was for sure. She placed everything on the special lap tray purchased from the website, with raised edges and a thick non-slip mat. Carrying it into the sitting room, she found Josh and Cal watching TV. She wondered why Cal was still in his wheelchair, when he would be much more comfortable in his recliner. Josh could have helped him, but maybe Cal had refused. Just leave it, she told herself, fearing another scene.

'Here you go,' she said, carefully placing the tray on Cal's lap.

Ahmed said she should encourage him to feed himself, but his hand–eye coordination was unreliable, and he struggled to get the spoon to his mouth. A combination of frustration and stubbornness meant he often refused to try, and she remembered Doctor Rudge telling her to choose her battles. She couldn't recall the context, but it seemed eminently sensible advice.

'Would you like me to help you?' said Josh, picking up the spoon.

Cal took the spoon from him and held it out for Grace, his eyes hard and unflinching. This was how it would be, she realised. The only person Cal wanted was Grace, perhaps out of love, perhaps out of malice. There really was no way to tell.

THIRTY

The chalkboard was Josh's idea. Yet another prop designed to help Cal, but which actually infantilised him. He resented being wheeled around like a baby in a pushchair, drinking from a toddler cup, needing help to stand and walk. *And don't even ask about the bathroom situation,* Grace had confided in hushed tones to her mother. Humiliation heaped upon humiliation, topped by his inability to make himself understood. The chalkboard went everywhere with him.

'Thank goodness it's his left side that's paralysed,' said Ruth. 'At least he can still write.'

Small mercies, thought Grace, thankful for even the unlikeliest triumphs. Ruth had a heavy cold, so hadn't visited the house since Cal was discharged from hospital. Grace kept her updated with daily phone calls, explaining how the chalkboard took the guesswork out of wondering what he wanted. Mostly he expressed himself with single words, always in capital letters: TEA, LUNCH, TOILET. One day when he and Grace were alone, he wrote WHORE. It confirmed what she had suspected, that Cal did indeed remember their fight. Doctor Rudge had said it was possible but not probable. Even with the odds in her favour, Grace had lost.

A new status quo had quickly emerged, with Grace expected to do everything for Cal, even things she knew he could do for himself. Ahmed had shown him a technique for transferring safely from the wheelchair to the Zimmer, from the Zimmer to a chair and so on. Cal had mastered it on the ward, but refused to even try at home. Instead, he put his whole weight on Grace, who strained her back and shoulder and had to take codeine for the pain. When the girls popped in for a visit (curiously, they never stayed long), Cal had her running around after them too, making cups of tea and sandwiches if anyone was hungry. They treated her like a servant, and an incompetent one at that.

When Beth arrived one lunchtime to take him out for a walk, she demanded to know why he was still in his pyjamas. Grace explained that he had refused to get dressed – his way of making it seem as though she was failing in her duties. Wife, carer, dogsbody – object of his derision. And on the day of Lydia's first visit, he refused to let Grace shave him or tidy his hair. He was perfectly capable of using an electric razor and a comb, but Cal looking unkempt made Grace look bad. He had developed a cruel cunning, always managing to make her seem wrong or deficient. In the bathroom, the morning of Lydia's visit, she pleaded with him to let her wash his hair. It hadn't been cut for months, and the greasy grey straggles aged him terribly. His obstinance had a bitter edge to it – sharp and unforgiving. She didn't remember raising her voice, but must have done because

Josh barged in and demanded to know what was going on. That was the moment Cal switched his demeanour from defiant to browbeaten, and Josh glared at her like she was the Antichrist. Later, when she confided in him about her aching back, he looked at her askance, as if how dare she complain when his poor dad was the one in a wheelchair.

It didn't help that she slept on a blow-up mattress on the floor. She had asked Josh to help clear out the spare room so she could sleep there, but Cal objected. 'PLEASE', he wrote on the chalkboard, and handed it to her with a beseeching expression. Grace wasn't fooled. She saw this as part of Cal's strategy to execute cruel and unusual punishments. He insisted on a commode next to the bed, so he didn't have to struggle to the bathroom in the night. Rubbish, thought Grace. Apart from a few 'accidents' early on, he managed to get from his Zimmer onto the stairlift, and then to a second Zimmer, waiting for him on the landing. If he could do it during the day, why not at night? It was a small house. The bathroom was less than ten feet away. His actions brought it home to her how brain-damaged he was. Cal had always been a proud and private man, who would rather die than debase himself in this way. Having to endure such indignities made Grace sad for them both. She held her breath when she emptied the commode, so as not to inhale the stench. Still it clung to her, like something dead and rotting.

Susan was too busy to visit, but phoned to see how Cal was settling in. 'Fine,' said Grace, because really, what more could social services do? In reality, Cal oscillated between resentment and dejection, and Grace once again sensed the darkness that had smothered her when Josh was small. She felt it stalking her – waiting.

Josh was polite, but withheld any expressions of love or affection. Their tenuous reconciliation had plateaued. When she asked about Millie he shrugged, which translated as 'mind your own business'. She wanted to say that what happened in his life *was* her business, but bit her tongue in case she made things worse. She wasn't sure which was more painful – Cal's simmering resentment or Josh's cool indifference.

A phone call from Christina was a pleasant surprise. She wanted to wish them all a merry Christmas, she said, sounding chirpy and busy. They were off to Verbier until the New Year, and she would have popped round but didn't want to intrude. A pal of Harry's had a ski chalet going begging, and she was up to her eyes in packing. Grace wondered if holidays were a thing of the past for her. She hadn't even managed to get Cal in the car – a plane was unthinkable. 'We must get together when I'm back,' Christina told Grace, who couldn't tell if she was being genuine or polite. It was only when the call had ended that she realised Christina hadn't asked how she was. She had asked about Cal and Josh, even Ruth, but not about Grace.

There was a queue to get into Sainsbury's car park – the last-minute Christmas rush. Grace sat patiently, hypnotised by the rhythmic back and forth of the windscreen wipers. The driver's side window was open an inch, letting in spits of rain. She didn't care about getting wet. It was a price worth paying to breathe cold, fresh air. At home Cal needed the thermostat ramped up to tropical levels of heat, and a faint but foetid odour persisted, no matter how much Febreze she sprayed around.

After some fraught negotiation, it was decided the girls would come for lunch today. Grace wasn't party to the discussions, merely informed of the outcome. Christmas Eve worked best for them, apparently, and they didn't want to overwhelm their dad with all the fuss and expectation of the big day itself. Grace had asked Ruth to come too. She badly needed to be smothered in one of her hugs. The only physical contact she had these days was when she helped Cal with his grooming, or manoeuvred him from A to B. Touching him repulsed her, although she imagined the feeling was mutual.

Grace had insisted her mum bring Charles, who seemed to have become a more permanent fixture in Ruth's life. His only daughter lived in the Algarve and this would be the first Christmas without his wife. 'Are you sure you want a houseful?' Ruth had asked, but Grace told her it would be nice to have a bit of a buzz around the place, especially as Christmas Day was just her, Cal and Josh.

The traffic crawled forward, but Grace wasn't in a hurry. Home felt like a prison, so even the stress of the Christmas food shop was akin to a whiff of freedom. She had made a list because she could hold nothing in her head these days. Her sleep-deprived brain was foggy and dull. When she finally found a parking space, she stood in the rain for a few moments, just to feel it on her skin.

The supermarket was crowded and chaotic, shoppers clearing the shelves like a plague of locusts. She filled her trolley with convenience food, and the obligatory turkey and all the trimmings. A rich coffee aroma drew her to the café, but just as she was thinking about taking ten minutes to herself, Josh texted to say Cal was agitated – how long would she be? Festive music played, barely audible over the chaotic din of desperate shoppers; songs about sleigh bells and reindeer and Santa with his sack of presents. This was supposed to have been their last Christmas together as a family, before she broke it to Cal that she was leaving. Now she could never leave.

Josh helped her unload the car, complaining that Dad had got upset because she was out so long. She could have explained about the traffic, the crowds, the long queues at the checkout, but mumbled an apology instead. Cal was leaning on his walker in the hall, watching them through the open front door. He had changed almost beyond recognition. Post-stroke Cal took little pride in his appearance, and his difficult, dishevelled old-man persona induced a combination of pity and distaste. The girls would blame Grace, accuse her of not looking after him properly, but what more could she do if he refused to cooperate?

She confined herself to the kitchen when they arrived, heating up sausage rolls and mini quiches for a buffet-style lunch. Cal's puréed chicken and sweetcorn would only take a few minutes in the microwave, and she made herself a coffee while she waited. Beth came in, ostensibly to get a bottle of water from the fridge, and proceeded to lecture Grace on how frail her dad looked, how little progress he was making. Grace assured her she was doing her best, before making the mistake of saying how difficult it was, looking after him by herself.

'Do you think I don't know that?' snapped Beth. 'I nursed my mother through cancer. Surgery, chemo, radiation, more chemo. I cleaned up her vomit, washed her when she was too weak to wash herself, sat with her all the nights she was in too much pain to sleep. For three years I watched her waste away – sacrificed my marriage, my son, to all intents and purposes, and my career.' She drew breath, eyes blazing. 'Well, now it's your turn, *Gracie*.'

The oven timer sounded, interrupting Beth's tirade. Their hospital détente had withered since Cal was discharged. The girls judged her for not doing a better job, no matter how often she told them she was doing her very best. There was a hint of triumph in Beth's voice, as if to say, *Now you know how it feels*. She seemed to relish the fact that Grace was struggling, as though she deserved it. Maybe she did. Maybe this was her penance for having strayed.

'Nan's here,' Josh called from the hallway.

Beth made a tactical retreat now that Grace had backup. Charles handed her a bouquet of carnations, tied with a festive red bow, and a bottle of champagne. She thanked him profusely, thinking what a sweet man he was – even envying her mother a little. Ruth squeezed her tight, telling her for the umpteenth time she needed to stop losing weight.

'It's not deliberate,' she said.

Josh was waiting to take their coats.

'You remember Charles?' Ruth said to him, diplomatically avoiding any mention of the fateful party where they had met.

'Sure,' said Josh, shaking Charles's hand.

He showed him into the sitting room, while Ruth followed Grace to the kitchen.

'You sure your cold's better?' she said.

'Much,' said Ruth. 'And I couldn't leave you with the three witches of Eastwick.'

It didn't matter that the reference went over Grace's head, she was just grateful to have an ally.

'You look exhausted,' said Ruth. 'I hope Josh has been pulling his weight.'

'Cal won't let him. He insists on me doing everything.'

'Well, I'm not having it,' said Ruth, concern turning to annoyance. 'And what about his precious girls? Do they help?'

'They work full-time, Mum.'

'Not evenings and weekends,' said Ruth briskly.

'Can you help me bring in the food?' Grace said, picking up a plate of sausage rolls. 'And you haven't seen Cal, so best prepare yourself. He's not the same.'

Ruth's expression was a mask of congeniality as she walked into the sitting room and deposited two plates of food on the table. Grace was sure the others wouldn't have detected the flicker of shock that passed across her face as she spotted Cal, hunched in his wheelchair. Ruth went right over and kissed his cheek.

'Good to see you,' she said, smiling warmly.

His own attempt at a smile was half formed and wet. She greeted the girls with equal warmth, belying the animus she harboured for the way they treated her daughter. When Grace went to get another bottle of wine from the fridge, Charles followed her into the kitchen, looking for a corkscrew. She took one from the drawer and handed it to him.

'It's very kind of you to invite me,' he said. 'I know your mother has been terribly worried about you.'

His brown eyes were rheumy and earnest.

'How did you do it?' said Grace.

'Do what?'

'Care for your wife after her stroke.'

It felt presumptuous to broach such a personal question, but he had been through what she was going through with Cal.

'I hope you don't mind me asking,' she said.

'Not at all,' he said. 'Although I'm not sure I can be much help.'

'Why not?'

He furrowed his brow, as if trying to compose the right response.

'What was important was to remember the person she was before the stroke, how much we loved each other.'

Grace nodded.

'Love,' she said. 'The missing ingredient.'

'I'm sorry,' he said. 'I didn't mean to be indelicate.'

'You weren't,' she said. 'You were honest.'

Back in the sitting room, everyone was eating, including Cal. It galled Grace to see him manage perfectly well, making a liar of her each time she told the girls he wouldn't even try. Lydia and Beth sat either side of him, praising his efforts. Julia, as always, was scrolling through her phone.

'While I've got you all here,' said Ruth, 'I think we need to have a bit of a chat about arrangements going forward.'

Grace looked at her in dismay. She had moaned about Cal's bitter resentment, the uncomfortable mattress on the floor, and how every time she tried to eat, the thought of his commode almost made her retch, but only to get it off her chest. Not because she wanted her hardships aired in front of the family.

'It's fine, Mum,' she said.

Confrontation made her anxious at the best of times, but the thought of the Wheelers ganging up on her again twisted her inside out. Their quiet contempt she could tolerate, but not a full-blown attack.

'No, it's not,' said Ruth.

'What do you mean?' asked Julia. 'Arrangements going forward.'

'It's not fair to expect Grace to manage on her own,' said Ruth. 'Haven't any of you noticed how thin and tired she looks?'

They all stared at her, as if to confirm Ruth's assertion.

'And I'm disappointed in you, Josh. You could do more to help.'

He looked like he'd been struck.

'That's not fair,' he said. 'Dad won't let me – he wants Mum.'

'You're right, it's not fair,' said Ruth. 'And it has to change.'

Grace already liked Charles, but his intervention made her like him even more.

'Ruth's right,' he said. 'I cared for my wife after her stroke, and there were times I felt I couldn't manage.'

'Who asked you?' said Lydia.

'I'm simply saying –' said Charles, but Lydia interrupted.

'Well, don't,' she said. 'It's none of your business.'

Ruth turned to him with an apologetic smile, as if to say, *Thanks, but I've got this*.

'Lydia,' she said. 'Your rudeness is uncalled for. You all

need to start doing more, and yes, I know you work, but you could give Grace a few hours off at weekends.'

'I come over every weekend,' said Beth, the colour rising in her face.

'Yes,' said Ruth. 'And expect Grace to wait on you, make your lunch, clear up after you. How does that help?'

Beth didn't answer.

'Grace needs a rest,' said Ruth. 'And if you won't pull your weight, I'll have to speak to social services about respite care.'

'He's not going into a care home,' said Beth defiantly.

'Absolutely not,' said Julia.

Even Cal managed an angry 'no', and wrote it on the chalkboard with three punchy exclamation marks.

'It's not your call,' Ruth said. 'I understand you're concerned for your father, but I'm concerned for my daughter and am not going to stand by and watch her being taken advantage of.'

Cal banged his fist on the tray and shouted 'no' again, clearer this time, as if putting all his strength into it. Spittle flew from his mouth, but whatever he tried to say next was unintelligible. When he wrote it down, he pressed so hard the chalk snapped in two. He threw half of it on the floor in frustration, and used the other half to write WIFE.

'Yes,' said Ruth, her voice measured but firm. 'Wife, not servant. She's sleeping on the floor, she's in constant pain from having to take your weight, and she's not eating. And before you all pile in, yes, I know it's nothing compared to what you're going through, Cal, but you're working her into the ground, and then what?'

'Are we going to mention the elephant in the room?'

asked Lydia. 'That his so-called wife left Dad to die while she spent the night with another man.'

Grace knew this was a mistake.

'Rubbish,' said Ruth. 'She did no such thing. Your father lost his temper and she ran from the house in fear.'

At this, all three girls piled in, vehemently deriding Ruth's version of events. She carried on regardless, speaking over them in a tone Grace hadn't heard before. She sounded like a teacher trying to control a rowdy class. Even Charles raised an eyebrow.

'She was a devoted wife and mother, who strayed once in twenty years of marriage. It happens, but then you know that, don't you, because your own mother did the same thing.'

'Don't you dare talk about my mother,' said Beth, stabbing her index finger in Ruth's direction.

'You got over it,' said Ruth. 'It's what grown-ups do.'

Cal's face was crimson and contorted, reminiscent of the grotesque paintings Grace had seen in a Francis Bacon exhibition Christina dragged her to. It was hard not to feel sorry for him. His family were quarrelling over one of the most painful episodes in his life, and he was impotent to intervene. He caught her looking at him, maybe even saw a flash of pity in her eyes, and with as much force as he could muster, he threw the chalkboard straight at her. Cal had always been a good shot. Decades of playing rugby and golf meant he rarely missed his mark. The corner of the board struck Grace's forehead, halfway between her eyebrow and her hairline. She yelped in pain and when she brought her fingers to the point of impact, they came away wet with blood. She reeled, thought she might faint, but her mother was on her feet to support her. Everyone had been momentarily shocked into silence. Josh was the first to react.

'Dad!' he shouted, on his feet too. 'Look what you've done.'

Cal's face was loose and pale.

'It needs stitches,' said Ruth, inspecting Grace's forehead. She grabbed a paper napkin and held it over the wound.

'I'm taking you to A&E,' she said.

'I'll bring the car round,' said Charles.

'Mum, are you OK?' said Josh.

Grace began to cry, not for herself, but for what Cal had become.

THIRTY-ONE

Christmas Eve in A&E was surprisingly quiet. Ruth sat in the back of the car with Grace, telling her not to fall asleep. Charles pulled up as close to the hospital entrance as he could, and said he would wait for them. The napkin had been replaced by a face flannel, now soaked with blood. As her mother led Grace inside, visceral memories of recent months hit all five senses. The stark fluorescent brightness, the smell of ether, so pervasive she could almost taste it. Sounds bouncing off the walls – voices, brisk footsteps, the squeak of wheels as patients were moved around. Ruth deposited her in a chair and told her to wait. A young child next to her stared at the crimson flannel, before snuggling into his mother. The woman moved a few seats along, as if Grace's injury was contagious.

A triage nurse called her name. After examining her forehead, she asked a series of questions, designed to establish if she was concussed. She wasn't, and the cut looked worse than it was. Head wounds bleed profusely, the nurse told her, and like most mothers, Ruth had panicked. It didn't need sutures – Steri-Strips would do fine. She showed Grace to a curtained bay where another nurse cleaned the cut, applied the Steri-Strips and covered the area with a large white plaster. The leaflet she gave Grace had a list of symptoms. If she experienced any of them, the nurse said, she should come straight back. Ruth wasn't happy that she had been fobbed off without seeing a doctor, but Grace was keen to leave. She had spent far too much time in this place.

A man walking towards them looked familiar, but it took her a few seconds to realise it was Doctor Rudge. He had a skier's suntan – brown face with panda eyes – and a neat haircut. No patched-up spectacles. She barely recognised him.

'Mrs Wheeler,' he said. 'What happened to your head?'

Grace didn't want to say, but Ruth blurted it out.

'Her husband threw something at her,' she said. 'Gave her a nasty cut. He's been treating her very badly.'

Doctor Rudge took a long, weary breath.

'I'm sorry to hear that,' he said. 'Does his social worker know?'

Grace shook her head.

'It's been escalating gradually.'

'And the violence?' he said.

Violence was such a strong word – not one Grace associated with Cal. But when she thought back to how furious he'd been the night of the party – the hateful name-calling, smashing her phone – that was a kind of violence too.

'This is the first time he's deliberately hurt me,' she said.

Doctor Rudge seemed troubled.

'Look, this is way beyond my remit,' he said. 'Other than to say the changes you're seeing in your husband are most likely due to brain damage as a result of his stroke. If it's escalating to the point where you're in physical danger, then you need to be protected.'

'Exactly,' said Ruth, her mouth set in a determined line. 'Grace is coming home with me tonight.'

'But what about –?'

Ruth cut her off.

'No buts,' she said. 'Josh can take care of his dad for once.'

'I'm sorry this has happened,' said Doctor Rudge. 'In theory, community support works well, but in practice, services have been cut to the bone. Which is stupid, because when carer networks break down, everything ends up costing more money.'

'What do you mean?' said Ruth.

'If Grace can't cope, or if she's at risk,' said Doctor Rudge, 'then her husband may have to go into residential care.'

'I suggested respite care,' said Ruth. 'But yes, we need to consider something more permanent.'

'I'm sorry,' said Doctor Rudge. 'I have to go, but please, speak to social services, tell them what happened. They're there to help.'

'I'll make sure she does,' said Ruth, as if Grace couldn't be trusted to do it of her own volition.

It did seem disloyal, though, conspiring to remove Cal from his own home, but he wasn't in his right mind – who knew what he was capable of? Doctor Rudge wished them a merry Christmas, which seemed far beyond the realms of possibility.

Charles was parked in the same spot. As soon as they

got in the car, Ruth told him Grace would be staying with her tonight.

'Of course,' he said. 'That seems very sensible.'

Grace wondered if he stayed over too. She hoped so. Her mother deserved to be happy.

Back at the house, the atmosphere was sombre. Julia had left, and Beth and Lydia were consoling Cal, who appeared very shaken. He was staring into the middle distance with glazed eyes. His skin was ashen, his hands trembling slightly. Both girls looked like they had been crying. Lydia stared at the dressing on Grace's forehead and welled up again.

'I'm sorry,' she said. 'I had no idea.'

Grace did what she had done a thousand times before when Lydia was upset, and hugged her.

'I've been so horrible to you,' said Lydia.

'You all have,' said Ruth tersely.

'Mum,' said Grace, not wanting her to spoil their much-hoped-for reconciliation.

She had missed Lydia very much. Beth stopped short of apologising, but at least she seemed contrite. She even offered to make everyone tea, but no one was interested.

'Where's Josh?' said Grace.

'In the kitchen,' said Beth. 'Doing the clearing up.'

'He didn't want to be in the same room as Dad,' said Lydia.

At this Cal lowered his head, as if in shame. He wouldn't look at Grace, who wondered if he had any insight into his behaviour. Doctor Rudge had talked about brain damage, and she chose to believe that was the cause of his outburst. The alternative – that he had deliberately hurt her – was too disturbing to contemplate. Josh came to see how she was. He looked shaken as well.

'We can't have a repeat of today,' said Ruth. 'Josh, you can look after your dad tonight. We'll get through Christmas and then talk to social services, but in the meantime, I don't want your mum left alone with him.'

Grace could tell Ruth was disgusted with Cal – couldn't even say his name.

'Charles is waiting,' she said. 'So Grace, why don't you throw a few things in a bag.'

She did as she was told, her head throbbing.

'Call me if you need anything,' she told Josh as they were leaving.

'He's training to be a doctor,' said Ruth. 'I'm sure he'll manage.'

Beth offered to stay but Josh declined, assuring her he'd be fine. Lydia hugged Grace again as she left, and said Ruth was right – she felt like a bag of bones. It was supposed to be a joke, but no one laughed.

'I really am sorry, Grace,' she said. 'I've been so angry with you, I didn't see what was going on.'

'Well, you do now,' said Ruth, ushering Grace out of the door. 'It's a pity it had to come to this, but at least it's finally out in the open.'

'And please tell Charles I'm sorry for being rude earlier,' she said, earning herself a conciliatory nod from Ruth.

'I hope I haven't ruined your plans,' Grace said, once they were in the car.

Ruth was sitting in the front next to Charles. They exchanged a look that hinted at intimacy, and he covered her hand with his.

'Not at all,' he said, smiling at Ruth. 'I'm sure your mother will love having you to fuss over.'

'You must think we're a very dysfunctional family,' said Grace.

'Is there any other kind?' he said.

She made herself scarce as Ruth and Charles said goodbye. The sight of a Christmas tree in the sitting room made her nostalgic for the simplicity of childhood. Her mum always insisted on a real tree, which they decorated together, singing along to cheesy songs. Ruth blustered in and told her to sit down, put her feet up. Grace knew better than to argue. She sank into an armchair, only then realising how exhausted she was. Her emotional and physical reserves were so depleted, she couldn't even summon the energy to talk. Ruth asked if she needed anything.

'A comfortable bed,' said Grace.

Ten hours of unbroken sleep was the best gift Grace could have imagined. Their actual gifts were sitting under the tree at home, waiting to be opened. The thought of going back made her nervous in the same way as going to the dentist or having a smear test. Unpleasant, but responsible and necessary.

'Merry Christmas, sleepy head,' said her mum.

She had made scrambled egg and smoked salmon for breakfast, and they each had a glass of Buck's Fizz. Grace picked up her phone to call Josh.

'Leave him,' said Ruth. 'You'll be home soon enough. It won't hurt him to take some responsibility.'

'I don't want to go,' said Grace.

'It's not for much longer,' said Ruth.

Grace held that thought close as they drove through the empty streets. The weather was grey and un-Christmassy, but it cheered her to see children excitedly riding new bicycles. She remembered Cal running along behind Josh as he learned to ride his first two-wheeler, steadying him, keeping him safe. It must hurt terribly to watch his strong, reliable dad, so cruelly altered.

This year Grace had intended to buy Josh a new fishing rod – the expensive kind David used – but that was out of the question. She got him an Apple watch instead, and a game for his PlayStation. They were under the tree, wrapped and ready, along with Ruth's presents and probably the girls' too. Yesterday had been so awful, exchanging gifts was the last thing on anyone's mind.

Ruth popped in to wish Josh a merry Christmas, but said she couldn't stay. Charles had booked lunch at the Royal Crescent Hotel and she had to make herself look presentable.

'Maybe this will help,' said Grace, handing her a box wrapped with silver paper and red ribbon. She told Ruth to open it now, so she could make sure she liked it.

'It's beautiful,' said Ruth, holding the amethyst necklace up to the light. 'You're such a thoughtful girl.'

Josh handed Ruth a book token from Waterstones and said he hoped it was OK – he never knew what to buy her. His tracksuit looked like it had been slept in. His hair was messy, and his face had an oily sheen. When Grace asked after Cal, Josh said he refused to get up. She knew how stubborn he could be but told Josh he was probably just tired.

'I feel guilty swanning off to a posh hotel while things are like this,' said Ruth.

'Don't be silly,' said Grace. 'You go and enjoy yourself. We're fine, aren't we, Josh?'

'Yeah,' he said. 'Course we are.'

Grace showed her out, and then it was just the two of them. She asked if he had eaten.

'Bit of toast,' he said. 'I'm not hungry.'

He slumped onto a breakfast stool, looking like he hadn't slept.

'Millie finished with me,' he said.

Grace was surprised to be taken into his confidence. Whenever she'd asked about Millie, he had shut her down. She resisted the urge to delve deeper, in case he did so again.

'I'm sorry to hear that,' she said.

'I mean, she knew everything that was going on, and at first she was, like, really supportive, but then she said she was on a different trajectory.'

He shrugged his shoulders.

'What does that even mean?'

'I don't know,' said Grace.

He ran both hands through his hair, as if trying to decipher the complexities of female logic.

'She was already with another guy, even before she told me.'

Grace felt the sting of judgement, as if all unfaithful women could be lumped together. She had often thought about trying to explain how she never intended things to blow up the way they did. Perhaps this was her opportunity.

'Not wishing to make this all about me,' she said, 'but my plan was to tell your dad after Christmas that I was leaving. I'd move in with Nan while he got used to the idea, and eventually I hoped he might move in with Beth.'

She marvelled at her own naivety, thinking the destruction of a marriage could be neatly planned and executed. Josh picked the dry skin around his thumbnail.

'I'm sorry I gave him your phone,' he said.

'I'm sorry I put you in that position,' she said.

Grace hoped he understood that between pitch black and pure white lay all the messy, murky greyness where people lived their lives, muddling through, making mistakes, and if they were lucky, being forgiven.

'I'd better go check on Dad,' he said.

Grace welled up again, although she didn't know why. All of it, she guessed. The whole sorry saga.

'Good idea,' she said, wiping her eyes.

He hugged her – the best Christmas present she could have wished for.

'See if he wants something to eat,' she said.

She wondered if it was too early for Prosecco. Surely one wouldn't hurt – not at Christmas. She poured herself a glass, feeling a faint flutter of hope gather in her chest. Lydia had forgiven her, and Josh seemed to be heading in that direction too. She would get help with Cal, and maybe, just maybe, the worst was behind them.

Josh called from upstairs, shouting for her to come quick. She gripped the sink to steady herself, because she knew from the sharp urgency in his voice that Cal was dead.

THIRTY-TWO

Overnight snow had been forecast, but it was still a surprise to wake up to such a pristine sight. The funeral was at eleven, the hearse and cars to the house forty minutes before – one for Grace, her mother and Josh, another for Cal's girls. None of them were bringing a plus-one. Was that the right term for a funeral, Grace had asked Ruth? It seemed a little too like a wedding invitation. Lydia refused to entertain the idea of bringing Kiara. She regarded Grace with disbelief for suggesting it.

In the corner shop, she had seen a shouty newspaper headline, warning people not to die at Christmas. It reported a spike in deaths over the festive period (a failed attempt at irony?) and a torturous wait to lay loved ones to rest. It had been twenty-five days since Cal's lethal second stroke. The family took comfort in the fact that he died in his own bed. His life had become a torment, and nobody wanted to see him wither away in a care home.

Grace and Josh had a quiet breakfast together before

getting dressed. Cal had always been a traditionalist, attending funerals in a black suit and tie. Josh looked so strikingly handsome in his own black suit and tie, it was as if Grace was seeing him for the first time. Ever since she and Cal had dropped him off at Exeter, she had been pining for her boy. It had taken time and tragedy to realise he was a man. Their roles had switched after Cal's death, Josh taking care of her rather than the other way around. He cooked her meals and made sure she ate them. He and Ruth redecorated the bedroom, bought a new bed and all the bedding. *Even a mattress?* Josh had asked Ruth. *Especially a mattress*, was her reply. Grace was deeply touched. They understood that she couldn't sleep there unless all traces of Cal's brutal decline were eradicated.

At first, Grace couldn't sleep at all. Her GP said that was perfectly normal and prescribed two weeks' worth of zopiclone, warning her about dependency and addiction. She managed without them now, and the diazepam that had dampened down the anxiety bubbling through her veins. She had saved the last two pills for today.

'Your dad was so proud of you,' she told Josh, straightening his tie.

Grace could tell he had been crying, something he never did in front of her. She tried not to cry in front of him either, but a few errant tears slipped down her face. She had composed herself by the time Ruth arrived, looking suitably solemn in a dark coat and leather boots. The snow had begun to melt, she said, so there would be no problem getting the funeral procession down the street. All three girls arrived together, clinging to each other like that first morning at the hospital. They would put that behind them today. Today was about saying goodbye.

The wake was held at the golf club, and was well attended considering the weather. It had started to snow again, which gave the mourners plenty to talk about once they had said all they could about what a great guy Cal was. Marty's anecdotes went back over thirty years. He became quite emotional, telling Grace how much he would miss his old friend, until his wife steered him to the bar for a stiff drink.

Adam had come with Christina – testament to his enduring friendship with Josh. More enduring than their mothers'. Christina had sent a card of condolence with lilies on the front and a few nice words, but hadn't phoned or visited. The first time Grace had seen her since those early days after Cal's stroke was in the line of mourners at the cemetery, waiting to pay their respects. Now she was standing alone.

'Thanks for coming,' said Grace, joining her. 'I wasn't sure you would.'

Christina blinked at that.

'Of course,' she said. 'Cal was a dear friend.'

'No Harry?' said Grace.

Christina seemed uncharacteristically subdued, but then they were at a funeral.

'Harry and I have separated,' she said. 'I asked him not to come. I'm sorry, I know that sounds selfish, but seeing him is too difficult.'

Grace's mouth gaped a little.

'I had no idea,' she said.

Christina took a sip from the wine glass in her hand. No wedding ring, Grace noticed. She looked around, aware that she was expected to circulate.

'Look, we can't talk about this now,' she said. 'Please call me.'

Christina said she would, but Grace wasn't sure she believed her. Josh caught her eye, as if he needed rescuing. Some of Cal's golfing pals had him pinned in a corner. She went over and asked if she could borrow her son for a moment.

'Thanks for that,' he said. 'They were trying to get me to join – apparently they need young blood.'

'Sounds sinister,' said Grace, smiling.

'I was thinking,' he said, 'how much Dad would have enjoyed this – all his friends and family together, saying nice things about him.'

Grace slipped her arm in his.

'He would have loved it,' she said.

As the snow got heavier, people started to drift away. They offered their condolences again, and wished Grace all the best. When Marty enquired about her plans, she realised she didn't have any. He intended to retire – 'at last', his wife chipped in – so they could travel, see more of the grandkids, spend more time together before it was too late. He apologised for his clumsy turn of phrase, but Grace assured him it was fine. He embraced her fondly – the last of the mourners – and then it was just family, pleased to have given Cal a good send-off, and relieved that it was over.

With Josh at university, and with no job to go to, Grace found the short winter days and long dark nights devoid of joy or purpose. She spoke to Lydia once or twice a week, but they were still treading carefully with each other. Whenever she asked about Kiara, Lydia was non-committal. *Don't push it*, was Ruth's advice. Trust had been broken on both sides, she told Grace, reminding her how nasty Lydia had been. Grace preferred not to think about that.

Beth had a birthday in mid-February, and sent a text thanking Grace for her card. She wondered if Cal's death might bring them closer together, but it didn't seem to. Still, thought Grace, cards and texts were better than nothing. Cal wouldn't want her to abandon his girls. Julia kept her distance, but then she always did swan around like a captain of industry – busier and more important than everyone else. Most days, Grace spoke to or saw her mum. She worried she was intruding on her flourishing relationship with Charles, but Ruth wouldn't hear anything of the sort. Grace bumped into him in Sainsbury's and commented on the bottle of suntan lotion in his basket.

'I'm going to visit my daughter and her family in the Algarve,' he said.

'Lucky you,' said Grace, thinking of the sharp slaps of wind that had assaulted her between the car park and the entrance.

'Mum will miss you,' she said. 'Can't you persuade her to go? A holiday would do her good.'

'I tried,' he said. 'But you know what she's like – always putting others first.'

'What do you mean?' she said.

For a second Charles looked flummoxed, as though realising he had spoken out of turn.

'Charles?'

'She's worried about you,' he said.

Grace blushed, embarrassed to have been cast in the role of middle-aged-woman-who-can't-cope-without-her-mum.

'Leave it with me,' she said, heading off to buy her own bottle of suntan lotion. She gave it to Ruth with a *fait accompli*. *Go to Portugal with Charles, or I won't speak to you for a month.* She meant it too. Ruth had sacrificed enough for her already.

Christina finally got around to calling, and invited Grace over for lunch. Evenings were difficult, she said, with the children around. She wanted to talk privately. Grace couldn't help feeling nervous, unsure how to negotiate this cut-and-paste version of their friendship.

'Come in,' said Christina, answering the door in faded jeans and a jumper.

She wasn't wearing make-up, and her hair was pulled back in a ponytail. By her standards, this was bag-lady territory. Grace felt silly, having put on lipstick and a dress.

'You look nice,' said Christina, leading her into the kitchen.

The table was set for two.

'Ellie's upstairs,' she said. 'Another tummy ache. The school nurse thinks it's psychosomatic, with all the stress at home. They pick up on things, however civilised you try to be.'

Christina's skin looked dry and papery, and the bright ceiling lights caught a few grey hairs.

'It's salmon and salad,' she said, getting a bottle from the wine fridge. 'Sauv Blanc?'

'Please,' said Grace.

She had taken an Uber on the basis that alcohol might help steer them through any awkwardness. Some topics were like fresh bruises – too tender to touch. Like why her closest friend had all but deserted her during the most traumatic time of her life. Grace had her suspicions. Ruth's voice was in her head – *you won't know if you don't ask*. Christina poured the wine.

'Do you blame me in some way for what happened between you and Harry?' said Grace.

The question didn't seem to surprise her, as if she had expected Grace to work it out sooner or later. She took a long drink before answering.

'I did,' she said. 'Partly, at least.'

She put a bowl of salad on the table, and two plates, each with a piece of poached salmon. There was bread in a wicker basket, and a white ceramic butter dish. She gestured for Grace to sit.

'I was angry with him for not coming to your party, when he promised that he would. The idea of being stood up for some nubile little intern made my blood boil. How dare he?'

She drank deeply, like she needed it.

'And when I saw those photos of you and David, something snapped.'

'Why?' said Grace. 'I mean, what did they have to do with Harry?'

'I wondered how many incriminating photos *he'd* taken. How many conquests I'd find smiling at me on his phone.'

The anger was still there – Grace could hear it. Christina took another drink.

'I waited up for him that night,' she said, her face hardening. 'Demanded to know where he'd been.'

She huffed, as if reliving the scene in her head.

'You should have seen him. So defensive. Such a fucking coward. I went through his phone – dared him to try and stop me.'

Her smile was tight and bitter.

'I found them on WhatsApp. I didn't even know he used it.'

She didn't go into specifics. She didn't have to.

'I'm sorry,' said Grace. 'That must have been –'

'Disgusting?' said Christina, topping up her wine. 'Yes. It was.'

Grace had barely touched hers.

'And when I heard about Cal's stroke – Ruth called me, said his daughters were being awful and you really needed a friend – I just couldn't. In my head, it was all wrapped up together – you and David, me and Harry. I told him to get the fuck out of my house, and he did. Can you believe it? Didn't even put up a fight.'

Her eyes were glistening. She sniffed back the tears and composed herself.

'Anyway,' she said, blowing her nose. 'Not wishing to wallow, but I've come to the conclusion that I have failed not only as a wife, but as a friend too. I feel pretty shit about that. I should have come to the hospital – been on your side.'

'Yes,' said Grace. 'You should.'

Christina's mildly surprised expression suggested this wasn't the reaction she expected. If it was absolution she was after, she would have to hear Grace out first.

'Harry's philandering was his decision,' said Grace. 'Nothing to do with me. And you looking the other way? Your decision – again, nothing to do with me, and yet somehow I'm the bad guy.'

She wanted a drink but her hand would tremble if she reached for her glass. Standing up for herself was a dauntingly unfamiliar experience. Christina opened her mouth to speak, but Grace pressed on regardless.

'Cal terrified me the night of the party – did you know that? And lashed out at me on Christmas Eve – I ended up in A&E.'

Christina's eyes widened in disbelief. She covered her mouth with her hand.

'His family held me responsible for his stroke, his suffering, and I took it on the chin because, truthfully, I thought I deserved to be punished. But not by you. Not by my best friend. You made me a scapegoat because you couldn't face what was going on in your own marriage, and that hurt me very much.'

She couldn't believe she had said all that. It just spilled out, like blood from a wound. Christina nodded fervently.

'You're right,' she said. 'I couldn't face up to it. I was humiliated. Four kids and a mortgage, and my husband bails the moment I tell him to stop screwing around.'

Grace spotted Ellie in the doorway, a teddy bear pressed against her chest, even though she was nearly twelve. The two women exchanged a look of horror. How long had she been there? How much had she heard? Her bottom lip trembled.

'Sweetheart,' said Christina, leaping into mummy mode. 'I was just chatting with Grace. I told you she was coming to lunch, remember?'

'Mummy says you have a tummy ache,' said Grace, as if speaking to a toddler.

Ellie nodded. Her skin was so pale it seemed translucent, and she had shadows under her eyes. Christina offered to make her a sandwich, but she shook her head.

'Why don't you watch *Frozen*?' said Christina.

'You said I had to read.'

'That was this morning,' said Christina. 'And you've been such a good girl, you deserve a treat. Off you go. I'll be in shortly.'

Grace felt awful for the poor child. She looked like a ghost, and Christina didn't look much better.

'Wait,' said Grace, suddenly remembering the ski trip she had told her about. 'You went to Verbier. I remember how excited you were.'

'Harry said he wanted to try and patch things up, but in truth, he just couldn't stand the idea of Christmas on his own.'

'He didn't make an effort?'

Christina let out a long sigh.

'He did, but too little too late. It all felt very half-hearted.'

'I'm sorry,' said Grace.

'I knew he was a lost cause when I caught him eyeing up the chalet maids. Couldn't help himself. And you're right – I should have faced up to it sooner.'

Their food was untouched, but neither of them seemed to have any appetite.

'I'd better go and let you see to Ellie,' said Grace. 'I hope she's OK.'

'So do I,' said Christina. 'I feel I've made such a mess of things.'

'Me too,' said Grace.

'Less than six months ago we were married,' said Christina sadly. 'And look at us now – a divorcee and a widow.'

THIRTY-THREE

There had been a flurry of activity around the house in the first few months after Cal's death. Grace had the ramp and stairlift removed, and a brand-new bathroom installed – bright, fresh, untainted by illness. Builders came and went during the week, and at weekends Josh was home. He had fallen behind at university and used the time to catch up. Too many distractions in Exeter, he told Grace.

But by early March the builders had finished and Josh was up to date with his studies, leaving the house still and lifeless. What had been obvious to Josh and Ruth – and they weren't shy of saying so – was now obvious to Grace as well. She needed to kick-start her life – get a job, do an evening class, volunteer, take up a hobby – anything that would give her days purpose and structure. She signed up with a recruitment agency, who said they had the perfect job for her – office manager for a firm of architects.

'I've got an interview,' she told Josh.

She had assumed he would be in a lecture and intended to leave a voicemail, but was delighted when he answered.

'That's great,' he said. 'Actually, I'm coming home this weekend so you can tell me all about it.'

'What, no parties to go to?'

His answer stopped her dead.

'Start of the fishing season.'

She breathed in sharply through her nose. Her nostrils might have actually flared a little.

'Sorry, have to go,' he said. 'Can you pick me up on Saturday? Train gets in at eleven.'

Grace didn't know what to make of it. Because of her, his beloved fishing was associated with sex, scandal and death. At Christmas she had decided against buying him a new rod for that very reason. Yet just now he mentioned it so casually, as if the whole David debacle had never happened. Did that mean she was forgiven? Or was the subject taboo – too painful to be spoken of ever again? She would have to wait until Saturday to find out.

The station car park was crowded and Grace had to drive around twice to find a space. She was early, and closed her eyes for a few minutes while she waited for Josh. Her thoughts turned to David, an indulgence she rarely allowed herself, but sometimes a memory would flash into her head and she let it play out. If she had never met him, Cal might still be alive and Josh might still have his dad. Christina had called her a widow – a word laden with loss and loneliness. The shameful truth was that Grace missed David more than she missed Cal.

Josh shocked her out of her reverie.

'Did I wake you?' he said, throwing his rucksack on the back seat.

'Just resting my eyes,' she said.

He got in next to her, looking student-scruffy but otherwise good. She had suggested he speak to a counsellor about losing his dad, but didn't force the issue. He was old enough to make his own choices.

As soon as they walked in the door, he dropped his bag and went to the kitchen to make a sandwich. Since food always seemed to be on his mind, she asked what he would like for dinner.

'Don't worry about me,' he said. 'I'm going out with a few friends from school. Not a late one. I want to be up early for fishing.'

There it was – the F word. She was nervous of saying the wrong thing, but had to say something. It would have been cowardly not to. How could she expect forgiveness if she didn't own up to her sins?

'I thought I'd ruined fishing for you,' she said. 'I hated myself for that.'

He carried on buttering his bread. Maybe he found it easier to talk if he didn't look at her.

'The counsellor says I shouldn't let what happened spoil the good things in my life. My memories of Dad before his stroke. Hobbies like fly fishing. All that stuff.'

'I agree completely,' she said, impressed by his maturity. 'And I'm glad you've got someone to talk to. Sounds like it's really helping.'

'You should give it a try,' he said, loading sliced ham and tomatoes onto the bread.

'I did,' she said. 'A long time ago.'

'Really?'

'I had a sort of breakdown, when you were five. Counselling helped me get better.'

'Why did you never tell me?'

'I suppose I wanted you to see me as unfailingly strong and reliable – someone who would never let you down.'

She gave him a sad, *mea culpa* smile. He eyed her suspiciously.

'You're not going to talk about that David bloke, are you?'

'No,' she said emphatically.

She was amazed Josh had brought him up, let alone referred to him by name. Out of nowhere, an idea came to her – a way of sealing off the trauma, symbolically at least.

'Remember the day before you left for Exeter?' she said. 'We went fishing on the River Frome – you in the water, me on the bank?'

'Yeah,' he said, spooning pickle onto the ham in a way that reminded her of Cal.

'Why don't we do that again?' she said. 'You know, a before and after. Bookend all the bad stuff. Does that sound stupid?'

She worried she had asked too much of him, and backtracked.

'I mean, I realise nothing can be undone, but –'

'Mum?'

'Yes?'

'Sounds good.'

The morning was bright and frosty, with a true-blue sky and gleaming sun. There were several cars parked along the lane – eager fishermen like Josh, Grace assumed. They picked their way along the footpath and found a secluded spot to settle. The grass was soft and dewy, the river shimmering silver in the raw late-winter light. A heron took flight in the distance, its cloak-like wings moving with balletic grace. Josh had finished setting up his rod and was putting on his waders. It made her think of David – the day they were meant to return his waders to the shop. The day they first had sex. Banishing him from her thoughts was a work in progress.

Josh strode out into the gin-clear water and made his first cast. Grace watched from the bank and remembered the empty-nest book Ruth had given her. She had dumped it into the recycling, unread. No great loss, she told herself. Nothing could have prepared her for the trauma of her empty nest. Even now, she could hardly believe everything that had happened.

It was a while before Josh got a bite. The fish he reeled in vigorously objected – a brown trout, from what Grace could see. He placed it in the landing net, where it continued to flap and thrash, desperate to escape.

'It's a beauty,' said Grace. 'What are you going to do with it?'

'Haven't decided,' he said. 'It can stay there while I eat.'

'You're hungry already?'

She had cooked him bacon and eggs for breakfast.

'Always,' he said, opening the hamper.

She had feared they might never do this again. Some family rifts endured for decades, but Josh had given her a second chance. It was such an ordinary thing, watching him tuck into a roast chicken baguette, and yet it filled her with joy.

'Why are you smiling?' he said.

'Dad told me your vegan phase would last as long as your Millie phase.'

They both laughed – the first time in a long time. When the heron landed gracefully on the opposite bank, she pointed it out to him.

'It's got its greedy eye on my trout,' he said.

She had momentarily forgotten that the poor thing was still imprisoned in the net.

'Can't we let it go?' she said, feeling the urge to save it.

They walked over to the water to find the fish was quiet now, as if accepting of its fate. She released it from the net and watched its glorious swim to freedom.

Acknowledgements

Writing a novel is a solitary endeavour, but bringing it into the world requires a team of talented people. Wanda Whiteley (aka The Manuscript Doctor) reads my early drafts and provides invaluable feedback and advice. Midas PR not only run brilliant publicity campaigns, but are a delight to work with. They introduced me to whitefox, who proved to be a breath of fresh air in the crowded and competitive world of publishing.

But none of this would have been possible without the love, support and encouragement of my husband. He is my biggest fan, and I am his.

Lightning Source UK Ltd.
Milton Keynes UK
UKHW011841230822
407726UK00004B/1086

9 781915 036575